Jack and Jill went downhill

R J Gould is published by Headline Accent and Lume Books. He is the author of five novels, *A Street Café Named Desire*, *The Engagement Party, Jack and Jill Went Downhill, Mid-life follies* and *The bench by Cromer beach*. He is a (rare male) member of the Romantic Novelists' Association. Having been selected for the organisation's New Writers Programme, his first novel was short-listed for the Joan Hessayon Award. Ahead of writing full time, R J Gould led a national educational charity. He has published in a wide range of educational journals, national newspapers and magazines and is the co-author of a major work on educating able young people. He lives in Cambridge, England.

www.rjgould.info

Jack and Jill went downhill

R J Gould

Part 1

1

For Jack it is love at first sight.

For Jill it is love at first sight.

Freshers Big Party Night at university. The hall is jam-packed with several hundred first year students, alcohol-fuelled to obliterate apprehension. The pre-party big news is that predatory second and third year boys have been banned following the previous year's behaviour which had been fully exposed in the local press. Britney blasts out of two giant speakers. A floodlit rotating silver ball, suspended from the ceiling, covers the dancers in a shower of white sparkle. As yet, there is little evidence of pairing off, unsurprising this being the first night. It's mainly girls dancing with girls, with the boys leaning against walls or at the bar. Looking on, weighing up the talent.

Jill has come along with the girls she's met on her corridor in the hall of residence. That afternoon they'd congregated in the kitchen within minutes of arriving and had nattered and drunk tea for an hour or so, planning their itinerary for the weekend. The party is a must-do and the four of them are now swaying as they karaoke to Craig David's *Fill Me In*.

Jack is alone, uncomfortable, weighing up whether it is where he wants to be, the *it* referring to the university as well as this event. Earlier that day, having unloaded the car, he'd remained in his room sorting his things, aware of the buzz in the nearby kitchen but unwilling to join his new housemates. That is, of course, assuming he stays.

Freshers Big Party Night is turning out to be a tacky affair. Standing by the bar, he looks down at his plastic beaker and swills the cloudy lukewarm lager before downing the remains and crushing the empty container. Commoners, that's the unpleasant word he can't help thinking of to describe the people around him. He watches as they jump up and down on the dance floor, dressed in tasteless cheap clothes. Probably from Primark or H&M or New Look.

Jack catches sight of Jill who picks up his gaze and their eyes lock. There follows the type of chemistry that no scientist has ever been able to explain, the instant drawing together of a man and woman without having spoken a word.

Jill abandons her newfound friends and approaches Jack. Unsure whether he is her target, he remains slouched against the bar.

'Dance?' she mouths, never shy when it comes to talking to strangers.

'I don't really,' Jack shouts in a vain effort to be heard above the volume of Pink's *Don't Let Me Get Me*.

'Come on,' she urges, extending her hand. Jack inadvertently presents her with the crumpled bit of plastic. He drops it to the floor then takes hold of her.

They dance and dance some more, bumping against a growing number of embryonic couples.

Their attempt to chat is futile.

'Something, something, something, something.'

'What?'

'Something, something, something, something.'

'Sorry, can't hear you.'

'What?'

'LATER!' this yelled down Jack's ear.

The absurdity of Bob the Builder's *Can We Fix It* is followed by the beauty of Lennon's *Imagine*. It is Jack who takes hold of Jill at this point, pulling her close, and it is Jill who instigates the first kiss, long-lasting and luscious.

'Let's take a break,' Jill yells.

Jack nods, lifting a hand to denote a pause as they reach the bar. He holds up a white and a red provided by the barman and Jill points to the white. Jack takes out a twenty-pound note, one of several in his wallet Jill can't help but notice. They continue walking and leave the hall.

Jack opens the bottle and hands it to Jill who swigs and returns it to Jack who does likewise.

'Thanks, I needed that. I'm Jill by the way.'

'I'm Jack.'

'Seriously?'

'Yes.'

Jill breaks into a smile that lights up Jack's world and surely would do for many others. He guffaws like a young schoolboy.

Standing outside the hall, they compare A-level subjects and grades, where they're from, where they're staying on campus, what degree course they're about to start – all the things Jill had chatted about with the girls earlier that day. A sudden realisation that sensual attraction risks being driven out by intensely boring dialogue seems to be mutual. All conversation abruptly ceases.

Jill instigates a second kiss, more long-lasting and more luscious than the first.

'Back inside?' they say in unison having paused for breath, the suggestion in tandem bringing on another world-beating smile and juvenile guffaw.

'My turn,' Jill calls out as they reach the bar. On the dance floor a second bottle of wine is drunk, this adding to the several pints previously consumed by Jack and approximately a quarter of the bottle of vodka shared by Jill with the girls in the kitchenette. They cling tightly together, regardless of the tempo of the song playing, though this is as much for mutual balance as it is for passion. Their hands grow ever more active in search of flesh.

'Had enough? Let's head off,' Jill suggests.

'What?'

'GO!' Jill informs Jack's left ear.

Jack nods and they proceed to the lobby where Jill picks up a copy of the freshers' edition of the university newspaper.

'What's that for?'

'I'll show you. Sit down a sec.'

'You're not going to read it now, are you?'

'Don't be impatient. Hang on a minute.'

She begins to make folds and within seconds has produced a pirate's hat.

'Da-da,' she exclaims, holding it up. 'I'm an origami nerd.'

'It's good, but…'

'…it's for you,' she says, placing it on his head. 'Your crown, as in Jack and Jill.'

Jack guffaws again. 'Now we need a hill.'

'Agreed. Let's find one.'

They step outside; it's mild for a late September evening.

'What about over there?' Jill says, pointing to an area some distance from any building, dimly lit by a near full moon.

She takes his hand and leads him onwards. They leap over twisted tree shadows on the lawn during an inebriated struggle to descend the gentle slope.

'Trouble is,' Jack says when they stop, 'we're at the bottom. If we wanted to stick to the plot we should have gone up a hill.'

'We can't do everything right, can we?'

'What are you doing?'

Jill is lying on the grass, her body stretched out. 'At least we can do the falling down and tumbling. Come on, lie down.'

Jack does as he is told.

'We need to be at least a bit accurate,' Jill adds. 'You have to go first and I'll come tumbling after.'

They shriek as they roll along, too busy laughing and too drunk to be aware of the potential for injury as they plough into a large oak tree. Having come to a halt pressed against each other, they are aroused.

Jill's dress has rucked up to the top of her thighs and she leaves it like that as she begins to undo Jack's shirt. His hand is soon in a place where Jill is happy for him to have found and she responds by undoing his trousers and

5

fondling him. Their lovemaking is clumsy and quick, intoxication creating a short blast of ecstasy ahead of dizziness and nausea.

~

Jill is woken by a tinny rendition of Bach's *Badinerie*, so terrible that she resolves to change the ringtone as soon as possible. She squints against the bright sunlight, momentarily confused as to why she's shivering in the middle of a field with a boy lying by her side. The caller is her mother, the purchaser of her Nokia 3310 gift. She was told that its alarm feature might prove valuable if intimidated by overzealous male students. Jill presses the phone icon as she looks down at Jack, her overzealous male student. He's still asleep, lying on his side, as cute as she remembers from the previous evening, despite the saliva trickling out of his mouth.

'Hi, Mum.'

Mum wants to know how the rest of the day and the evening had gone after she deposited Jill and her possessions. Jill talks about the afternoon tea party with the lovely set of girls on her corridor, her mother having met a couple of them. The evening event had been alright, Jill explains, but she was tired so didn't stay that long. And today is for unpacking, walking around to get to know the campus, and probably a pop into the library to take out some of the books on the reading list. Yep, well remembered, American Literature, the Victorian Novel and Romantic Poetry are this term's topics.

Jack stirs, opens his eyes and looks set to say something.

'Must go, Mum, one of the girls is nagging me to head off for breakfast. Speak soon.'

6

'Breakfast! More like brunch, it's already…'

Jill presses the end call button just in time.

'Christ, we slept outside,' Jack says.

'We fell into subconsciousness outside!'

'I'm freezing, my legs have gone numb,' he adds as he stands.

Jill sits up and rubs her own aching limbs. 'Me too. Pull me up, will you.'

Jack helps her stand and they set off towards the halls of residence, at first hobbling along like a pair of frail old age pensioners, but their muscles soon loosen up. The ground around them is strewn with empty beer and wine bottles. When they reach the first of the buildings, the residence where Jack lives, they exchange phone numbers and agree to meet up for lunch in the main food hall.

Jill decides against a kiss, put off by the encrusted deposit that might possibly be dried vomit on Jack's chin. Instead, she gives him a friendly wave like the way Diane Keaton does in *Annie Hall*.

On reaching her corridor there is a reception party waiting for her. Morag grabs her arm and drags her into the kitchen. The last thing Jill wants to do is chat, a shower is top of her list, possibly followed by something to eat, some sleep, and after that, there is unpacking to do. But she accepts that she can't shun her new friends.

'Tell us all,' Morag orders, but with a friendly tone.

'There's not much to tell,' Jill begins ahead of *Badinerie* striking up again.

'That's Bach,' Charlotte exclaims, 'the most awful rendition possible. I don't think I'll ever be able to enjoy listening to it again.'

7

'Aren't you going to answer?' suggests Annie, as if that option wasn't apparent to Jill.

She presses the icon and the room falls silent in anticipation.

It is Jack and there's no point pretending otherwise. 'Hello, Jack…Yes, you've got my number right…I'm looking forward to lunch, too…it was great, everything…yes, even that. Look, I must go now, I'll see you later.'

Her three new friends are looking at her, no questions asked, instead the expectancy that she will do as ordered and tell all. So she does, even the part they most want to find out about. Jill wonders whether they're shocked that she's had sex with the first boy she's come across and so soon after they'd met. Their questions suggest otherwise, they are seeking guidance on how to do likewise. Their assumption, presumably discussed ahead of her return, is that Jill ended up in Jack's bedroom for the night. She informs them that this hadn't been the case.

'Under the stars. That's so fucking romantic,' Charlotte ventures.

'Not really, it was more a case of us passing out.'

'Making love until you were too exhausted to move,' Morag adds.

'No, just passing out.'

Annie is emerging as the motherly one. 'You poor thing, I bet you're starving. I'll pop out and get you a croissant. What would you like with it, tea or coffee?'

Jill is all set to say it's unnecessary but has a change of mind, appreciating the goodwill of Annie and for that matter, all of them.

'Coffee, please. Black.'

She stays with the girls for a further half hour or so, deflecting increasingly sexually explicit questions. She'd only met them about sixteen hours ago and has no inclination to reveal how many boys she's slept with, her most outrageous sex act, whether she possesses a sex toy, and exactly what she did with Jack the previous night. By the end of the inquisition, she is looking forward to the familiar safety of Bronte's *Wuthering Heights*, this being the topic of her first lecture and seminar.

Jack also has a group in the corridor to contend with at his hall of residence. He staggers past them with no more than a cursory nod as he makes his way to his room. He looks in the mirror and is appalled by the image confronting him. There are marks on his chin that could be dried vomit. His utter exhaustion brings to mind a jet lag experience. Slumping down onto his bed, he is all set to sink his head into the pillow before springing up with the realisation that a shower is a far better idea. He has en suite accommodation, but the size and quality of the bathroom leaves much to be desired. At least the water is hot and his Lynx Africa is a welcome home comfort, the tangy fragrance restoring some energy. He steps out of the cracked shower basin onto the lino floor, its edges stained and detached from the wall, curling upwards. The bitterness at ending up at this university resurfaces, an anger that has been growing since the day he'd reluctantly accepted a place through clearing. Then he remembers Jill and his heartbeat accelerates at the thought of her.

Dripping wet, towel round his waist, he dials, eager to hear her voice. 'I'm just checking that I got your number right…is lunch still on?...I can't wait to see you again…I thought last night was brilliant and I'm including the sex even though it was a bit quick…OK, I'll see you at one…Jill?'

Jill has hung up without a goodbye, in fact throughout the short conversation she'd seemed distant. Maybe she isn't into long-term relationships.

On his bed is a pile of documents about his courses, including pages and pages of background reading for his first lecture and seminar on Business Basics. He assumes it's preparatory work for students who know nothing about business; fortunately this isn't true in his case. His father has fostered his interest in the subject quite possibly since he was in nappies. He pushes the papers out of sight under the bed, postponing the decision whether to attend the first week's sessions or not until the next day.

He takes hold of his absolute prize possession, an Apple iPod. He'd bought it when he was in New York for a long weekend over Easter, the $400 price tag considerably lower than what he would have had to pay in England. He lays in bed listening to *Murray Street*, the new Sonic Youth album, contemplating university life so far. He's at the wrong one, he's about to take a subject that he probably already knows as much about as the lecturers, his room is worse than his school dorm and the boys on his corridor are absolute plebs. But there is Jill, though judging by the telephone call, perhaps not for much longer.

2

Jack sits in the vast food hall watching indecisive individuals and small groups enter with needless bewilderment. It's hardly a complicated set up, there are big signs indicating which areas serve hot food, salads, sandwiches, pizza and pasta, KFC and Mexican.

The over-polite conversations he hears as students tip-toe around embryonic friendships are beyond belief.

'Where shall we eat?'

'I don't know, where would you like to go?'

'Maybe the pizza and pasta place?'

'If that's what you'd like.'

'I didn't say we had to, only that it's a possibility. I really don't mind, I'm happy for you to choose.'

'Are you sure?'

'Yes, absolutely.'

'I wouldn't mind a pizza then.'

'Oh. That's a problem for me, I'm gluten-free.'

Jack overhears variations of this conversation ten or more times and is surprised by how much anger it has brought on. Don't they realise the way a food hall is organised? Groups can split up, get whatever they fancy and then meet to sit at a table together. If there was a microphone at hand he'd happily stand up to announce the obvious.

In walks Jill. Goddess Jill, wearing a canary yellow T-shirt and a short brown skirt embroidered with a white and cream leaf design. Yesterday he hadn't noticed just how stunning her legs were. She lights up the room. He returns her wave then glances around expecting to see all other male eyes upon her. They aren't, everyone's too preoccupied with the trauma of deciding what type of food to select.

If the first minute of today's encounter is anything to go by, he's got it completely wrong about Jill wanting to dump him. In front of everyone, even though no one's looking, she flings her arms around him and kisses, her tongue pushing into his vigorously toothpasted and mouthwashed mouth.

'I needed that,' she says as she edges away. 'I've been telling the girls on my corridor just how sexy you are and I wanted to check that I've got it right.'

'Have you?'

'Seems like it.'

They kiss again. 'I'm so pleased I've found you,' Jack says, this uncharacteristic and somehow clumsy show of affection bringing on a self-conscious reddening.

'That makes two of us. Let's get some food, I'm starving,' Jill suggests, looking around. 'Where shall we eat?'

'Actually we could go to different…'

'…I'm not that fussy, you choose.'

'No need, you see we can…'

'…what about the pizza and pasta place?'

'Well, if that's what you'd like.'

'Do you know what, we don't have to queue together, we can just grab whatever we want and then meet up at a table.'

Jack smiles: this girl is smart. 'Good idea. I think I'll go for Mexican.'

'Salad for me. See you in a few minutes.'

~

They sit and chat, conversation flowing as easily as the previous evening.

Jack wades through a mountain of enchiladas. Jill watches as the strips of cheese, shreds of chicken, lumps of guacamole and black beans fall back onto his plate whenever he lifts the envelopes of corn. She picks at her mackerel salad with coleslaw, lettuce and tomatoes. Jack watches with fascination as she cuts her food into tiny squares.

He looks up to her face, it is truly beautiful. Her hair is long, straight and blond. He and his friends back in school had taken to ridiculing the fake blond Essex girls they'd seen in television shows like *Essex Invades Ibiza* and *What my Mum Would Like to Know.* One evening they'd googled "How to spot a fake blond". Having established that the giveaway was dark roots against the scalp, they'd embarked on late-night pranks in the town centre. Carrying binoculars and magnifying glasses, they would approach a girl, inspect, then cry out "Fake" or "Real". This activity came to an end when the boyfriend of a fake victim punched Jack's best friend in the face, knocking out two teeth.

'Jack, why on earth are you leaning half way across the table and staring at my hair?' Jill asks.

13

'Oh, was I? Sorry.'

'But why?'

'I thought I saw a spider in it.'

Jill springs up. 'God no! I hate spiders!'

'I was wrong, there's nothing there.'

'Sure?'

'Yes, positive.'

Jill remains standing. 'Well, finish your feast then let's grab a coffee.'

Jack is convinced Jill is a real blond. He looks down at the mishmash of food congealing on his plate and decides enough is enough. He takes note of the baby tomato, four weeny squares of lettuce and half the piece of mackerel left on Jill's plate. There was hardly anything there to start with. Could she be anorexic or bulimic? Although unsure of the difference between the two, he fears for Jill, having watched a documentary on Sky Living about a girl who died from one of them.

He gets up and they head towards the coffee counter near the exit.

'Just popping to the loo,' Jill declares.

'Why?' he asks. He has remembered from the documentary that secret vomiting in toilets is a commonplace symptom.

'Why? Do I really have to answer that?'

'I just wanted to check you were alright. Not feeling sick or anything.'

'No, I'm fine, see you in a minute.'

The documentary had also exposed lying as a feature of the illness. He'd have to keep an eye on things.

14

When Jill comes back he kisses her, nobly checking for vomit on her breath. There is no indication of this, nor the taste of a tell-tale mint. The girl in the documentary was as thin as a rake – Jill is gorgeous, slim but with curves in all the right places.

She buys take-away coffees and mini muffins and leads them round the campus with map in hand to help locate places of importance. She takes hold of Jack's hand and they walk past the library, Faculty of Humanities, sports centre and computer suite. She's on her third mini muffin, a good sign.

It's mid-afternoon and Jill informs Jack that she has loads of work ahead of her first seminar the next day. If she gets everything done perhaps they could meet up that evening.

A disappointed Jack heads back to his room, ignoring the boys chatting away on his corridor. He pulls out the stack of Business Basics documents from under his bed. He flicks through texts that are blindingly obvious, the titles alone making it unnecessary to read on.

Why businesses need a customer focus.

So they can sell stuff, stupid!

Why companies must look after their employees.

Duh! Because if the workers are ill they won't be able to make any money for you.

Why the bottom line matters.

Something to do with finance. Hopefully there won't be too much of that on the course.

He decides that he might as well go to the first seminar to show his face. At the very least it will be a chance to get to know people in addition to Jill. Who knows, one or two might be OK. He remains devastated about where he's ended up. The day after the results came out, he and his father had met the headmaster to instigate an appeal against his abysmal grades. The man refused to support this option. "All the fees I've been paying, what has that been for if not to guarantee success?" his father had demanded. "If one doesn't make any effort how can one expect to do well?" the patronising idiot had replied.

Now Jack is left with a simple choice, either stay put at this second-rate place or not go to university at all. Jill might be the deciding factor.

He lies on his bed listening to Elbow's *Asleep in the Back* and before long he's doing what the album title suggests.

~

It looks like afternoon tea is becoming a tradition on Jill's corridor, though whether a tradition can be set after just two days is open to debate. At any rate, the gang of four are there, now joined by Priya. Boys are once again high on the agenda. There is a Freshers Frolics Fancy Dress event that evening and Morag makes it clear that she is out to catch or get caught, her terminology generating a discussion on attitudes towards feminism. Jill indicates she'll be doing something or other with Jack.

'Is it wise to adhere to only one person so early on in your time here?' Little Miss Serious Annie asks.

'Well, I've got you lot, too, and I'm sure I'll meet more people tomorrow in my seminar. In fact, talking about seminars, I haven't quite finished all the prep reading. I'll see you later.'

16

Jill does have more reading to do, though she's already covered the compulsory part and a fair amount of the additional recommendations. More to the point, she wants some thinking time away from everyone. Annie's comment hit a raw nerve. Maybe she has been hasty in grabbing the first male available without sizing up the alternatives. So what though, Jack's lovely and that's that.

Yes, Jack *is* lovely she reiterates that evening as they walk down to town to eat at an Italian. Jill chooses a ricotta and spinach cannelloni and Jack opts for the beef lasagne. She thinks it's so sweet that his thoughtfulness extends to asking her if she's got enough to eat every few minutes.

'You must have a dessert,' he says when the waitress is clearing up their plates.

'I really couldn't, Jack, I'm full.'

'Please, for me.'

'No honestly, I couldn't eat another thing.'

'Stomachs contract if you don't eat a lot, then it's a vicious circle and you end up eating less and less. Did you know that?'

'I can't say I did, though I'm not sure I've missed out.'

'It was in a documentary I saw a while back. Look, I'm going to have a tiramisu, will you at least have a bite?'

When it comes, he divides it into two almost equal portions and is beaming by the time Jill lifts her last spoonful.

Her intention had been not to drink more than one glass of wine bearing in mind work was starting the next morning, but Jack orders a bottle and she consumes her half. They are well and truly "merry" as her mother would have put it, by the time they head back to campus and Jack's

17

bedroom. Sex is great, a mix of passion and laughter, the passion as their bodies press together, as he slides into her, the laughter due to the emergency stops to reposition to prevent falling out of the narrow bed.

Lovely as it all is, Jill informs Jack that she won't be staying the night, not with her first seminar early the next morning. Soon after eleven Jill takes the short walk back to her own hall of residence. Sweet Jack has offered to escort her; she's declined.

~

Jack is late arriving at his first study session, having finally decided that he would attend only minutes before the scheduled start. The lecturer has begun without him and doesn't pause to welcome the new arrival. Jack sits at the back of a room housing twenty or so students, this quantity far exceeding the number in his lessons at school and not comparable to the one-to-one tutorials on offer had he got his place at Oxford. However, he is able to take advantage of the large group, he can drift off and no one will notice. He can think about last night with Jill, of all the nights to follow, of days together too, trips out, concerts, cinema, meals.

He's doodling while deep in such thoughts, 3-D boxes drop down onto a tree-covered landscape. He senses scrutiny before seeing it; when he looks up all eyes are upon him.

'If you please, Mr Ashley-Lovett,' the lecturer says.

'Yes?'

'I asked if you could provide an overview of one of the papers included in your preparation reading. Since you're

18

the first name on my register you can choose which one to cover.'

Although he hasn't read any of them, Jack isn't fazed. After all, at school he blagged it often enough and since these titles are so simple, he's confident he can do a fair old job. Finance is best avoided as it can get tricky. The employees article might involve some understanding of law which he knows nothing about. So the one about consumers is the best bet. After all, he's a big time consumer himself so can speak from first-hand experience.

It doesn't take long to recognise that speaking from first-hand experience isn't working. The laughter of his fellow students is a clear sign, as is the probing by the lecturer.

'All very interesting, Mr Ashley-Lovett, but your own experience represents a survey of one which might not be deemed statistically significant. Perhaps you could draw on the findings in the 2001 Meyers and Shaw report?'

He can't. Nor the Clarke and Timms, Drake and Franks, Dubois and Moreau, Li and Han, and Albertssom and Lindholm ones.

Other students pick up the pieces, enthusiastically chatting about why companies succeed or fail based on the degree to which they are customer focused. The lecturer doesn't chastise Jack as had often been the case at school; he simply ignores him, which is somehow worse.

~

Jill's first seminar starts at the same time as Jack's. It's ten to ten and she's arrived early to bag a seat near the front. The background reading has been completed and her obsession with highlighter pens is evidenced by stripes of luminous colour on each printed page.

Carole is the lecturer's name and having introduced herself, she invites the class to do likewise – name, place of origin, why they've chosen this module and the best book they've ever read. Jill's answers are London; because to her the Victorian novel reflects the excitement and tensions of the move from an agricultural, rural society to an industrial and urbanised one; *The Yellow Wallpaper*.

'What an interesting choice,' Carole says. 'Why that book?'

'Well, in part because I only read it a short while ago and I suppose more recent books come to mind quicker than old favourites. But I love the brave challenge to male domination. You want her to win but she's so vulnerable.'

'Some people identify this as the first feminist novel. Feminism will be a central part of this module and I expect we'll come back to *The Yellow Wallpaper*,' Carole informs.

Jill glances around the room. With only two boys present there may not be much challenge to the significance of feminism. She smiles with that thought. Jack probably has no concept of the need for it – he'll soon find out!

They discuss Brontë's *Wuthering Heights*, Jill discovers it was slated when first published. *How a human being could have attempted such a book without committing suicide before he had finished a dozen chapters, is a mystery. It is a compound of vulgar depravity and unnatural horrors...*wrote one critic. She has highlighted this quote in orange, noting that the reviewer was male and he'd assumed the novelist was, too.

The great thing about the lesson as far as Jill is concerned is that, unlike at school, she isn't the only contributor. Others are having their say, with loads of great ideas. All agree, even the two boys, that the Victorian Age was a man's world.

'Was this the first feminist work?' Carole asks as the session draws to a close, 'or did we have to wait until *The Yellow Wallpaper*?' she adds, looking across to Jill and smiling.

The ten girls in the class stick together for the rest of the day, comparing literature likes and dislikes as they drink coffee, take an early lunch, and then head off to the library.

Life is great, Jill reflects. After only a couple of days at uni she's already feeling comfortable. She senses she's liked by those in her class and in all probability by the lecturer, by the girls on her corridor, too, and of course by Jack. It's a pleasant thought.

~

Jack has tried to call Jill several times during the day but she hasn't answered. When she finally does so it's late afternoon. She chats about the seminar and her new friends. When she asks how he's got on his answers are monosyllabic.

'Is everything OK?' she asks.

'Yeah, I suppose so.'

'You've hardly told me a thing about your first seminar.'

'I will when we meet up. You set for tonight?'

'Do you mind leaving it 'til tomorrow? I'm meeting up with a couple of the girls from the course. We're going to have a bite to eat then a group read and discussion about that book I told you about.'

He does mind, he has nothing to do unless work counts as something. Unlike Jill, who seems to be getting to know

21

everybody at the university, he has no one else to hang around with, in fact no one he wants to hang around with.

'OK. I'll see you tomorrow then,' he states with manipulative pathos, but Jill has already terminated the call.

3

It's no surprise that Jill is rapidly making friends at university, she's always been popular without having to make a concerted effort. From an early age she's been at peace with who she is, possessing a natural self-confidence that is devoid of any big-headedness. She is, quite simply, *a good girl*, polite and sociable, devoid of the adolescent hostility towards parents and teachers that had been common among her friends as they struggled to establish their identities. She loves her family life, a feeling shared by all its members. There has always been an openness at home, with discussions about politics, literature, music, cinema and science commonplace. Along with her brother, Dan, who is two years older and in the final year of his degree course, she's been encouraged to put forward her opinions from an early age.

Even the big S has been tackled candidly. Her parents sat her down the day after her fourteenth birthday to cover sex.

'Jill, Dad and I would like a chat with you about the facts of life.'

It had been an effort not to burst out laughing. Even her teachers called it "Sex" when introducing the subject during Personal Development classes, the topic slotted in among a seemingly random list including bullying, drug taking and the world of work. Discussions with friends were a far better source of information.

Despite their odd choice of title, she was impressed by her parents' guidance, the warning about the risks tempered by their message that sex was actually enjoyable, something her teachers hadn't quite got as far as admitting.

Jill accepted her mother's request not to lose her virginity until she was sixteen. She didn't quite instigate a countdown, but equally didn't wait long after she'd reached that age to give it a go. Before Jack there were four relationships, all with boys at her sixth form college, two in Year 12 and two in Year 13. She opted for boys her own age, unlike some friends who went for older men. Jill liked the youngsters' immature bravado, a good counterbalance to her own behaviour. She was the sensible one, putting up with misdemeanours while making sure the boys didn't get out of hand.

Glen was the first college boyfriend, one of the in-crowd, though by the time she dumped him, Jill reckoned his popularity was more to do with him playing lead guitar in the rock band rather than possessing any endearing personality trait. In her first term at sixth form college she spent far too many afternoons and evenings at band practices which frequently comprised of more arguing than playing. The rehearsals were in Glen's garage. She would sit for hours on a threadbare leather couch that had seen far better days, listening to the squabbling and the occasional triumph of reaching the end of a song. Their lovemaking took place on this couch after a frustrating wait for the drummer to dismantle every cymbal, stand and drum before

24

packing each one in a tailor-made case and chatting for a while before finally departing.

Initially it was an enjoyable enough mutual journey of discovery, both being virgins. Glen was a computing buff, keen to use his laptop to check on chords and lyrics during rehearsals. He discovered another application and Jill had to admit that at first their sex was enhanced by the thrill of the pornographic guidance available on the wonderful worldwide web. But before long she got the impression that Glen was more interested in the internet than in her, so she called it a day. Her boyfriend didn't seem bothered. A week or so later, Jill overheard a girl tell her friend what she and Glen had been watching together on the laptop in the garage.

With first term marks mediocre, Jill knew that she had to take her studies more seriously. There followed hard work and a highly successful second term ahead of boyfriend number two. This was Andy, a likeable though lazy boy from her history class. The relationship started when she bumped into him during late-night shopping in town one Wednesday evening. She took up his invitation to go to a pub and it turned out to be a fun evening. She liked the fact that Andy saw the funny side of everything, even the potential embarrassment of having to show his fake ID to get served when Jill wasn't even asked. That evening he rapidly downed several pints of lager and Jill soon discovered that high volume drinking was habitual. Andy looked young and acted it, always game for a prank with mates. The girlfriends would look on as the boys played, often mildly amusing at the time but less so on reflection afterwards.

Like the time when Andy unearthed a full-sized female mannequin from a skip. He and his friends took it in turns holding the thing's hand as they strolled through town, dragging it along, stopping to chat with it, sometimes even planting a kiss. The purpose was to film people's reactions using the oversized video camera borrowed from Andy's father.

Jill discovered the camera weighed a ton when they were in a supermarket car park and it was her turn to do the filming of another setup, this one ending their relationship. Andy and two friends targeted a man who'd parked well away from other cars. After he'd entered the store, the boys charged round collecting shopping trolleys and surrounding his vehicle with them. Jill stood some distance away filming as the man came out, but he caught sight of her and wasn't amused. Having chased her, he insisted that she remove all the obstacles or else he'd call the police. Andy and his mates were nowhere to be seen and the failure to come to her rescue was the moment when she decided enough was enough. Silliness was one thing, but cowardice was inexcusable.

She'd had enough of childishness. After a summer of boyfriend dormancy, she picked up again at the start of the next academic year with Clive. He was well and truly different to the first two, a studious intellectual from her French class, rather good looking though he didn't know it, which in itself was sweet. She convinced herself that there had to be hidden passion behind the serious front. He was like the flawed hero in a Victorian romance what with his deep dark voice and fierce frown when faced with the simplest of questions. They started dating a little before

Halloween, providing an opportunity for Jill to test her theory regarding latent lust. It fell on a Saturday night during a weekend when her parents were away. She invited Clive to her house and greeted him clad in damsel in distress gear, a damsel with see-through outer clothing and no underwear. She teased him about her need for neck bites and wild lovemaking.

This was not to be. In its place, while undressing, and even more astoundingly, during sex, Clive instigated conversations about Camus, Sartre, Baudelaire and the May 1968 riots.

'The thing about existentialism, Jill…'

Unzip.

'…is its lack of credibility. It simply doesn't reflect how people think and act.'

Untie.

'Of course I appreciate it was preceded by the Dada movement which makes you realise that…'

Unclasp.

'…the French intelligentsia…'

'Clive, now that I'm naked don't you think it would be a good idea if you took off your shoes and then maybe more? We can continue the conversation later this evening or even tomorrow.'

He conceded and they got going, only for Jill to suffer from the coitus interruptus of "By the way, have you finished the translation yet?"

There was so little on offer once the undressing had taken place that they might as well have returned to covering twentieth-century French culture, literature and society. The hidden passion she'd anticipated simply wasn't there or was so well hidden she couldn't find it. Sweet though he was, the relationship had to come to an end.

The poor boy was devastated. Despite his love of the subject, he dropped A-level French soon afterwards, a friend telling Jill it was because he couldn't bear to be in the same room as Jill, his beloved ex-girlfriend.

Sean, her fourth boyfriend, was the final one at college. She liked him loads. He was super confident, good looking, popular and kind-hearted, this latter quality in her view rare for a sports fanatic. In her experience, members of this set tended to mock those less proficient. The trouble was, he spent most of his time either training or travelling to venues all over the South of England to compete. Jill trekked along to some matches, but three hours on a coach, followed by standing for an hour and a half in the freezing cold, followed by the tea provided for the away team, followed by another three hours on the coach, she soon recognised all this to be a waste of a day. As summer approached it was bound to get worse since cricket matches went on for ever. She concluded that dating a sports mad boy wasn't for her and terminated the relationship. Lovely Sean was understanding and they remained good friends.

With examinations nearing, that was it with boys for the time being.

~

Jack's path to a relationship with Jill had been rather different. He'd attended an all-boys boarding school with girls incessantly talked about but rarely seen. The male schoolmasters were a throwback to an ancient era, wearing gowns and addressing pupils by their surnames. The only females visible were the waitresses in the dining hall, often

28

as dumpy as the suet pudding they served up. However, with no other options, they were the objects of the boys' fantasies, their comments lewd and immature.

'I know what I'd like to do with her…'

Masturbation was a frequent though usually private affair.

However, during the fifth-form after lights out one evening, privacy wasn't on the cards after Freddie declared "I bet I've got the biggest one in the dorm."

He coerced the others to show theirs, bribing them with a bar of Cadbury's Dairy Milk if they dared and a Curly Wurly for the winner. Jack was reluctant to join in but was teased until he did so and ended up with a degree of pride having been awarded third place, as measured and judged by Freddie using a ruler. With the exception of Freddie, the boys chatted about the waitresses as they stroked, thereby maximising chances of victory. Meanwhile, Freddie was content to do the measuring with loads of double-checking. When it later emerged that he was gay, this and future behaviour was put into perspective.

Future behaviour kick-started rather quickly. Mr Frobisher was doing the rounds that night and when he entered the room to check all was quiet, he was confronted by torch beams and groans. Switching on the lights, he witnessed five boys standing in a line rubbing their things, while a sixth, Freddie, was crouching down in front of one of them assisting.

'What on earth's going on?' Frobisher yelled. 'Stop immediately! Pull up your pyjama bottoms now!'

'Please sir…'

'Don't even begin to offer excuses. I will not have boys in my house doing such things, do you understand?'

'Yes sir.'

'All of you?'

'Yes sir.'

'Yes sir.'

'Yes sir.'

'Yes sir.'

'Yes sir.'

Frobisher continued to observe after the boys had pulled up their trousers, virtuously ensuring that all erections were subsiding. 'Who started this disgraceful act?' he asked.

'Me sir,' Freddie Warburton volunteered, following the unwritten code in public schools that boys must own up.

'I'll see you in my office after assembly tomorrow morning, Warburton. I'm not putting in a report tonight, I want time to reflect, but I warn you, if anything like this happens again you'll have the book thrown at you, all of you. To bed, I don't want to hear another sound.'

The boys did as they were told.

'Did you see the lump in his trousers?' Zak whispered as soon as the door was closed. Actually Jack had, but kept quiet.

Freddie went to Frobisher's study as requested the next morning. No report of their misdemeanour was forthcoming and Freddie became a regular visitor for extra tuition. This might have been valid during the GCSE years because Frobisher was a history teacher and Freddie was taking history. It was harder to comprehend when the visits continued at the start of the A-level years because Freddie was studying the sciences. He came out as being gay at the end of the first term in the sixth form and all but told his friends what had been going on in Frobisher's office. Jack could only assume that the school authorities picked this up because the history teacher disappeared without explanation over the Christmas holidays.

An opportunity for sex emerged at the start of the A-level years because girls were enrolled into the sixth form for the first time. There was only a sprinkling of them in his year, eighteen out of over ninety in the year group. With this ratio the girls had the pick of the bunch. Although Jack was good looking and had a pleasant enough personality, the competition was simply too intense and he was left at the starting gate by boys who were either more sporty, cleverer or more experienced at chatting up girls.

The girls had gained entry based on their GCSE results and were meant to be intelligent. Somehow Caroline Curbishly got in despite being stupid, an attribute exposed beyond doubt during the first few lessons. Her father was exceedingly rich and the rumour going around was that he had promised to fund a theatre auditorium if she was given a place.

Teachers adopted deep sarcasm in dealing with Caroline.

'Miss Curbishly, since this is a Spanish lesson, could you explain why you are answering in French?'

'Miss Curbishly, have you read the book or was your essay merely based on the film?'

'Miss Curbishly, are you only taking Psychology to enable you to carry out self-analysis?'

Caroline seemed oblivious to the abuse which classmates were increasingly prone to imitate.

One summer evening towards the end of the school year, Jack found himself walking by her side into dinner. Until then, he'd hardly acknowledged her.

She looked across with a nod which he returned. 'I fucking hate this place,' were her first words. 'Everybody thinks I'm a retard but actually they're the ones who are, for toeing the line. The creeps.'

They sat together at dinner exchanging no more than a word or two in front of his friends, but left together as an unspoken arrangement, Jack curious to find out more about the girl. As they walked Jack concluded that she was anything but stupid. She hadn't wanted to change schools, she didn't want to do A-levels, and she was utterly pissed off being in the shadow of her super brainy elder sister. Her parents' favouritism was one of a host of other issues that had resulted in her hating her father and mega loathing her mother.

'As soon as I get the chance,' she told Jack, 'I'm off to California to be an artist.'

They sat on the lawn in a remote part of the school grounds, chatting away with the conversation turning to Jack. He spoke of the pressure his father had put on him to follow in the family tradition – going to Oxford to study Classics ahead of working in the City. He was expected to behave like his younger brother Seb, which he assured Caroline, was even worse than pressure to be like an older sibling. As he spoke he realised he was articulating such thoughts for the first time, they'd been unspoken at the back of his mind for ages.

He told Caroline about his own interest in art, but unlike her, he had no talent for it.

'I bet you would be good at it if you were given the chance. As my tosspot father would say,' at this point Caroline's voice became deep and gravelly, '"You are at one of the best schools in the country. You aren't there to paint, you did enough of that at prep school."'

She looked across at Jack who was smiling.

'Should we have sex?' she enquired, right out of the blue with a could-you-pass-the-salt-and-pepper-please tone of voice.

They did so, there and then, and it was apparent even to virgin Jack, that it wasn't a first for Caroline.

With the end of the academic year arriving, their nascent relationship was put on hold, to be revived as soon as they returned to school. It continued during the whole of the upper sixth year, a term-time only affair given the distance between their two homes.

The possibility that Jack would be going to Oxford was short-lived. It soon became clear that the old boy network no longer held sway, even for a family providing funding for an endowed professorship. Jack wasn't called for interview and he failed miserably to get the grades required even for his league division two university offer. It was third division or nothing for him.

Meanwhile, Caroline dropped Psychology and took up Art, this done without telling her parents. She put together a portfolio that Jack thought was fantastic, a view clearly shared by admissions tutors. She had the pick of the art colleges and opted for Glasgow, her decision based on this one being the furthest from the family home on the south coast.

The day results came out Caroline phoned Jack to see how he'd got on and he told her his awful news.

'I'm sorry you didn't get the grades you needed but listen, I've been thinking. It makes sense for us to split now that I'm off to Glasgow. I can't promise I won't get another boyfriend up there and it would be simply awful having to lie to you.'

Her three-sentence termination of their year together was followed by a jolly enough 'Good luck' and that was that. This experience, admittedly limited, had made Jack wary of girls abruptly ending relationships. Was this the norm?

~

A preliminary judgement of the relationship with Jill is that this might be different. The reason for this belief is that she has suggested that they meet each other's families. Why say this if a breakup is imminent? Having checked dates with his parents, he invites Jill to his home. Meeting his mother and father poses huge risks but that's one for the future.

4

They leave campus midday, Jack obsessing about having to get a move on to beat the Friday afternoon build-up of traffic. 'We live in a tourist hotspot, it's always jam-packed,' he informs her as he strides towards his car, Jill all but running to keep up with him.

'Even in late October? You do realise I've had to skip a seminar.'

'Sorry about that, but yes, it's always busy.'

His Mini Cooper is parked on the far perimeter of the campus. Jill has been in the car twice, one short trip to the nearest off licence when the university supermarket was closed, and the second time to the town centre and back for dinner. He'd drunk more than was sensible or legal for a driver.

The car has cream leather bucket seats and a dashboard with controls that wouldn't be out of place in an aircraft cockpit. 'Everything's controlled by the press of a button,' he tells her as he sets the temperature on a digital display.

'Not the steering,' she says, removing his roaming hand from her thigh.

He drives too fast for her liking, racing down the outside lane of the motorway, frequently little more than a car

35

distance from the vehicle in front. When they turn onto a single lane road, Jill considers his driving to be reckless as he shoots past cars, darting back in as oncoming drivers hoot and flash their lights. After two and a bit hours of high tension he enters a winding country lane, smacking into low hanging branches at high speed, seemingly oblivious to the possibility of cars approaching from the opposite direction.

Jill has had enough. 'For God's sake, slow down will you?' she urges as a tree branch snaps against her side of the windscreen with a thud loud enough to make her duck.

'I'll get someone to cut down all this overhang.'

'Who on earth do you think is going to do that for you?'

'One of the gardeners. It's our land on that side.'

'All of it?'

'Pretty well.'

'The way you're driving I doubt whether we'll reach your house. We're bound to hit a car head on.'

'Not much chance of that, the road's virtually private. Didn't you see the no through road sign back there?'

'I did, but that doesn't make it *your* road.'

'Actually it does,' Jack says as they swing into a narrow tree-lined gravel drive. They round a bend and Jill gasps as she catches sight of a four-storey Georgian mansion, reminiscent of those used in films of Jane Austen novels.

'Like it?'

'Jesus, is this yours?'

'Yes. Well, the family's, though as the eldest son I suppose eventually it will be mine.'

'I knew you were rich, public school and all, but not this rich.'

They park, get out and take their backpacks from the surprisingly large boot for a car named Mini. Jill lifts the flowers she has bought from the back seat. They approach a huge bottle green front door flanked by impressive columns. Jill studied Classical Civilisation at school – these are textbook Ionic with fluted sides and elaborate scroll-shaped tops, called "volutes" she is pleased to recall. She touches the left column, stroking it with affection, enjoying the roughness against her smooth palm.

'Cool aren't they. They're Ionic,' Jack tells her.

'Oh, really?'

Jack places his hand on the polished brass knocker just as the door is opened by a woman who, Jill reckons, fits the phrase "mutton dressed up as lamb" to a tee. She is caked in make-up including a Panda bear layer of black around her eyes and harlot-scarlet lipstick that has smudged beyond her mouth. Her silk blouse reveals considerable cleavage, some sort of wonder bra uplifting her breasts.

'Darling,' the woman exclaims, ignoring Jill as she hugs Jack and deposits a kiss on his cheek, leaving a red imprint.

'Mamma, what a joy to see you,' Jack responds, using an accent and indeed terminology not evident at university.

'And you must be Gillian,' the woman says with a fake smile.

Jill hates being called Gillian, her name is Jill.

Mrs Ashley-Lovett steps back to inspect his son's girlfriend. 'I can never comprehend why girls wear tops that don't reach their trousers these days. Don't you feel the cold on your belly, my dear?'

'I'm fine, we've been in the car with the heater on. I do have a jacket with me for later.'

'And that piercing, it must have been ever so painful to have done, all in the name of fashion.'

Jill's been brought up in a New Labour household, not out and out socialists, but defiantly resentful of snobbery and the flaunting of class. She's naturally polite but has taken an instant dislike to this woman and a bolshie button has been pushed.

She feigns downmarketness. 'Misses Ashett-Lovely, I'm honoured to be 'ere, Jacko's told me bucket loads about yer,' she Eliza Doolittles. Jill has starred in amateur dramatics at college and is gifted at reproducing accents.

'Actually we are Ashley-Lovett.'

'And actually I'm Jill. It ain't no abbreviation, it's me proper name. Oh and I've brought yer these,' she adds. Suddenly concerned about creating an awkward situation for Jack, she passes over the bouquet of lilies with her sweetest of smiles.

'Absolutely lovely, my dear,' Mrs Ashley-Lovett exudes with barely a glance before placing the bouquet on the table to her side. 'I'll get Mary to put them in a vase. Now, no doubt you'll want to freshen up and get changed for dinner. I'll get Mary to show Gillia…Jill her room.'

'No need, Mamma, I'll show her.'

'Very well. We've put her in the green room. Come to the library for six. I'm afraid Father won't be joining us, he's had to stay overnight in London.'

Jack lifts up his backpack and Jill does likewise. She follows him towards a staircase wide enough to house three Mini Coopers.

'What's with the accent, Jill?' Jack asks as soon as they are out of earshot.

38

'Likewise Jack. *Mamma*.'

'Oh, it keeps her happy. I'm still her little boy really, I play up to it for an easy life.'

'Now that you've left home, don't you think it might be time for her to see the real you?'

Jack nods in agreement as they proceed down a long corridor lined with paintings of bucolic scenes.

Jill stops abruptly. 'Is that…isn't that a Constable?'

'We're not that rich. I think it was painted around the same period though.' They carry on walking. 'I suppose you're right about Mamma, my mother. She lives in a bit of a dream world, I'm afraid. I feel sorry for her, for a start she knows full well that my father being in London means he's spending the night with his mistress.'

'That's terrible.'

'I agree, though I can't see what I can do to help.'

'Tell your father his behaviour is unacceptable?'

They stop having reached the end of the corridor.

'Here we are – the green room,' Jack announces as he opens the door, revealing a room with, not surprisingly, green wallpaper, a William Morris print which Jill rather likes. The top end of the bed is piled high with brightly coloured silk cushions. The furniture, a wardrobe, chest of drawers, dressing table and two bedside cabinets, are dark wood, as is the floor.

'Like it?' Jack enquires.

'Yes, lovely.' There is no sarcasm in her reply, the room is tastefully decorated and has a nice feel to it.

'It's about the furthest room from mine which I'm sure is a deliberate tactic, but we can sort that out when everyone else is asleep.'

'Can I see yours?'

'Sure, follow me.'

They walk back along the corridor, Jill once again pausing to inspect paintings. They pass the staircase and end up at the furthest room on the opposite wing. The last vestiges of autumn sunshine are filtering through the sash window in Jack's room which is kitted out for a schoolboy rather than a young man, right down to the model aircraft suspended from the ceiling.

'My bed's bigger than yours so let's sleep here tonight. Mother's relocated her bedroom to the ground floor so we won't have to worry about getting interrupted.'

'You are an adult, Jack, surely sleeping with your girlfriend is acceptable? Especially a sexy one like me,' Jill adds as she puts her arms around Jack's waist and pulls him tightly against her. They kiss.

Jack is the one who pulls away. 'We'd better get ready for drinks in the library, let me take you back to your room.'

'No need for that, it's just straight ahead for a couple of miles.'

She's already by the door when Jack calls out. 'Thanks, Jill.'

'What for?'

'For coming home with me and putting up with my family.'

'Families – they're all the same.'

That isn't the case she thinks as she heads back to her room. There's no way her mother would treat Jack the way she's been spoken to.

Having been instructed to freshen up and get changed, she considers the options. The former is easy enough; her room isn't en suite, but Jack has pointed out the bathroom directly across the corridor. Changing is more of a challenge. She travelled in jeans and a T-shirt and all she's brought with her are two spare tops, a cardigan, a pair of just-in-case pyjamas, and some sexy underwear as a surprise for Jack. She takes a shower in an art deco bathroom with stunning black and white décor. The towels are super soft, a pile has been stacked on a stool and it crosses her mind to pinch one for use at university. Back in her room she puts on her uncomfortable skimpy underwear, jeans and a clean top. She sits on the bed reading a novel as she waits for Jack to fetch her. At six fifteen there's still no sign of him so she makes her way downstairs.

She meets the maid standing at the foot of the staircase. She'd wondered whether Mary would be a Mrs Danvers lookalike, hopefully without the malice, but she turns out to be young and pretty.

'Good evening, madam. I'm Mary. I'm to show you to the library. Will you be wanting me to prepare your room before bed this evening?'

'What do you mean by prepare?'

'Pull back the covers, tidy it if need be.'

Jill struggles not to laugh, this house is an *Upstairs, Downstairs* parody. She adopts her Eliza Doolittle accent. 'No fanks, Mary, I fink I can do it all meself.'

Mary looks confused and Jill feels guilty directing her sarcasm at the girl.

Jack and his mother are sitting close together in the library, Jack not responding to Jill's "Why the fuck didn't you come and get me" look. He is wearing a suit and tie, which generates a "Why the fuck didn't you tell me I needed to bring smart clothes" look. It is a vast room with ornate cornices and high ceilings. Shelves run the full length of one wall, filled with leather bound books apart from a small area of paperbacks.

A wafer thin, long-haired boy leaps up from a cavernous armchair. 'Hello, I'm Seb, Jack's brother,' he says with an unexpectedly deep voice. They shake hands.

'Hi, Seb, Jack's told me all about you,' Jill says, a lie as Jack has never spoken about his family. 'Nice to meet ya,' she adds for good measure, to preserve her pretend accent.

'I see you've decided not to get changed, my dear,' Mrs Ashley-Lovett observes, clearly intended as a dig.

Us poor gals we ain't got no smart togs is the first thing that comes to mind, but no, enough of that game, Jill decides to cease the play acting.

'Well, this is a clean T-shirt, but your dear son failed to mention I needed to bring something smarter.'

'We do like to dress for dinner, he really should have told you.'

'That's what I thought.'

'Consideration for others never has been his strong point.'

'I wouldn't go as far as that.'

'Well of course you haven't known him as long as I have.'

Confident, often mouthy Jack is sitting there like a sheepish little infant as they speak about him.

'No need to fret about dress code, I'll call for drinks,' Mrs Ashley-Lovett continues.

Jill gasps because yes, there really is a pulley cord by her side, which Jack's mother yanks once, and within half a

42

minute or so an elderly man shuffles in. He's wearing a tailored black jacket with a thin pinstripe and Jill is sure he gives a half bow as he approaches. 'Drink for you, madam?'

Jill is so preoccupied with gawping she fails to realise that the question is directed at her.

'Madam, may I ask what you would care to drink?'

She would be happy with a glass of any wine, but assumes they expect her to suggest Domaine Cote de St Something or Other 1966. If she'd still been in a taking the piss mood, she would have made up a convoluted name. She settles on 'Let the others choose, I'll take what's going.'

'We'll have a bottle of the red we had last night,' Mrs Ashley-Lovett requests, followed by an order for the man to light the fire after he's brought the drinks.

This elderly man is their manservant or butler or valet, and Jill is struggling to come to terms with that. It's like being in an early twentieth-century time warp, a hundred-year difference between this experience and the real world.

There follows conversation that resembles an interview, covering the degree Jill is taking, which school she went to and where her family live. When she owns up to Islington there's a gasp as Mrs Ashley-Lovett comes to terms with the pronouncement. This gives Seb the opportunity to take over. What A-levels did Jill do, what is her favourite film and which bands does she like? All this time Jack remains silent, switching his gaze between interviewer and respondent.

The elderly man returns with a tray and adds a drop of wine into Jack's glass. Jack swishes, sniffs and tastes ahead

43

of allowing the butler to pour. Jill takes a substantial gulp and is about to set the glass down on the table by her side.

'Stop!'

This outcry from Mrs Ashley-Lovett gives her such a fright that the wine shoots up out of the glass then down onto her clothes.

'It's mahogany, you need a coaster,' Mrs Ashley-Lovett explains. She yanks the cord twice and within seconds Mary appears. 'Gillian has had an accident, could you take her upstairs and find something for her to change into? Perhaps from the bag I've put together to give to charity.'

~

Five or so minutes later, Jill is back downstairs in a shapeless long beige dress with a high neckline. There are folds of material around her bust, waist and hips, to be expected when wearing something two or more sizes too big.

'Welcome back, my dear,' is Mrs Ashley-Lovett's jolly greeting, 'That's better, you look lovely. Doesn't she Jack?'

'She is lovely, but what she's wearing isn't.'

'At least she's now dressed suitably for dinner.'

Jill is livid. She isn't going to take it, she goes on the attack. 'I don't know your first name, Mrs Ashett-Lovely. Pray tell.'

'Sabrina.'

'How quaint. May I call you Sab, then it can be Sab and Seb.'

'I would prefer you to use my full name.'

'Pity, it has a nice ring to it, like Starsky and Hutch or Pinky and Perky. Anyway, thank you for lending me this wonderful dress, you must have once looked stunning in it

44

though I can see why it's going to Oxfam now. Mary's kindly offered to wash my jeans tonight. They're all I've brought because us poor students, we can't afford loads of clothes. Luckily it's only wine to wash off, not like a couple of weeks ago when we were knocking back Baileys which stains like fuck. I doubt whether Jack remembers anything about that night though, he was so drunk he had to be carried home.'

Seb laughs raucously. Jack seems detached from the proceedings.

The manservant reappears and announces dinner is served. They are led into a room that makes the library seem like a cupboard, admittedly a large one, but this room is vast. In the centre, under an elaborate chandelier with cascades of cut glass beads, is a beautifully inlaid mahogany table. They are seated at the far corner which has been laid out with napkins, lines of cutlery and several glasses, fit for a banquet.

During the meal Jack perks up a bit, describing his degree course with enthusiasm, a complete fabrication because he is more disengaged than anyone Jill knows at university. She describes her own studies and there follows at last some rapport with Sabrina who, it turns out, has an interest in and it seems a good knowledge of English Literature.

Dinner is asparagus, venison and crème brulee, each course accompanied by a different wine which Jack is asked to judge for suitability, in contrast to at university where he simply opens the first bottle he can lay his hands on and glugs.

Somewhat unsteadily they return to the library, the coal fire still blazing. For an instant the cosy ambiance tempts Jill to stay put, but no, enough is enough. She announces the need to go to her room, claiming she has her *The Portrait of a Lady* essay to finish.

Jack escorts her to the staircase. 'I'd better stay put for a while, but come to my bedroom at eleven. Everyone else will be in bed by then.'

'You've been so distant, is everything all right?'

'I'm embarrassed by the whole situation. Coming home is strange, it's so different to what I've got used to over the last few weeks.'

'You go back down.' Jill kisses him. 'I'll see you later.'

She lies on her bed and reads. She must have dozed because it is approaching eleven when she next looks at her watch. She's drunk too much and considers abandoning Jack and sleeping. However, the attraction of being in a full-sized bed with him is strong, and it would provide a two fingers up act of defiance against Queen Sab.

She gets into her pyjamas and sets off, her head fuzzy from the alcohol. It's pitch black and eerily silent, but all she has to do is keep going until she reaches the far end of the corridor. She smiles, it's like being a naughty pubescent pupil on a school trip.

She pushes open the door and hears light breathing ahead of catching sight of the bed, weakly illuminated by a shaft of moonlight.

She takes off her pyjamas and climbs in, no messing about, going straight for Jack's penis. He jolts then keeps perfectly still apart from the bit of him that is growing as she rubs. If size is anything to go by, he is more turned on than he's ever been at university, the weirdo.

'Nice?'

'Mmm.'

'Come on, you are allowed to touch me.'

His hand dives between Jill's legs and he starts to rub, fast and furious.

'Hey, slow down, will you?'

She moves closer to kiss him, lifting up her spare hand to stroke his hair, he likes that. She's confused. The hair is long, thick. Jack's hair is short, not thick.

'Jack?'

There is no response other than the still growing erection. Perplexed, she proceeds to kiss him. Her tongue brushes against metal, there is a brace across the lower teeth.

Is this a drunken dream? 'Jack?'

'Seb.'

'What!'

Jill lets go of him and springs up. 'Why didn't you say?'

The light on the bedside table is switched on and Seb is sitting up too, looking at her breasts when he should be looking at her face.

'I was enjoying it.'

'But you knew I'd got into the wrong bed.'

'I wasn't certain, strange things can happen when it comes to sex, can't they?'

'Not this strange, well not with me anyway.'

'Now that you're here, would you stay?'

'Of course not.'

'Just to touch me a bit.'

'Absolutely not.'

'You're turned on, look, your nipples are hard.'

'How do you know about nipples getting hard?' Jill asks, glancing to the floor to locate her top. 'You're only a child.'

'I'm not an idiot.'

'How old are you?'

'Fifteen.'

'Bloody hell. I was in danger of having underage sex. I could have gone to prison.'

'I wouldn't have told. Please stay.'

'Absolutely not,' Jill says as she stands. She grabs her pyjamas, puts them on and heads towards the door.

'You're ever so pretty,' Seb calls out as she closes the door behind her.

Jill stands in the corridor for a while, trying to work out what had gone wrong. Her head is still fuzzy though the recent shock has restored a degree of sobriety. Having reached the end of the corridor, she must have entered the room on the opposite side to Jack's. Now she has no desire to be with her boyfriend, she's had enough adventure for the night, and heads back along the corridor.

~

Jill is woken by a knock on her door. Jack enters and swishes the curtains open.

'And where were you last night?' he asks.

'With your brother.'

'Very funny. Seriously, what happened?'

'I was tired and wasted so I just came up and slept. I'm wide awake now though,' she says, unbuttoning her pyjama top.

'No time, we mustn't be late for breakfast.'

'Surely we don't have to eat with the others,' Jill says as she removes her top.

'We do. It's cooked just the once to fit in with the staff's duties.'

'Jesus, Jack, you're posh beyond belief. Is fitting in with staff a higher priority than sex with me?'

'We'll be off tomorrow morning then it'll be back to normal.'

'But isn't being here your normal?'

'It was, but being with you is what matters to me now.'

Jack sidles up to Jill but she edges away and starts to dress. 'Go on, breakfast calls. You head down and I'll join you in five minutes.'

The dining room is laid out as grandly as the previous evening with the addition of a line of silver terrines resting on the sideboard. Jill is greeted by Mrs Ashley-Lovett, Jack and Seb. They already have plates in hand and as soon as she has collected one, they proceed to lift lids to release an aroma of oozing fat as they help themselves to lashings of food. Jill follows, rejecting the kidneys, kippers, black pudding and bacon on offer.

'Aren't you hungry, dear?' Mrs Ashley-Lovett asks.

'Do you have any muesli? And fresh fruit?'

The aged servant is standing by the coffee pot. He offers to see what cook can provide, returning a couple of minutes later with porridge and a banana.

Once seated, Seb avoids eye contact, Jack remains silent, and it is left to Mrs Ashley-Lovett and Jill to carry the conversation. Something odd has happened, they are beginning to communicate having discovered the common interest in literature. Jill appreciates the woman's knowledge and their shared favourites. Not just the classics, but also all the twentieth century stuff that Jill loves. Angela Carter, Margaret Attwood, Philip Roth and surprise of all surprises, Jack Kerouac.

'You didn't!'

'I certainly did.'

'You named your Jack after Kerouac!'

'Yes, dear.'

'And Seb?'

'Sebastian Barry, do you know his works?'

'His poetry, yes, of course. I love it.'

'It wasn't just poetry, you should read his plays and novels, too. There's a family connection, it goes back to when Jack's grandfather was stationed in Ireland in the army.'

The conversation continues in the library where Jill is shown first editions through the ages, some signed. Merely touching the books is exciting. Jack is hovering restlessly so with reluctance Jill accepts his invitation to go for a walk to see the grounds.

It is a crisp frosty morning with a bright blue sky. Jill enjoys treading on the crunchy carpet of brown, orange and golden leaves, holding hands, prising out details of Jack's past. Until that point, their time together had centred on sex, drink and parties. Jill thinks this conversation is taking their relationship to a new level.

'Love you, Jack,' she says as they approach the house.

Jack stops and looks across to Jill. For a short while he appears lost for words then he beams his lovable smile. 'You are my only reason for staying on at university. I love you more than you can possibly imagine.'

A passionate embrace is on the cards, but instead there's the scrunch of a car travelling at speed along the gravel, a skid to a halt, and a Morse Code beeping of a horn. It doesn't take a high level of intuition for Jill to realise that Jack's father has arrived. With difficulty, the man is edging out of his red Porsche – fat middle-aged men should not drive sports cars. He shuffles across with arms outstretched, ignoring Jack and making straight for Jill. He bear hugs her, his hands dropping down to rest on her bottom which receives a fondle. She's enraged and pushes him away with enough force to make him stumble.

Throughout that afternoon and evening, Jill's first impression is confirmed, the man is obnoxious. It is evident that Jack doesn't like him and Sabrina doesn't like him either. Jill becomes a temporary teetotaller to counter Mr Ashley-Lovett's massive consumption of alcohol – whisky in the library, sherry before dinner, wine with each course (admittedly they'd done likewise the previous evening), dessert wine with cigar after dinner, and then back to whisky.

Sex with Jack that night is a much needed release, a blissful reminder of her love for him. She can sense Jack's tension oozing away as they caress. During this lovemaking she catches sight of the bedroom door opening a touch and fears the detestable Mr Ashley-Lovett is about to storm in. No one enters, it's the wind playing tricks in the draughty old house. No, it's a face by the door, Seb is peeping. She's far too much in a state of ecstasy to protest.

The next day, during breakfast, Jack announces that he has to set off early due to a huge work commitment. Jack and work commitment do not sit comfortably together, but clearly he is every bit as keen as Jill to flee.

5

Standing by the front door, Sabrina Ashley-Lovett waves them off. She pulls from her cuff a handkerchief embroidered with a flower and the letters S A L and wipes away an unwanted tear. She hates herself. What an awful thing to think, but it's quite true. Why on earth has she play acted the mean spirited lady of the manor in front of Jill? Why did she want the girl to dislike her? This Jill is a breath of fresh air, articulate, free-spirited and a wonderful mix of self-confidence and modesty. The very qualities she would like to possess. Perhaps she did once, long ago. And theirin lies the problem, she's jealous, the years of intense unhappiness have made her bitter and resentful of those who might have some joy in their lives.

The Ashley-Lovett name, the mansion and the estate, the servants, the possessions, all result from a marriage to a man she now has nothing in common with beyond an intense mutual hatred.

Lately she's been doing a lot of reminiscing, rueing the choices she's made. She must have been about Jill's age when she fled her sleepy Yorkshire village home to follow her dream of becoming an actress. She had talent, at least that was what she'd been told, but the competition in

London was ruthless. With little money and few contacts, she was betrayed time and time again by casting directors who promised her parts only if she slept with them. What an idiot she'd been to go on believing despite the countless broken promises. She ended up with minor roles in dull regional playhouses rather than in the West End.

Sabrina thinks back to possibly her most successful role, acclaimed by reviewers, and this brings on a rare smile – it was the very same Eliza Doolittle that Jill had impersonated so well. She watches Jack's car turn the corner and then it's out of sight. There had been no return wave from Jack or Jill, and of course the way she'd behaved, why should there be.

How lucky they were to have such youthful optimism. Hers died long ago and she remembers the exact moment when it did. It was during a bleak March in Skegness when she had a chorus role in *Oklahoma*. Standing in the wings dressed up as an early twentieth-century cowgirl, she was watching Curly sing *Oh, what a beautiful mornin'* with a poor attempt at a Midwest accent.

Now, as she closes her front door, she breaks into song: 'Oh NOT such a beautiful morning, Oh NOT such a beautiful day – NOT! NOT! NOT!'

Mary comes running out the kitchen. 'Is everything alright, Madam?'

'Yes thank you, Mary, I'm just being playful.'

The girl frowns, nods, and returns to her duties.

Back then, in Skegness during the very first scene with Curly belting out *Ev'rything's goin' my way*, she realised it wasn't and never would be going her way. That was that. She walked off the set, went back to her digs, packed her bags and headed out of the inappropriately named Sunny Skegness. More like Pissing Down Constantly with Gale Force Winds Skegness.

Perhaps she should have returned home there and then, but what was there to go back to? Employment at the local jam factory or the petrol station with the pretend French café by its side? She stayed in London and when a similarly redundant actress suggested escorting, she agreed to see her friend dance at a Soho strip joint one evening. She hated the place, she hated watching her friend slink off with one of the punters, her wan smile as she left oozing discomfort.

There followed a sleepless night. Go back home or copy her friend? In the morning she met the revolting manager with the pockmarked face. He expected favours like the casting directors before him. The job was hers.

Sabrina remains by the door lost in thought, Jack's car long gone. She shivers, the vestibule is always draughty. Returning to the library, the fire is burning ferociously. She pulls her favourite armchair close to it, savouring the warmth as she sinks down.

Whenever she thinks back, the month or so working at the club is hazy, blanked out to escape memories of the beyond belief depravity of some of the customers. But one night does remain as clear in her mind as if it were yesterday. Four rowdy young men at the Soho club asked her to join them at their table after she'd finished dancing. She was ignored while they shared experiences of working life in the City. It became evident they were holding a public school friends reunion when they began reminiscing about schoolmates, teachers and pranks. As the alcohol kicked in they took to fondling her, not a word spoken. They laughed when she protested and laughed louder as she stormed off.

To this very day, Sabrina can feel the anguish she suffered sitting in that tacky changing room with its sickly smell of cheap perfume and body odour, her dreams vanished, the jam factory in Yorkshire her destiny because she was not going to continue to be humiliated.

The club owner had pounded on the locked door, but she refused to let him in.

'That's it then, you're fired,' he yelled. 'And don't expect to get work at any other place round 'ere.'

Sabrina, now pleasantly warm, is looking at the untidy pile of books on the table that Jill had taken from the shelves, the choices near identical to her own favourites. She lifts up Flaubert's *Madame Bovary* and rests it against her cheek. She kisses the picture of the feisty independent woman depicted on the front cover before setting it back down.

She used to be called feisty, that was before she made her biggest mistake that fateful evening.

She had stepped out onto the dimly lit narrow street behind the club. The beauty of the late June evening – mild, still with a touch of twilight, the buzz of Central London on a Saturday night, the bright lights, the crowds – all this passed her by. Despondency descended as she contemplated the return to her Yorkshire birthplace where a stray fox would provide the most exciting action on the late evening high street.

She heard him before she saw him, a meek 'Excuse me.'

It was one of the awful men at the club. 'Get lost, will you.'

'Please, I would like to apologise.'

'Go away!'

Henry pursued her. 'Pray stop, I urge you to give me a few seconds of your time.'

She knows now that she should have run a mile, but instead she smiled at his posh voice and the words he used. She slowed and faced him. 'A few seconds is all you get. Starting now.'

'I…how many seconds?'

'Not many and you're wasting them.'

'I…I'm…look you see…you see we've not met up for ages, not that that's an excuse, but…'

'Time's up.'

'Surely not.'

'You've not said anything of value.'

'Well, I would like to most humbly apologise for our rudeness and effrontery and for all the discomfort our behaviour must have caused you.'

Sabrina's smile turned to laughter, the first time she'd laughed for a long time. 'If you are genuine, which I doubt, can't you simply say sorry?'

Sabrina hasn't noticed Mary enter the library. 'Sorry for what, Madam?' the maid enquires.

'Goodness, I must have been thinking aloud, just ignore me.'

'Are you ready for coffee to be served?'

'Not yet, thank you. I'll let you know when.'

Mary gives a little curtsy before leaving and Sabrina thinks for the umpteenth time how absurd it is to have someone at her beck and call to make coffee. She hardly ever goes into the kitchen, Henry insisting that's servant territory.

He did say sorry that evening and she remembers thinking he was quite sweet as she watched his clumsy fidgeting, unable to keep his hands still. At the club he'd not behaved as disgracefully as his companions so when he suggested the coffee bar close by, she agreed.

Once seated, Sabrina talked about her failure as an actress and Henry was a good listener. It was a short taxi ride to The Ritz where she spent the night with him, more to see what luxury looked like than wanting this man's company. She'd expected instant dismissal in the morning but to her surprise, while they were eating a scrumptious full English breakfast, he asked if she would like to spend the rest of the day with him.

They strolled round the sites of Central London, stopping at the British Museum to visit an Anglo-Saxon exhibition. They wandered down New Bond Street en route back to Henry's hotel. Being a Sunday, shops were closed. Henry patiently watched as Sabrina gazed at the grand window displays. As they walked on he explained that he had a flat in Chelsea to return to once he'd collected his bag, the stay at The Ritz having been for a single weekend with his friends.

'Where do you live?' he asked as they stood in the hotel lobby.

'Harlesden,' she replied with some degree of embarrassment.

'Take a taxi home, will you,' he said, lifting his wallet from his back pocket.

'No need, I can catch a bus.'

'Please get a taxi, it's safer than a bus.'

She was set to contest his view about safety in Harlesden when he continued. 'I want you to look after yourself this week. I'd like to see you again. No more work at that club and please, would you get the outfit you fell in love with.'

He handed over a bundle of banknotes and a business card with his name, address and telephone number on it. Henry Ashley-Lovett. On leaving the hotel he hailed a taxi and waived her off.

The outfit he referred to was a two-piece blue silk costume. It had been the sole garment displayed in an exclusive boutique window and cost over £50. The notes in her handbag were twenties, enough to cover the purchase, a meal at a top restaurant every evening if she so wanted, and considerably more.

Sabrina pulls the cord to summon Mary. It's time for a coffee. She looks down at the *Madame Bovary* cover. What would that character have done in her situation? Probably not what was already under consideration in the taxi that afternoon, give up futilely striving to be an actress and instead pursue Henry's interest in her. She stayed at his Chelsea home the next Friday evening and most weekends thereafter. On Sunday afternoons as she was about to leave, he gave her exceedingly generous sums of money to pay for clothes, food and something he regarded as a London necessity – taxis.

'Buses never turn up, the tube is filthy, and both are dangerous,' was his repeated mantra when she questioned the need. The giving grew increasingly lavish: expensive jewellery, visits to the theatre, opera and concerts and trips abroad. During a rollercoaster Easter she saw the Eiffel Tower one weekend and the Colosseum the next.

Five months after their first encounter and with Henry down on one knee, she opened the box he'd handed her. There was a huge diamond on the silver band. Having accepted his proposal, he suggested a visit to his family home to break the news in person.

'They'll love you,' she was told.

Of course they didn't, they made her feel thoroughly uncomfortable and unwanted, all too similar to how she'd behaved on meeting Jill. Sabrina had a toughness back then and played a game of not noticing their disapproval. This pretence continued as she acted the perfect bride during the wedding ceremony and reception, but as soon as that day had passed she had as little contact as possible with his loathsome family. By the time Jack was born, Henry's father had been murdered while serving in Northern Ireland and his mother was in a rehab clinic for alcoholics. Good riddance to both of them. By the time she was pregnant with Seb, Henry had inherited the family home, their home.

Now the Madam Bovary on the book cover is looking up at her. "OK (did people say OK in the nineteenth century?) you made a mistake marrying him, but you didn't have to stay." Bovary's imagined question is spot on because it didn't take long for the real Henry to be found out. He was a selfish, greedy, lecherous man who thought it perfectly reasonable to have a wife at home while embarking on affairs in London. At first Sabrina had been dismayed, but grew to tolerate the situation, sucked in by the pull of so much wealth. By following the news about Lady Diana right up to the tragic end, she believed it was par for the course for rich and powerful men to treat their women abysmally.

Sabrina turns the book to its back cover. She's unusually twitchy this morning as she sits by the fireside, unable to do anything other than look back with regret. Jill has sparked something in her, something counter to the indifference that has become her norm. She admires Jill's self-confidence and vibrancy, her strength of character to address the nastiness front on, just as she had once done. Not any more though, in its place a cowardly acceptance of the status quo. She wants to be like Jill. Their encounter has triggered the notion of escape from the husband she loathes. Poor Jill because she fears that Jack is as uncaring as his father. Seb though, he's different, such a sensitive and considerate soul, still her little boy.

At that very same moment, Seb is in his room masturbating as he fantasises about Jill. He is imagining her stroking him, not stopping as she'd done the night before last, rubbing him harder and harder as his face rests on those gorgeous breasts. This climax is less intense than the one last night when he'd stood by Jack's bedroom door watching them do it.

As he mops up with tissues, he plots how he can get to see Jill again and soon. There might be a Christmas holiday visit, but he doesn't want to wait that long. He'll invite himself to see Jack at the so-called university; his thicko brother could only get into an ex-polytechnic. If he sleeps in Jack's bedroom, might there be the possibility of the two brothers sharing Jill? Things like that did happen, in fact Jack has told him stories about escapades at school when sixth form girls offered themselves to groups of boys. He

61

can't wait until he's in the sixth form, only a few months to go. Jack isn't good enough for Jill and if the opportunity arises, he'll have a heart-to-heart with her, pointing out his brother's many deficiencies. Jill could well ditch Jack for him, bearing in mind that she had shown some passion when in his bed if nipple erection is anything to go by.

And also at that very same moment, Henry is sitting on the edge of the bed, phone in hand. Sabrina now sleeps in a downstairs room so he has sole possession of the vast master bedroom. It has the best view of the grounds and he is admiring the magnificence of the autumn foliage as he speaks to Lucinda, his P.A. and lover of late. She's extremely attractive, but his thoughts are not entirely of her.

He picks up the gist of Lucinda's request and tries to placate her. 'I don't think I'll be able to make it back to London for dinner, darling, it's going to be difficult to get away early…I'll see what I can do, I just can't promise…You go to the restaurant and I'll try to join you there. Why not take that friend of yours?'

The friend, possibly called Tanya, is who is on his mind. She is gorgeous beyond belief, her voluminous breasts staggering considering such a thin frame. Her hair makes him think of Cleopatra – jet-black, straight, touching her shoulders, with a low fringe that reaches her eyebrows. It's possible that Cleopatra didn't have hair like that, but Liz Taylor certainly did in the film. Henry is desperate to see more of Tanya, if that is her name.

Lucinda is taking liberties and he isn't happy. 'If you must have a new handbag go ahead and buy it, you've got the credit card I gave you,' he tells her. 'I'll never understand how a bit of leather can cost over three hundred pounds though, you could probably buy a whole cow for that.' For an easy life he relents. 'But nothing else, please...yes, of course I didn't mean the meal when I said that.'

Lucinda has become a burden. She is, nevertheless, a stunning blond and fabulous in bed. Her work in the office is decidedly less fabulous, but her assistant covers for her. He's considering asking Lucinda how she'd feel about having her friend join them, he reckons she might well be game for it. The thought of having a blond one side of him and a raven-haired beauty the other is most appealing.

Sabrina calls out. 'Coffee, Henry?'

'I have to go, Lucinda, there's so much work to do on the estate and one of the men is waiting for me. I'll see you later.'

He replaces the phone and shouts down. 'Yes please, dear. I'm coming.'

They sit in the library as Mary serves the coffee, small-talking civilly enough about it being cold out, though no colder than one would expect for this time of the year; the autumn leaves are a delight, perhaps even finer than last year's showing, though perhaps not; the kippers that morning seemed smaller than usual, though perhaps not.

'What do you think of Jill?' Sabrina asks.

'Charming, Jack's a lucky lad don't you think?' he replies, thinking about her looks alone.

'She's very nice, but I let myself down. I was disagreeable.'

'I thought you were pleasant enough,' Henry says. 'After all, it was only the first meeting with her and we do need to make sure she isn't money-grabbing.'

'Like me?'

Henry doesn't want to engage in such dialogue, which inevitably ends up with Sabrina bitter. What he most requires is a compliant wife who manages the house and its staff and is willing, every so often, to organise a social event. Usually Sabrina plays the game, but sometimes she challenges the status quo. He can tell from her body language, leaning forward on the edge of the chair with a determined look, that today is threatening.

'Darling, I really must head back to London, I've work to do ahead of a meeting tomorrow morning.'

'I'm sure you have lots to do,' Sabrina says as her husband heads towards the door.

6

Back on campus after the visit to the Ashley-Lovetts, autumn has arrived with a vengeance. During the early weeks of term it had been unseasonably mild and students had sat on the grass reading, glancing up to admire the view of the city. Now the hilltop campus is a far less attractive site, shrouded in a damp mist and bleakly windswept.

The weather may have worsened, but Jack and Jill's love for each other has intensified and they spend as much of their free time as possible together. There is no shift in their attitude towards their studies – one of them inspired, the other indifferent or even antagonistic.

'You'll get into trouble with your no shows,' Jill says one Monday morning as she clings onto Jack to prevent falling off his narrow bed. His room is the venue of choice. The one time they'd spent the night in her room, the corridor girls had shown a little too much interest in Jack for Jill's liking, prancing around like models on a catwalk in their skimpy nightwear.

'My lectures are recorded so I don't have to go, I can watch them whenever,' Jack informs Jill.

This isn't a hundred percent accurate. Jack has never been online to check the validity of the statement, but had he done so, he would have discovered that for each lecture only a few key points are listed within a document.

Jill persists and he relents to her pressure, agreeing to take part in the ten o' clock seminar on marketing.

'Have we met?' the lecturer asks as Jack enters the room.

'I was present in Week 1.'

'How considerate, but why haven't you appeared since then?'

'I've not been well,' Jack explains, unaware that he is a regular topic of conversation during Faculty of Management staff meetings. Similar excuses to other lecturers have been checked and exposed as blatant lies.

'Ah yes, you must be Mr Ashley-Lovett.'

'That's right. I'm Jack.'

'I'm delighted you're feeling better, Mr Ashley-Lovett. As you will know, during my lecture yesterday – you were there, I assume.' Jack nods. 'I introduced the concept of the product life cycle. Perhaps you could start today's proceedings by reminding the class why the duration of the cycle varies.'

This is a challenge for Jack since he hadn't attended the lecture. He reckons there has to be a link between life cycles and life, so is clueless why something to do with Biology is featured in a Business Studies class. He remains speechless.

'Are you able to provide us with an answer?'

'No, I'm afraid it's gone right out my head.'

'Then let me take you through the process. Would you care to start by naming two products?'

'What, any two?'

'Yes, be my guest.'

Jack has sussed out this man. He's like one of those sarky teachers at school who set out to show him up. He sees no choice but to play the game. 'OK. Mini Cooper and – a Ted Baker suit.'

'Which would you expect to have the longer life cycle?'

Bearing in mind what appears to be the character of the questioner, this could well be a trick question, Jack reasons, but it's hard to see how the answer is anything other than the obvious. 'A car lasts for about three years whereas a suit goes out of fashion in a season. So it's got to be the Mini Cooper.'

Other members of the class adopt different degrees of smiling, sniggering and laughter. This, too, brings back memories of school.

'Cars last longer than three years,' a girl calls out.

'Maybe,' Jack replies, 'but you wouldn't want to go more than three years before getting a new model. For a start there's the prestige of the new number plate. Unless, of course, you've got a personalised one.'

'Like TOSSER 1,' another classmate calls out.

'More to the point, Mr Ashley-Lovett,' the lecturer intercedes, Jack feels with over-emphasis on his name, 'you haven't quite grasped the concept of life cycles. It's not related to a single unit, it's the longevity of the product *type*. Surely you understood that when I compared cornflakes to mobile phones during my lecture?'

Jack decides to nod emphatically.

'So you were at my lecture?'

Another vigorous nod.

'Then you'll know my conclusion.'

'I didn't quite catch it.'

There is widespread laughter.

'Even though I stressed, stressed twice, that this is the most important influence on corporate marketing strategy. Someone rescue Mr Ashley-Lovett please. Yes, Abdul.'

'A company can't wait until a product has reached its mature stage before having researched and developed new goods, they need a portfolio of items at different stages of the life cycle. By chance, my fellow student has given the correct answer. Ted Baker will need to be producing new fashion on a regular basis while the car would stay in the showroom for longer. But he has completely misunderstood the broader issue.'

'Well put, Abdul. Are you with us on that, Mr Ashley-Lovett?'

Jack is too busy thinking about foreigners coming to England to study at our universities, even foreigners with perfect English accents like this one. And why is he being addressed by his surname, unlike nerdy Abdul?

Meanwhile, Jill's seminar is an altogether different experience. The passion that she and her friends share for literature makes for exciting classes, their enthusiasm enhanced by the knowledge they've accumulated as avid readers ahead of going to university. Now into their eighth week, the lecturer can get a discussion going then sit back and admire the dialogue.

The American Literature module is taught by Harvey Crowe, a white-haired, furrow-faced professor who studied and taught at Harvard.

This session is covering the works of Raymond Chandler. The consensus view is that his novels are wonderful with Philip Marlowe the perfect detective.

'Unlike the texts we've covered in previous weeks, these novels sit firmly in the crime category. Is this a genre for the female reader?' Crowe asks.

'I think yes,' Jill replies. 'Why shouldn't it be? The plots are good and the style of writing is gripping for the female reader, for any reader.'

Other students join in the praise.

'For me, it's the blur between good and evil: Marlowe is no saint.'

'That's evident in the film extract you gave us to watch, that film noir trick of using shadow to capture the dark side of human nature is so clever.'

'And even though the main character is male, there's always an important female in the plot.'

'But usually a dangerous one, the femme fatale,' Crowe contributes.

Jill is buzzing by the end of the seminar. She meets Jack for an early lunch. 'Jack, I'm going to be sitting in your room watching films for hours and hours, there are so many I want to see. Chandler didn't only write novels, he also did screenplays for greats like *Double Indemnity*. He was a genius.'

'Yeah, OK. Big deal.'

'What's up with you?'

'Look, can we get away this weekend? You said you'd set up a visit to your parents.'

'Maybe, though I've got tons of reading to do. I suppose I could work for a bit while we're there.'

'Whatever.'

'Is everything alright, you're as dark as Philip Marlowe today?'

'Who's he?'

'I've just been telling you about him. Never mind, how was your seminar?'

'I'd rather not talk about it.'

'Don't be silly.'

'It was fine, thank you.'

Jill decides not to pursue the questioning. She tries a new tactic. 'Tell you what, come to the library with me for a couple of hours this afternoon then we can go into town so I can rent *Strangers on a Train* or *Lady in a Lake* from Blockbusters. They're bound to have one of them. We can stay out for a meal which I'll be paying for. And after that, we can watch the film, then who knows, it could be a night of lust.'

She takes hold of his hand and her smile lightens his mood. This, plus her plans for the evening and the offer of a weekend escape, is enough to tempt Jack to go to the library with Jill. They sit opposite each other in a booth with pine desk and chairs, enclosed on two sides by high bookshelves, all so functional compared to the alluring dusty chaos that he'd seen when visiting friends at Oxford colleges. With a book open but unread, he passes the time reflecting on what he's missing. He watches the rain form irregular patterns as it races down the large windowpanes. Jill is unable to do much, she's distracted by Jack's idleness.

They rent *Strangers on a Train* and watch it on the state of the art DVD player and portable TV in Jack's room.

'Great, great, great!' Jill declares as the titles roll. 'I wonder what we'd do in a similar situation, who we'd kill if we thought there'd be no chance of getting caught.'

'I'd arrange to get my father murdered,' Jack suggests.

Jack remains poker-faced as Jill laughs. 'You're not serious?'

'No, but I'd happily never see him again. I enjoyed that film, maybe I should be taking what you're studying.'

'It's not all about watching films, you'd have to read loads if you took English, which, let's face it, is not your strong point.'

'At least I'd be in the same class as you,' he says as they undress. Jill shivers, she loves his touch, the perfect balance between gentle and firm. He knows exactly what she likes – the sex is great.

When she rolls out of bed the next morning, Jack tells her he is staying put, he has no interest in Business Law. Jill doesn't attempt to persuade him otherwise and they agree to meet in the coffee bar at twelve.

~

As soon as they meet he hands over a letter. It's from his personal tutor, an official warning based on the widespread dissatisfaction with his work, or more to the point, lack of it. There's a second sheet listing all the classes he's missed that term. He is to be put on a six-week trial extending into the Christmas holidays and the start of the next term, during which time he's expected to complete all outstanding work. He's been summoned to a Monday morning meeting to discuss the proposal.

'Bloody hell, this is terrible. What are you going to do?'

'Maybe leave.'

'That's silly.'

'Or maybe do what they've asked. I've been in situations like this at school and made it through.'

'God Jack, university's meant to be a pleasure, not a burden.'

'I think I'm doing the wrong subject, but let's drop it for now. We're visiting your family this weekend, right?'

'Sure, that'll help you chill out.'

'That's hardly likely during a family visit.'

'It will. Remember, my lot are normal.'

~

The journey to Jill's home begins with a race down a motorway just like the start of the one to his house. Jill's nervous as Jack drives too close to the not quite as fast-moving vehicles ahead of him. Once they reach the outskirts of London the similarity to the journey to the Ashley-Lovetts ends. There are no gently rolling hills within which isolated farm buildings nestle; there are no broad expanses of woodland; there are no tiny villages traversed in a flash; no winding lanes; no mansion at the end. Instead, there's a bumper-to-bumper crawl and endless roundabouts and traffic lights to contend with as they pass through neighbourhoods with lacklustre lookalike houses. The parades of shops are run down with To Let signs in abundance. They journey through an industrial estate with squat windowless buildings and garish signage.

'You should live in the countryside,' Jack comments as a break in oncoming traffic allows them finally to pass a stationary lorry with its warning lights flashing.

'Nothing happens in the countryside,' Jill replies.

They come to a halt when the lights change by a pedestrian crossing. Jack restlessly taps his fingers on the steering wheel as a woman with pram saunters across the road, speaking on her mobile as she goes. By the time she's reached the other side, the pedestrian light has turned red and Jack sets off, drawing to a sharp halt as a cyclist shoots past on his outside then veers to the left across him.

'I could have killed him, the idiot.'

'Yes, but you didn't. Calm down will you, we're nearly there. That's my local cinema,' Jill says, pointing to a multiscreen. 'And there's the nightclub I used to go to,' she adds. 'Bet you don't have a nightclub near where you live.'

'There's a pub in the village.'

'No doubt full of old men in tweeds, drinking whisky and complaining about high taxes, immigrants and the opposition to fox hunting.'

'Oh, you've been there, have you?'

They laugh as Jill directs him to take the next left.

The congestion and the brute ugliness have vanished. Here there are well kept Victorian houses with imaginative variations in design and brickwork.

'Not this turning, but it's the next on the right.'

They enter another street of pleasant houses. 'Anywhere round here will do to park, there aren't reserved spaces,' Jill informs Jack.

'No garage or driveway?'

'Victorian?'

'Oh, I see. Maybe not.'

'I'll dash in and get you a visitors parking permit,' she says as they stop. 'The wardens don't take prisoners.'

Jack watches as Jill walks on; he loves her. She passes elegant semi-detached houses and enters the first in a line of three squarish concrete and glass buildings that seem totally out of place for the street. She's back a moment later with a card and a pen, she writes down the date and car registration number and places the permit on the dashboard.

'Coming?'

A wave of nervousness hits Jack. What would her parents make of him?

'Yours is rather different to the rest in the street,' he says as they stop in front of Jill's house.

'Blame the Blitz. There was a lot of bombing round here and these were put up to fill a gap quite a time later. I think in the 1960s.'

Mrs Cross is at the door waiting for them. 'Hi Jack, I'm Vanessa, Jill's mum.' She takes hold of him and plants a kiss on each cheek. 'Take your bags up and I'll get drinks. What would you like?'

Jack follows Jill into a room with a large picture window providing a surprising amount of light for a late November afternoon. The sea blue walls are decorated with posters of an eclectic mix of films – *Gone with the Wind*, *Pulp Fiction*, *The Godfather*, *Barbarella.*

'Our bed,' she says, looking across at one that's somewhere between a single and double in size. The bed linen is navy.

'Ours? What about your parents, won't they mind?'

'They know we're in a relationship, that we share a bed.'

They drop their bags and return downstairs to sit in the lounge with Vanessa, eating chocolate muffins with their coffee. Though the room isn't large by his own house standards, it's deceptively so compared to what he'd envisaged when he'd stood outside. A line of French windows runs across the wall facing the garden, Jack notes a decked patio with olive and bay leaf trees in pots, a mosaic table and four chairs are visible beyond.

'This is a lovely room, Mrs Cross.'

'Do call me Vanessa. We've done loads to change things since we moved, my husband's an architect. We're rather fortunate though. Our neighbours in their Victorian houses aren't allowed to alter anything, but since ours is a carbuncle amidst the beauty, we can do what we want. From here on,' she says pointing up to a cross beam, 'is an extension that's virtually doubled the size of the room. Come over and see the garden.'

Jack follows Vanessa. Dusk is approaching and low-level spotlights come on as they step out onto the decking. The garden is narrow and deep, there's a summerhouse at the far end. Vanessa sees him looking at it. 'That was Jill's hideout. We were banned from entry and she even kept her older brother out. The place was crammed full of books.'

Jill approaches. 'Talking about me, are you?'

'Only good things,' Jack says as he takes hold of her hand, draws her close and kisses her.

'It's cold, let's go back in,' Vanessa suggests. 'We're getting frosts at night so we really should put away the table and chairs and wrap the trees. Maybe you can help tomorrow, Jack.'

'I'd like that,' Jack replies, and he means it. On his estate, jobs like this are left to the staff. He remembers as a child how much he'd wanted to help plant the vegetable patch and had been told by his father, in no uncertain terms, that it wasn't for him to do such things.

'Fancy a tour of the rest of the house?' Vanessa asks.

'Sure,' Jack replies and Jill joins them as they wander round. The kitchen has a black and white tiled floor with a stylish mix of stainless steel and red appliances resting on a wooden work surface. It's uncluttered as is the case throughout, so different to his own antique and knick-knack laden home.

The tour reaches Vanessa and her husband's bedroom. Above the bed are two paintings of an entwined nude couple.

'Do you like them?' she asks, noticing Jack's look.

Jack thinks of an appropriate answer; he's momentarily embarrassed, blushing.

She continues. 'A friend painted them. As you can see, we were rather more attractive then.'

Jack reddens further, the woman is unmistakably a younger Vanessa. The paintings aren't pornographic, not like the stuff he's seen on the internet, but they're hardly family portraits.

'Mum and dad used to go nudist on holidays,' Jill explains. 'These were done in Crete, weren't they mum?'

'Yes, that's right, the same place we all visited a couple of years ago.'

Was Jill nudist on holiday, Jack wonders? Had she brought a boyfriend along?

'Jesus,' he whispers to Jill as they head downstairs. The mood in this house is substantially different to his own.

Paul, Jill's father, returns from work and the laid-back atmosphere is preserved. How different to when his own father steps through the door, when everything becomes strained and intimidating. Here the conversation jumps from topic to topic in chaotic fashion, with much laughter when covering anecdotes about Jill's childhood. Apparently her parents dragged their son and daughter round the country and abroad in search of architectural wonders.

'It drove us mad,' Jill pipes in, her tone indicating that it did anything but, 'though it kept Dad happy.'

'It must be so rewarding creating buildings, Paul,' Jack says with genuine enthusiasm. 'What about you, Vanessa? Do you work?'

Vanessa is deputy head at a local primary school. It's a fascinating mix of wealthy children from the streets around them and the desperately poor from the council estates across the main road, she explains. Jack reflects on her consideration that she is rich. Clearly Jill's family aren't going short what with Bose speakers, a Miele washing machine, a Sony state of the art television, but no way would they be regarded as wealthy in his social circle.

The four of them watch an episode of *Morse* then head upstairs to their respective bedrooms. Jack wonders whether all four would be making love, one couple under the paintings of the entwined nudes. He's never thought about his own parents having sex, in this household it all seems so natural.

7

The two days with Jill's family are enjoyable beyond expectation for Jack. On the Saturday morning they work in the garden then after lunch walk round the corner to an open market with stalls selling beautifully displayed foods from far afield. Vanessa buys things Jack's never eaten, a fruit called kumquat, a vegetable called kohlrabi, a spicy sausage called knackwurst – and that's just the foods beginning with k, he jokes. That evening, Vanessa cooks a delicately flavoured Thai curry using produce from the market, then together they watch *Crouching Tiger, Hidden Dragon* on TV.

Sunday is a lazy day, up late for brunch then a stroll to the local park on a bitterly cold though clear afternoon. Jack's surprised to see so many people out and about given the weather. He takes note of the diversity – age, colour of skin, dress code – all mixing in and enjoying themselves. He grasps Jill's hand and kisses it. 'Love you,' he declares.

As they are about to leave late afternoon, Vanessa hands Jack a parcel wrapped in Santa Claus cartoon paper. 'I know it's a bit early for a Christmas present, but I thought you should open it now in case the size is wrong or you don't like the style or colour, then we can exchange it.'

It's a navy sweatshirt from Gap, Jill's told her parents he likes the shop and it's his favourite colour. He slips it on, it's perfect. 'That's so kind of you. I've had a lovely two days, thanks ever so much for everything.'

He's hugged by Vanessa and Paul as they leave, he can't remember having ever been hugged by his own father in such an affectionate way.

As soon as they are seated in the car Jack's reaching across to put on a CD.

'Let's not have music for a while,' Jill says. 'There's something I'd like to talk about.'

'All right, I'm all ears.'

'Work.' There is a deliberate pause. 'Your work at university. I'm not lecturing you, but to put it bluntly, you're a bloody idiot not doing any.'

At this point Jack would very much like to put on some music. He considers what would be appropriate if he had the bravery to reject Jill's demand for full attention. He smiles, it would be Minor Threat's *I don't wanna hear it.*

Jill catches his look. 'It's not funny, Jack, it's serious. That letter you got.'

She proceeds to tell him what he already knows, that this is his last chance to turn things round, that he must get into a routine to cope with work, that it would be a mega black mark on his cv if he was kicked out, that…'

Jack's reflecting on the kindness shown by Jill's parents. His thoughts drift to those pictures in their bedroom. In each one, two substantial clumps of pubic hair are visible. Was their friend painting what he saw or was it an impressionist take? Jack has an erection.

'Jack, you aren't listening.'

79

'No.'

'Do you mean no, I'm not listening or is it disagreement with my accusation, as in yes, I am listening?'

'The latter, I am listening. I just had to concentrate on driving for a sec, some idiot looked like they were about to leap across the road.'

'I didn't see anyone. If you're not interested, just say so. I'm staying on at university for three years, don't you want to be there with me?'

'I do. I don't like what I'm studying, that's the problem.'

'From what you've told me, you don't like studying, full stop.'

'I loved history at school until we had a new teacher at the start of Upper Sixth, he was an idiot.'

'Why not ask to change subject, to take history. You'll only have missed a term.'

'I'll consider it.'

'Yeah, I bet.'

'No, I will, honestly.'

'Jack! For God's sake watch out, you nearly killed that pedestrian. He was already on the crossing.'

'I didn't see him, he shouldn't be wearing black when it's dark. Can I put on some music now?'

Radiohead's *Amnesiac* plays as they drive on, Jill despondent due to Jack's lack of interest in the conversation. Hardly a word is spoken for the rest of the journey and as soon as they arrive at university, she pecks him on the cheek and heads off to her hall of residence with the excuse of having loads of work to do.

~

That night is a sleepless one for Jack as he thinks about his future, balancing what his father expects of him with what he wants to do. By the morning he's made a decision and is outside his personal tutor's office well ahead of the nine o'clock appointment.

At first the conversation with Professor Appleton is confrontational with his tutor outlining the misdemeanours in meticulous detail. When Appleton pauses to drink a glass of water, Jack grabs the opportunity.

'May I suggest something, sir?'

At first Appleton is dismissive of his suggestion but Jack persists. 'You see, it was my father who decided what I should study, not me. I love history. Please may I change, I implore you,' he urges, utilising the method acting technique he'd learnt at school.

His acting wins the day. Appleton agrees to make a call, requesting that Jack leaves the room while he speaks. He is summoned five or so minutes later and discovers that it may be possible to switch courses though there is a proviso – he will have to undergo an interview with the Head of the History Faculty before a decision is made. It has been set for two o'clock the next day. Jack readily agrees to this and the conversation with Appleton becomes much more convivial. He talks about his father's expectations and is told that a history degree is as good as a Business Studies one for a career in finance. In truth he already knows this, after all, his father studied Classics at Oxford and that hadn't prevented him from embarking on a career in banking.

Jill calls to find out how the meeting with his tutor has gone.

'I'm in with a chance,' he informs her.

'What do you mean?'

'I'll explain later.'

'Shall we meet for lunch then?'

'Sorry, can't. There's something I need to do that's going to take up the rest of the day and tomorrow morning.'

'What?'

'I'm not going to say, it's a surprise, a nice one. I'll see you tomorrow afternoon when it's all over.'

'What are you on about. When what's over?'

'Coffee bar at four tomorrow.'

'Why the secrecy? They aren't thinking of letting you join MI5 just because you went to public school are they? God help the nation!'

'Very funny. Be patient. I must go, I haven't got a moment to spare.'

He joins the medics in the library, deliberately sitting in a section where Jill and her friends never go. History books covering the French and Russian revolutions and the War of the Roses are in front of him. He skips dinner and works on until ten. The following morning he is back in the library by nine, amazed that there are already others there. He reads up on the Romans and Greeks, pleasantly surprised that knowledge acquired at school years ago has resurfaced.

Professor Dawson would have fitted in well as a teacher at his old school, he's a conservatively dressed serious man with half-moon glasses balanced near the bottom of a prominent nose.

'Tell me, Mr Ashley-Lovett, why should we take you on bearing in mind your poor performance so far?'

Jack has prepared well, anticipating the first question and having his answer ready. He looks down, his face the epitome of sorrow, this all part of the rehearsed performance.

'Because sir,' he says with as much pathos as is humanly possible to muster, 'my father gave me no choice. He told me that if I wanted to go to university it would have to be to undertake a degree linked to the world of business. I love history so much, from the bottom of my heart, but it was to no avail.'

At this point Jack would like to shed a tear or two but is unable to manufacture them. He makes a mental note to ask Jill if she has any tips about this based on her acting expertise.

'What exactly do you find so attractive with history?' Dawson asks.

Jack has expected this question, too. 'There are many reasons, sir. Perhaps the most important is that studying it gives us a sense of place in the world. A society without history is like a person without a memory.' He cites several examples to hammer home the evidence.

'Do you have a favourite era?'

Yet again he is prepared. 'I'm interested in the whole lot, but I suppose some periods are of particular significance because of their huge impact on future generations.' He is able to manipulate the conversation to discuss the topics he's chosen to read over the past day or so – the Greeks, the Romans, fifteenth-century England, eighteenth-century France, twentieth-century Russia. Keep well away from Hitler, he'd decided, everyone goes on about the Nazis.

'And that in itself is fascinating,' he concludes. 'The fact that we can see parallels time and again over the centuries when men, and I do mean men as opposed to women,' (this populist statement courtesy of previous discussions with Jill), 'make the same mistakes.'

Jack looks across to Dawson with a smile, the professor is not returning it. 'I note you went to a public school,' he says, flicking through the papers in front of him. 'They certainly taught you how to bullshit, I'm saying that off the record of course. All right, I'll take you on probation next term. I'll instruct my staff to monitor your progress fastidiously and subsequently I'll make the decision as to whether you stay or not. Are you in agreement?'

'Yes, sir. And thank you, sir.'

Jack shakes Dawson's hand, softly chanting *wanker, wanker, wanker* as he leaves the building.

By the time he gets to his room there's an email from Dawson providing him with a full page list of background reading together with details of four assignments he needs to complete for submission by the start of the following term.

~

Jack and Jill are sitting in the coffee bar. He waits for her to finish her muffin, he wants her full attention.

'Are you actually ever going to tell me what's going on? This is ridiculous.'

'OK, here goes.'

Jack describes the events of the last day or so, boasting about his smartness at the interview, though omitting the professor's suspicion. 'So,' he concludes, 'I'm in with history on a term's probation.'

'I'm disappointed, I expected to hear that you had actually been recruited by the secret service. I've always wanted to go out with a spy.'

'That opportunity could well follow, I think they take on History graduates.' Though not from this place, he laments. His spirits are too high to dwell on not getting into Oxford, he's succeeded in changing courses and he's with a beautiful woman. 'The thought of making love to foreign agent Jillena Crossavich is extremely tempting, enough to turn me into a double agent.'

'I say, what a grand idea, Mr Ashley-Lovett.'

They make their way to Jack's accommodation block. 'You've been a massive help, Jill, it was your idea for me to change courses.'

He stretches across and kisses Jill as they enter the building. Once inside he gives a cursory nod to a couple of boys chatting in the corridor.

As soon as they're in Jack's room they drop onto the bed and clumsily race to unbutton and unzip. 'Stop!' Jack orders as Jill is tugging at his shirt. 'I've got a better idea. Go and get a night bag and come straight back.'

'Why?'

'A celebration.'

Jill does as she's told and when she returns they drive into town. Jack's booked a room in Tower Plaza, the swankiest hotel. The next sixteen hours consists of sex, shower, dinner, tv, sleep, sex, breakfast, then back to campus. Then it's library, lunch, library, dinner, early night.

~

Jack's a changed man. He hasn't become the hardest working student overnight, but he is making a considerable effort during the last couple of weeks of term.

'We've only been together for ten weeks, but it feels like I've known you for ages,' Jill says as they leave the library on the penultimate day.

'It's been a wonderful ten weeks.'

'Yes, it has.'

'I'm going to miss you loads. Are you sure we can't meet up over Christmas, even if it's just for a weekend?'

'We've had this conversation about a hundred times. It's not doable, not with you off skiing the day after Boxing Day.'

They're tramping through an unexpectedly thick covering of snow that fell overnight, deep enough to soak Jill's feet even though she's wearing ankle boots.

'Maybe I should cancel, I can ski here.'

'Very funny! It'll be soggy slush by tomorrow. Go and enjoy it. Just make sure you don't break a leg or get over-plastered with your public school chums and then get off with some chic Val d'Isere French girl.'

'There won't be any French girls, it's virtually an English colony during the skiing season.'

'And remember you've got assignments to do.'

They have one last night together before Jack sets off at the crack of dawn.

Jill returns to her hall of residence to finish packing ahead of Vanessa collecting her and the ton of books. The corridor girls have already departed and there's an eerie quietness – no laughing, kettles boiling, calling out if anyone has a spare teabag, pen, notebook, tampon or battery. She's made plenty of holiday plans of her own. She'll miss Jack, but will be more than busy socialising with family and friends. Everyone will have stories to divulge about their first term at university. She'll tell them about Jack, including gossip about Mr and Mrs Ashley-Lovett, their house, their servants and the incident with Seb, which could well become the story of the year.

~

The holiday flashes by. On their first night back together, the day before the start of term, Jill bursts out laughing as Jack removes his clothes. 'You look like that game kids play, the one when you build cardboard people with a mix of hats, heads, bodies, legs and shoes.'

'I assume the cut-outs have clothes on.'

'You assume right though this might be an interesting new version for an adult game. Tanned or even burnt face. Milk white body apart from little fluffy bits around that thing. Red blistered feet. Pity you haven't got a hat to add.'

'Just come to bed will you, Jill.'

They're as close as ever during the second term, with Jack sticking to his resolution to make an effort. He gets good enough grades to be allowed to continue with history and Jill once again excels in her studies.

Over Easter they spend a week in rainswept Peak District, returning wet and cold after long walks to the comfort of an open fire in the lounge of their small hotel.

'We're like a middle-aged couple,' Jack declares as they head up to their bedroom.

'Do middle-aged couples do this?' Jill asks, pulling off his jumper as they climb the staircase. 'Or this?' as she unbuttons his shirt on the landing. 'Or for that matter, this?'

she adds as she takes off his shirt as they approach their bedroom.

At this point a white-haired couple open the door next to theirs. Jill thinks fast, unsure whether the looks she's receiving are ones of disdain, tolerance, humour, or in the case of the woman, envy, because Jack does have a fine torso. 'He spilt his soup, he's soaked through and probably burnt. I'll dab some cold water on and get him changed.'

The couple nod in disbelieving unison and Jack and Jill rush inside.

'Why on earth did you say that? They'll think I'm either your son or a moron.'

'You're neither, but don't you think these had better come off just in case you've burnt yourself down here,' Jill says as she undoes his belt, unzips, and yanks down his trousers and boxers in one fell swoop.

They return to university a couple of days ahead of the start of their third term, nominally Summer Term, but by name only because it looks like ending up the wettest April and May on record. Their campus is muddy and windswept.

At last Jack is making friends, socialising with the students taking his courses, at times he even hangs out with the boys on his corridor.

Jill continues to be Little Miss Popular. Every Tuesday she has a late afternoon tea, cake, alcohol and Doritos session with the corridor girls. Their experiences are a microcosm of what goes on at university. Morag is having an affair with one of her lecturers, over twice her age but rather dishy. She has mixed emotions because she babysits for his delightful children and thinks his wife is really nice, too. It's getting serious, she tells the others, the man is talking about leaving his family. Charlotte favours one-night stands, or in exceptional cases a couple of nights. She seems in danger of running out of fit boys studying Psychology and may have to shift her attention to another faculty. She chain smokes, drinks a lot and does weed. Somehow she remains on top of her work and is one of the star students in the department. Priya doesn't socialise beyond the corridor events, she works incredibly hard and goes home every weekend to be with her boyfriend. Annie has joined the Young Conservatives and the Christian Union. Her mission appears to be to convert others to her beliefs. If the corridor girls are anything to go by, she's having little success.

They're discussing favourite chocolate bars when out of the blue, deadly serious, Annie says, 'Jill, have you ever thought that it would have been better to have delayed consummation until after marriage?'

Although the others spend a fair bit of time with Annie, her comments regularly generate a shocked silence.

'Well, it's too late, Annie, but I can't say I agree with you. I like sex and anyway, who's to say that I'll end up marrying Jack.'

'You're pretty well married now, you're like a middle-aged couple,' Morag quips, the comment hitting a raw nerve as Jill assesses the validity of the statement. They met on the first evening at university, they're together every day and most nights, they even sit next to each other in the library, they've met the parents, and they're planning to live together during their second year.

'You wouldn't say that if you saw us in bed. Sorry, Annie, no intention to embarrass you.' Should she be seeing

89

less of Jack? Surely not, she loves him. And she has plenty of friends, male and female.

The next day she's having lunch with Jack in the food hall. Old habits die hard, he has a mountain of enchiladas and she's opted for a mackerel salad with coleslaw, lettuce and tomatoes.

Jack has some good news, he's arranged for them to see a couple of one-bedroom flats the next day. 'It's a fabulous new development overlooking the river. Luxurious.'

'Jack, do you ever think we're a bit too close?'

'Close? What do you mean?'

'Maybe we are too much like a middle aged couple.'

'No, not at all.'

'But what about mixing more with other students?'

'We do, we've got loads of friends.'

'Listen, I've been thinking. Of course I want to live with you next year, but I'd prefer a shared house.'

'I thought it would be good just the two of us.' He looks forlorn as he stands, his enchiladas unfinished. 'I've got a seminar, we can talk more later.'

In response to Jack's disappointment, Jill calls Vanessa for a second opinion. Her mother seems distracted, her recommendation is merely of the "it's up to you" nature, that is to say, hopeless. It's unusual for her not to dive in with advice.

'Are you OK, Mum?'

'Yes fine, but I really must go. Let's speak tomorrow.' And the call is terminated before Jill has a chance to say goodbye.

8

Vanessa has reason to be distracted.

It had all started late afternoon the previous Friday when Paul called to let her know he wouldn't be home until late. Her husband and his partners were off to a pub to commiserate, having failed to gain the contract for thirteen new toilet blocks in local authority parks. The council planner had assured Paul that the job was theirs for the taking, but when it came to the crunch their bid was rejected as being too modern.

'That's not logical, how can something for the future be too modern?' Paul had demanded.

'People don't want avant-garde toilets, we've done a survey.'

'A survey! What did you ask? Would you prefer a traditional toilet or an avant-garde one? They wouldn't have any idea what you were on about.'

It was pointless continuing the conversation, the decision had been made.

Paul had got home late, Vanessa was half-asleep. 'Everything alright?' she'd mumbled.

'Just work. Nothing to worry about.'

Saturdays were stay in bed mornings for the Crosses. The ritual involved taking it in turns to make coffee and toast with marmalade and bringing it upstairs with the mountain of *Guardian* sections and supplements. That Saturday, Vanessa was on kitchen duty.

Paul was groggy and not in the best of moods. He had yet to tell Vanessa, but the discussion with colleagues went far beyond the contract to build toilets. The failure to acquire that work together with the declining London property market meant big trouble. After a miserable hour or so at the pub the partners had switched their attention to evaluating the quality of wine on offer, so Paul's Saturday morning mood was as much a hangover as to do with work worries.

'Breakfast,' Vanessa announced cheerily on her return to the bedroom.

They munched, drank and read in silence for a while and Paul began to feel better – the coffee had done the trick. He dropped the newspaper onto the floor and leant across to lift off Vanessa's nightdress. Like toast and marmalade, sex was a traditional Saturday morning activity for the Crosses.

Vanessa glanced at the two paintings done by Lawrence, Paul's best friend from university. The men had started an architecture degree together, but Lawrence packed it in for art, painting for pleasure and teaching for income.

Paul and Vanessa had gone on three naturist holidays with Lawrence and his girlfriend Carol. Their first trip was to Yugoslavia, a memorable one because they'd had to flee as war in their Croatian resort threatened. The following year they travelled to the South of France, but had to return early because everything was so expensive. Their final holiday together was to Crete, with the hope of no war and low prices. They were on the beach when Lawrence suggested making sketches to use for paintings. Paul, a good artist in his own right, reciprocated by drawing his friends. The combined effect of the nakedness and the men visibly turned on brought on a torrent of arousal for Vanessa, she felt as sexy as she had ever done. Carol must have felt the same if her suggestion as they were heading back to the hotel was anything to go by.

'No way,' Vanessa had replied, there were limits to what she'd do.

'Why not? Don't you fancy Lawrence?'

'That's beside the point. I'm with Paul.'

Vanessa didn't know that Lawrence was asking Paul the same question and receiving the same rejection. However the seed was sown and on a drunken last night the four of them were in bed together, not exactly a swap, but probably enough to constitute infidelity.

Soon after the holiday, Lawrence had presented them with the two paintings. Over twenty years later they were still hanging in their bedroom and Vanessa often had a pang of guilt when looking at them. She'd never told Paul how Lawrence had pestered her for sex for months afterwards. Once, just once, she was unfaithful.

She didn't enjoy the lovemaking that Saturday morning, uppermost on her mind were the hints Paul had dropped about difficulties at work.

He remained dismissive throughout the weekend. 'Honestly, there's nothing to worry about,' he assured her.

When he got back from work on the Monday she suggested they went to see a film. 'It'll take your mind off things,' she said.

'I'd like to but I can't, I've got stuff to do.'

Paul never turned down an offer to go out. 'Will you please tell me what's going on?' Vanessa implored.

'I need to sort out what we've got in the pipeline now that we've lost the toilets bid. Three of the team were earmarked for that project and there's nothing lined up to replace it.'

'Can I help? At least talk it through?'

'Not now, let me do the sums first. You go to the cinema and by the time you get back, all will be resolved.'

As soon as Vanessa left, Paul began his slog through spreadsheets. He hated spreadsheets, he'd much rather be working with design software. In advance of doing any calculations he knew it wasn't looking good, with insufficient work to keep the team occupied more than a couple of months.

Paul switched from Excel to Spider Solitaire, taking a break from spreadsheets to play the computer game was his norm. Before he knew it, half an hour had raced past. He switched back to Excel but was soon solitairing again to avoid facing up to the reality the figures were bound to reveal. His company was in danger of going bust.

Reflecting on the family's finances, he was sure they could cope. Having both children at university was costing a fortune, but Dan was about to graduate. They had Vanessa's good salary, so even if he was jobless for a while, they would hardly be poor. In fact, if the value of the house was taken into consideration, they were probably millionaires what with daft London house price inflation.

He completed a successful round of Spider Solitaire with the cards lined up in neat stacks. One last game then back to Excel. It crossed his mind, having thought about the millionaire tag, that selling the house was an option, something smaller would do now that Dan and Jill were away. But it was the family home, the place where the children and their future families could visit. He and Vanessa had put so much energy into making it right, it would be criminal to pack it in at the point when the project was finally complete.

Paul had won again when he heard the front door open. He clicked out of the game, shut down Excel and switched off the computer.

He greeted Vanessa. 'Good film?'

'*Frida*. The Mexican artist. But I couldn't concentrate. What's going on, Paul?'

Over the next couple of days Vanessa was relentless in extracting the truth from her husband. There followed two sleepless nights, her thoughts were all over the place and she was a waste of space at work.

In addition to worries about the financial circumstances, a deep sense of loss had surfaced. Why now was anybody's guess, but after over twenty years of caring for her children, she was desperately missing the buzz of activity in the house.

"Don't forget your games kit."

"I'll pick you up after the rehearsal."

"Text me as soon as you get your results."

All so hectic, so wonderful.

All change because Dan was about to start work in Manchester, living with his girlfriend. Her son, her first born, would have well and truly flown. Although Jill might come home during some of her holidays, she had already planned to "do Europe" with Jack over the summer.

Vanessa was surprised about Jack, she wouldn't have thought he'd be Jill's type. But she could tell they got on well. He was a nice boy, more than that, on first appearances exceptionally polite. Good looking, too.

She'd be spending the rest of her life alone with Paul which surely would be fine. He was a wonderful husband and they shared loads of interests – art, theatre, cinema and of course travel. They'd be able to visit all the places they'd talked about but had yet to see, the Alhambra in Grenada, the geysers in Iceland and everywhere in Australia. Or would they? Not without money. Maybe Paul's idea of selling up and moving somewhere smaller and cheaper wasn't a bad one. By coincidence, she'd recently thought about going part-time or even packing in work. She loved the teaching but not the administration she'd taken on since becoming deputy head. The lowlight of the week had been constructing the risk assessment for using glue sticks in the classroom. But if Paul's company went under, early retirement wasn't going to be possible.

That Wednesday Vanessa got home after school exhausted, the lack of sleep having caught up with her. A glance in the bathroom mirror was so uncomfortable that she put on eye liner and lipstick, a pointless gesture when all she'd be doing that evening was cooking, eating and watching television.

By the time Jill phoned late afternoon to ask her something or other to do with the following year's accommodation, Vanessa was unreceptive. She had been in the middle of cooking, though it was her mood rather than the task in hand that made her put off any discussion. She felt guilty as soon as she ended the call. The children would need to know about the financial state of affairs though there was no urgency. It was better if they were told in person rather than during a telephone call.

'You look fabulous,' were Paul's first words on returning from work. He put his arms round her waist, pulled her close and kissed. 'Fabulous. Let's go to bed.'

'What, now?' They hadn't had sex outside of early morning or late evening for years. Vanessa made a mental note to put on make-up after work more often.

In the bedroom she quickly undressed and was already naked while Paul was still fiddling with his shirt buttons.

'You're slow,' she said as she helped him undress.

Paul was looking at the two paintings. Occasionally, just occasionally, he had a rush of guilt as a result of his brief affair with Carol soon after that holiday. Vanessa had been working flat out during her first year of teaching while he was still a student with loads of time on his hands. There were three months of afternoon liaisons to feel guilty about.

The business was on his mind, too. If it went under surely he could find a job with another architect. A daft iteration of Forrest Gump's philosophy sprang to mind. "Architecture is like a box of chocolates, favourites come and go". Were Parsons & Cross no longer a favourite and about to go? And bloody Spider Solitaire, was he addicted?

Some nights he dreamt of shifting cards and woke up twitching. He should delete the game.

'Earth to Paul, I'm not getting any response here.'

'Sorry, Vanessa. Would you like me to…?'

'…no, never mind, let's forget it. Oh, by the way, Jill phoned. She was on about where she should live next year. I wasn't helpful, I'm afraid.'

'It's up to her to decide.'

'That's basically what I said.'

9

Jill gets her way with accommodation. The luxurious penthouse with state of the art fittings and a rooftop balcony overlooking the river has been swapped for an unattractive inter-war semi in a far less salubrious part of town, though as Jill points out, it is near Blockbusters and a great Indian take-away.

'We can advertise for people to share,' Jack suggests.

'We could do that, but I've asked the girls on the corridor if they're interested. I thought it was a start, we know they're trustworthy and loads of fun. Only if you're happy with that though.'

'Good idea, I like them. The biggest bedroom's going to be ours and the others are quite a bit smaller, too small for sharing. So we can only take three of them.'

'That works out fine. Morag, Charlotte and Priya are happy to join us and Annie's already said no. She told me, and these were her actual words, that intoxication, fornication and general debauchery were not things she wanted to be party to. She's wangled a second year in halls of residence as a mentor for first year students, the poor things.'

They're chatting as they walk from library to the accommodation blocks.

'Talk of the devil,' Jill declares as Annie comes striding towards them, the new look Annie. She's wearing a T-shirt with a near copy of the GAP logo, underneath which is the slogan *God Answers Prayers*. Round her neck is a giant cross that could well have a detrimental effect on posture. Attractively wild hair has been tamed into a tight bun that cuts into her forehead.

'My dear friends, guess what,' she says. 'I'm off to a Jesus camp in America.'

'That's nice,' maximises the enthusiasm Jill can muster. 'We're inter-railing in Europe.'

'I know, you told me when we were in the kitchen a while back. Surely you remember.'

Annie has lost the ability to smile and gained the ability to reprimand. Jill considers suggesting that her own intoxication, fornication and debauchery are combining to adversely affect memory, but settles on 'Well, we'd better dash, loads of packing to do. See you next term, Annie.'

'Yes, see you.'

As they walk on, Jack and Jill could bitch, but there's no point.

~

Inter-railing was an inspirational holiday, but now it's back to university at the start of the second year. Everyone is settled in the house, the atmosphere's good. The common areas have been luxuriously furnished thanks to Jack's generosity. The landlord had been happy for him to ditch everything – ripped curtains on dangling pelmets; stained velour sofas with cigarette burns on the arms; Formica tables with edges snapped off; chipped crockery; a broken microwave. He was told he could replace it all provided the new stuff remained in the house when he moved out. Ikea products predominate along with an impressive television, DVD player and sound system.

Jack and Jill's bedroom boasts a top of the range double bed and the visual highlight is an original *Strangers on a Train* poster that he bought for her birthday.

The other occupants have made their mark, choosing colours, fabrics and an eclectic mix of posters for their own bedrooms. Morag is a heavy metal fan. Her door, window frame and skirting board are painted black and the walls are puke lime. She possesses two posters advertising gigs. When she visits to see how Morag is settling in, Jill's passing comment about not having heard of any of the bands on display results in being coerced into listening to *Children of Bodom* and *Blind Guardian* at high volume. She beats a hasty a retreat with the excuse of having masses to do.

Charlotte's room colours are lilac and dove grey and her posters are attractive black and white photos of Freud, Adler and Pavlov.

Priya has white paintwork and off-white walls which house three posters with uplifting quotes.

Out of difficulty arises opportunity.

If I persist long enough I will win.

Your greatest success is one step beyond your greatest failure.

Clichéd quotes aside, Jill wants to tell Priya to line them up against their top edges rather than run them diagonally down her wall.

It doesn't take long for the residents to discover Jack has a trait that even Jill had no idea was so severe until they are living together. It's more than a trait, it's an obsession, an obsession to keep things ordered. He sorts DVDs in alphabetical order. Morag deliberately disarranges them so she can watch Jack repairing the damage. He's good natured about her teasing and the whole house join in when they realise that food, cutlery, crockery, saucepans and other kitchen utensils are all meticulously stored to conform to Jack's wishes. The fixation extends to the bedroom where Jill is politely but firmly discouraged from going near his side of the wardrobe or putting anything away in his drawers.

The bathroom presents the greatest challenge, always untidy despite Jack's request that everyone should do their bit to keep it in good order. The residents are called to a meeting one evening and the defendants playfully account for their lack of care.

'I was late and in a rush to get to a lecture this morning.'

'I was drunk and with a boy.'

'I'd forget to put it on if I stuffed it away in a cupboard.'

Jack buys a small lockable cabinet for his toiletries which, after negotiation, Jill is allowed to use, though on trial for the first month.

Beyond Jack's good-humoured obsession with household pristineness, life for the tenants is progressing in typical student fashion.

Morag has terminated her relationship with the lecturer and by all accounts the man is devastated. One drink-fuelled evening she relates the story of how it all came to an end. The lecturer's seven-year old son had seen the pair on the sofa engaged in what the father claimed was artificial resuscitation due to Morag feeling unwell. Seven-year olds recognise kissing when they see it and he'd screamed which had resulted in his twelve-year old sister charging down the stairs as Morag was getting dressed.

'You've been doing it,' the daughter yells.

'Doing what?' her brother enquires.

'We haven't been doing anything,' the lecturer claims.

'Then why isn't Morag wearing all her clothes?' asks the daughter.

'She was hot and feeling faint, you know your mother's forever turning the heating up too high. That's why I was resuscitating her.'

'But why did she have to take these off,' the girl persists, lifting up a pair of very skimpy knickers she's seen on the floor.

There can be no valid explanation and the lecturer resorts to pleading. 'Please don't tell Mum, she'd be so upset.'

'What's in it for me?'

'What do you mean?'

'What can you offer as a bribe?'

'Do you really mean that?'

'Yes.'

What do you want then?'

'An iPod.'

'Why on earth would you want an iPod?'

It's a silly question and the girl ignores it. As Morag is buttoning up her blouse, she notices the victorious smirk.

'Alright, I'll get you an iPod,' the lecturer concedes with a sigh.

'That's not fair, what about me?'

'What do you want?' he asks his son.

'Can I have some Lego please, Dad? A space station.'

'I suppose so. Now will you two go back to bed?'

The lecturer walks Morag to the door. 'I'll call you tomorrow, I can sort this out.'

'Maybe you can, but enough is enough. It's not fair on your family, it's over,' Morag announces, now telling her flatmates that her biggest regret is the loss of babysitting income.

Charlotte is smoking less, drinking less, taking fewer drugs and counter-intuitively, her work seems to be suffering. It may be because she's in love. Having done the rounds with the Psychology Faculty fit boys, she's back with her first date and it's lasting; he spends most nights at the shared house and Charlotte is talking about the need for a bigger bed. She goes as far as to suggest that perhaps Jack could purchase it. Jill cuts that cheeky request short.

Priya returns from the Christmas break with an engagement ring. The wedding is on hold until she finishes university though her fiancé has questioned the need to carry on studying. The girls in the house insist she must continue, but Priya is wavering.

There is gossip about Annie who failed to reappear at the start of the new academic year. The story doing the rounds is that she has stayed on at the Jesus camp as a volunteer. Apparently, one of her emails stated that Jesus definitely had spent some time in America, the Mormons were right all along.

~

All is fine for Jack and Jill. They are secure and comfortable in each other's company yet retain the spark evident from the moment they first set eyes on each other. Jill is excelling in her studies and Jack's doing well, too.

Sometimes Jill reflects on what Morag had once said about them being like a boring middle-aged couple. Did Morag include the word boring? Maybe not and anyway, it wouldn't be true because they've done a bungee jump to raise money for a hospice, had a Eurostar weekend trip to Paris, and slept rough to draw attention to the plight of the town's homeless. Jack wasn't over the moon to take part in that, he agreed on condition that Jill would never tell his parents and that he could book a room at their favourite hotel for a shower and hearty breakfast the next morning.

Visiting families has been an ongoing topic for discussion, with Jack far more enthusiastic to see Jill's parents than both he and Jill are to see his own mother and father. And brother, Jill could add.

Towards the end of the first term they journey to London where Jack is warmly welcomed by Paul and Vanessa. He meets Jill's brother, Dan, and the three of them head off to the pub together on the first evening.

Dan's a good talker, friendly and welcoming, he shares the Cross family's sociability.

Out of the blue he gets serious. 'Jill, have you noticed anything odd about mum and dad?'

'Odd, in what way?'

'They seem stressed. I've asked if everything is OK and they've said fine, but I'm not so sure.'

'What do you think it could be? They're happy enough together, aren't they?'

'Yeah, I don't think it's that. I'm not sure what, but there's definitely something going on.'

Jill spends the weekend looking for evidence to back up Dan's claim but can't detect anything, nor can Jack. They return to university confident that all is well.

The next visit to her parents is a fleeting one without Jack, allowing him to see his own parents which Jill is happy for him to do alone. By the time she returns to university she's convinced something's wrong but her usually open parents have continued to claim all is well.

'I'm not convinced that's the case,' she tells Jack.

'If it is anything, they'll talk to you when they're ready.'

'I suppose you're right.'

'Mine are as bonkers as ever. Seb didn't stop going on about how insulted he is at having never been invited here, my father ordered me to investigate careers and my mother urged me to get you to visit again despite how she treated you last time. Apparently she really likes you.'

'Hell, I wouldn't want to be someone she disliked!'

'Would you come to my place again?'

~

It's midway through the second term. As their car scrunches along the gravelled drive, pulling to a halt by the grand door, Mrs Ashley-Lovett emerges and waves. As soon as they step out, she's by their side greeting the pair with smiles and hugs.

Once inside, Sabrina addresses Jack. 'I'd like a word with Jill please. Alone if you don't mind.'

Jack nods in agreement and carries their bags upstairs while Jill follows Sabrina into the library. 'I want to apologise,' she says before they have even sat down.

'For what?'

106

'You must know. For being so unpleasant last time you were here. I don't think I need to provide details other than to say that was the case.'

'There's no need…'

'There absolutely is, I liked you from the word go, but did anything but show it. I think Jack is a lucky boy.'

Jill blushes, she's unsure what to say, but is saved by Seb entering.

'Jill, great to see you again.' He all but sprints across the room and hugs her.

He's changed, Jill notes, he's losing his boyish looks. The brace has gone as have the spots on his face, apart from one on his chin that he's tried to camouflage with a pink paste that's made it more noticeable than if he'd let it be.

'You can chat with Jill later, Seb, I'm talking to her now.'

'I won't be a nuisance, I'll just sit down and listen quietly.'

'Go!'

Seb does as he's told, his exit far slower than the entrance.

'You must have thought I was the most unpleasant stuck-up bitch imaginable. It's a bloody act that's become a habit and I hate myself for it. It's only when I meet people like you that I realise what a fraud I am.'

Henry bursts in, matching Seb's speed across the room to reach Jill. 'My dear, my dear, what a delight to see you.'

He takes hold of her hands and lifts her out of the armchair before placing his arms around her and planting a kiss smack on the lips. Jill smells whisky. If his hands stray onto my bum he's for it, Jill resolves. They do and she shoves him off her.

'Honestly Henry, you'll suffocate the girl if you aren't careful,' Sabrina says, her accent decidedly different to the one when speaking to Jill a short while earlier. 'We're talking about something private if you don't mind. Could you leave us alone?'

'With pleasure. Until later, ladies.' Henry kisses Jill's hand and gives a sort of bow before leaving. Jill wipes her hand on the side of her jeans, Sabrina notices and smiles.

'That's what arrogant and lecherous looks like,' she says. 'I need to apologise as much for him as for me.'

'I'd say more. A lot more.'

'You'll never get an apology from him, it's not in his genes to say sorry. Fortunately I don't think Jack is like his father.'

As if on cue, Jack knocks and enters. 'Hi you two. Chat over?'

'I suppose so, at least for now.'

The weekend is weird, the tensions in the family apparent. Henry tries to touch Jill at every opportunity, with increasing boldness as he consumes more alcohol. Jack and his mother are well aware of Henry's appalling behaviour and marvel at how Jill deals with it. She's treating him like a pleasant enough geriatric who can't help what he's doing.

'I think it would be best if you removed your hand from my bottom, Mr Ashley-Lovett.'

'Could you take a step back, it might make breathing easier.'

Then there's Seb to deal with. He endeavours to manipulate a private conversation and her counter is to avoid being alone with him. She fails on the Saturday morning when Jack has been ordered to go for an early morning walk round the grounds with his father.

Seb enters her bedroom. She's dressed, sitting at the desk taking notes for an essay. He's still in his pyjamas.

'Jill, I have to tell you something. Since you were last here I haven't been able to get you off my mind. I think about you constantly.'

'Well, then it's time you stopped thinking about me constantly.'

'I can't. Look.' The boy pulls down his pyjama bottoms.

'Stop it! If you don't pull them up immediately I promise you, I'll tell Jack and your mother.'

Seb does as he's told but remains in the room. 'There are a few things you might like to know about Jack.'

'I think I know quite a lot already thank you very much. And I like what I see.'

'You've only seen one side of him, I've known him for a lot longer than you have. I know how spiteful and devious he can be. He only thinks of himself, of what's in it – '

' – I'm not going to listen to this bollocks. You can stay in here and talk to yourself if you want.' Jill gets out the chair and pushes past Seb; she despises him for his disloyalty. 'I warn you, any repeat and I'll tell Jack, so I suggest you watch it.'

'I'm not scared of him.'

'It's nothing to do with being scared, you immature little tosser, quite literally no doubt. It's about acting with decorum.'

'Decorum, what does someone like you know about that?'

109

Jill leaves him in the room and spends the rest of the day ignoring Seb and avoiding Henry.

On the Sunday morning she jumps at Jack's suggestion of a drive to the seaside.

'Shall we ask Seb to join us?' Jack asks.

'No, absolutely not,' Jill replies, declining to offer a reason.

They walk for miles along a near deserted beach in contented silence, returning to the house late afternoon.

After tea, Sabrina requests another chat alone with Jill. She talks about her failed career as an actress and how everything changed once married to Henry. Although not all for the worse because there had been benefits, the negatives outweighed the positives. Her so-called friends are no more than acquaintances, she has nothing in common with them. And she's lost contact with those from her youth, quirky, fun-loving people with a passion for theatre, literature and art.

'I'll tell you what, let's meet up in London,' Jill suggests. 'We could see a play or visit a gallery. I'm sure Mum would be keen to join us, you'd like her.'

A single tear appears and slowly makes its way down Sabrina's cheek. She flicks it away brusquely with the back of her hand. Jill has noticed and takes hold of Sabrina's other hand. 'I'm serious,' Jill continues, 'let's set the date before we leave.'

10

Jill keeps her promise and meets Sabrina in London for a matinee and meal one Saturday in early May. She hasn't invited her mother, having decided to test Sabrina's behaviour ahead of an introduction. After all, faced with hostility on one visit and repentant tears during the second, who is the real Sabrina? Living with Henry would be enough to drive anyone crazy she concludes and thanks the high heavens that Jack is so different to the other males in the household.

Their day together is a delight. It turns out that the play they see, a Restoration comedy, is one Sabrina has performed in. Over dinner they laugh loads as Sabrina shares her acting experiences, some of her stories are shockingly funny.

'Next time we meet I'll make sure Mum joins us, you'd definitely get on.'

'I'd like that. And Jill, thanks for today, I've enjoyed it so much. I don't remember when I last laughed such a lot.'

'I've enjoyed it too. God, some of the things you got up to, just wait until I tell Jack! That is a joke by the way.'

Sabrina's light-heartedness, more or less non-stop for the last couple of hours, abruptly ceases; she looks on the verge of tears. 'Today's made me realise I must change things.'

'What do you mean?'

'I can't go on pretending life's fine when it's so bloody awful.'

Jill's unsure what to say, this is a dramatic disclosure to make to your son's girlfriend during only their third meeting. 'Why not speak to Jack about how you feel, he's a good listener.'

'Perhaps you're making him a better one, but he's still not the right person to talk to. But hey, let's not end on a sad note. I'm fine.'

They travel in opposite directions on the Underground with Jill staying at her parents for the night. She senses that Dan had been correct in suggesting that all is not well. Her attempt to find out what the problem is falls on deaf ears. 'Problem? Of course not, we're fine.'

Returning to university none the wiser about her mother and father, she notes a new seriousness with the house occupants revising for end of year exams. Despite this, there remains time for socialising.

Morag has met her dream man, a townie who left school with no qualifications aged sixteen and has played in unknown heavy metal bands ever since. The current one is *Cadmium Lake* and Morag assembles the housemates to listen to their demo CD.

'Not bad at all,' from Jack.

'Yes, there's definitely potential there,' from Charlotte.

'I think the singer's good,' from Priya, aware he's the band member who is Morag's boyfriend.

Jill is speechless, the music is absolutely awful.

Priya is committed to finishing her degree but has had to accept a list of terms and conditions set by her fiancé, including that she must return home to be with him every weekend and she is not to consume alcohol at university.

Charlotte's relationship with the boy of her dreams is over. She is now experimenting with women, Jill suggesting to Jack that this is because she's exhausted the supply of fit males in the Psychology Faculty. Jack's showing an interest in this lesbian phase because the women that Charlotte brings home are stunning. He's taken to prancing around each morning only in boxers, justifying his dress code to Jill as being due to the exceptionally hot weather. She doesn't make a fuss because it's turning him on big time and she's the direct beneficiary of his arousal. And it's not as if the stunners pose a threat.

Humour is at the heart of Jack and Jill's great relationship, they can laugh at each other's foibles. He buys her a bumper set of highlighter pens in honour of her obsessive use of them to mark key points in documents. She takes all the socks out of his drawer and lines them up in alphabetical order by colour with black first and yellow last. They share the mundane tasks of everyday life. They're in the bathroom together as she vigorously flosses. She smears hydrocortisone cream on the rash in the centre of his back that he can't quite reach. In the supermarket they debate what toilet paper to buy.

~

It's a lazy Sunday morning, Jill's in bed reading a novel and Jack's by the wardrobe contemplating what to wear.

His phone rings, it's Sabrina. She instructs him to read the newspapers.

113

'Why, what's up?' Jack asks.

'Just take a look then phone me back.' Sabrina terminates the call without further conversation.

'What is it?' Jill asks.

'I'm not sure. Mother wants me to see the newspapers,' he replies as he throws on some clothes.

He's back within minutes and drops a heap of Sundays onto the bed. Jill lifts the one with left of centre political leanings.

How the Rich Live is in large type splashed across the front page, then in smaller font: *One wife, two mistresses, three in a bed.* To the right is a photo of Henry Ashley-Lovett in evening dress.

Inside, across pages four and five, are the lurid details. There are photos of two scantily clad women, one blond, one dark-haired. The page is cleverly constructed with the blond on the left, the brunette on the right, both looking across at a profile photo of Jack's father, his unflattering smile distorted by the fold in the paper.

Jill scans the article and quickly picks up the gist. Henry is having an affair with Lucinda, a work colleague, this taking place behind the back of Sabrina, his long-suffering wife and mother of his two children. Lucinda has introduced him to her best friend, Tanya, and he has had sex with this woman behind his lover's back. The women often chat about their love lives and discover that Mr Ashley-Lovett has been two-timing, three if you count the poor wife. When they confront him, he readily owns up to his misdemeanour. Not only does he fail to show remorse, he suggests the three of them could have sex together and he's willing to pay. Foolishly the friends do as asked, just the

114

once, before recognising their mistake and deciding to expose his appalling behaviour.

Jill drops the paper onto the bed.

'There's plenty more,' Jack indicates, holding up one of the tabloids.

They flick through headlines.

Ashley-LovesIt!

When One or Two isn't Enough.

A Tale of Depravity.

The most serious of the broadsheets has a different slant. The scandal is one thing, but Ashley-Lovett is currently doing some consultancy for the Bank of England and the accusation is that he's claiming fees for work during times when he's having sex. There's the possibility of a charge for misappropriating taxpayers' money.

'What now?' Jill asks.

'Well, first of all, I need to call Mamma, er, I mean Mother.'

'Call her Mamma if you like. God, I feel so sorry for her.'

Jack phones and does far more listening than talking as a surprisingly cool and collected Sabrina describes how Henry had come home a few days earlier to inform her that the story was about to break. She tells Jack that's it, she's going to file for a divorce.

'Can I speak to her?' Jill asks.

'Mam…Mother, Jill would like a word with you.' Jack hands her his phone.

'Sabrina, this is terrible, is there anything we can do to help?…that's true…I think that's sensible…OK, I'll let Jack know. You take care, bye.'

She replaces the phone.

'She said she's glad this has happened because she's been thinking of leaving him and this is the final straw. I don't blame her.'

'I'd better phone Father.'

'Why, he's a rat?'

'Maybe, but he's still my father. It's only fair to get his side of the story.' He dials and leaves a message.

Seconds later the phone rings.

'Hello Father, I've read today's newspapers.'

Jack sets the phone onto speaker so Jill can hear the conversation. Henry's booming voice is boomier than ever, his arrogance and pomposity have not been diminished by the exposure. He admits to having been in a relationship with Lucinda, that's well and truly over now. He reckons right from the start she was scheming how to make money from their liaison. Although vague about the two in a bed incident, Henry admits, as the papers have indicated, to suggesting to Lucinda that he was up for a night with the three of them together.

'She's a damn pretty young thing, that Tanya,' Henry tells Jack. Had this conversation been in person, Jill would have been sorely tempted to punch him.

Tanya agreed to join Henry and Lucinda. She turned up with a new device, a mobile phone that was also a camera. 'Remarkable that a tiny thing like that can take such splendid pictures,' Henry continues without second thoughts about the subject matter – neither stunning scenery nor striking buildings, instead the three of them in highly compromising positions.

Henry chuckles as he reminisces about how the three of them laughed when they viewed the pictures. He's enjoying telling the story, boasting. Jill really does want him in the room so she can get that punch in.

'The next day I received an email from Lucinda with a photo attachment. She suggested ten thousand pounds would be a fair amount to hand over if I didn't want her to send this and other photos to your mother. I was livid, Jack, I had no intention to pay up. No one is going to blackmail an Ashley-Lovett, just you remember that.'

Henry suggests to Jack that his mother might not have kicked up too much of a fuss. Jill wants to get dressed, set off, track him down, punch him. Hard. Or whack him with a stick. She's hoping Jack might say something in protest, but he remains quiet.

Henry relates how he stormed into his office on the Monday morning and ordered Lucinda to leave immediately. He would never be blackmailed, he told her, he threatened to show the correspondence to the police. Two days later he got his first call from a newspaper, asking if he would care to make a comment.

'I told them what they could do with their story. That very same day I got a text from the dreadful woman. Just a minute, I think it's possible to send it on to you so you can read it yourself. Let me see.'

'It doesn't matter, Father.'

'I'd like you to see it. You'll notice she can't even spell properly. I think I have to press this.'

Jack's mobile pings, he glances at the screen before passing it over to Jill. *Glad u didn't send pics to wife, we got more money from papers. Thanx.*

117

'Have you received it?'

'Yes, Father.'

'Marvellous these new contraptions, eh.'

'Yes, they are good.'

A seething Jill is waiting for Jack to pass judgement, to indicate his disgust at the way Sabrina has been betrayed, but something else seems foremost on his mind. 'What about the accusation that you were, were doing things, when you should have been working for the government. Is that true?'

'That's sorted. I've got too many friends at the Bank to cover for me.'

Jill wishes she was recording the call to pass on to officials.

Henry is outrageously confident that everything will blow over. 'These things happen, all will be fine,' are his final words.

As soon as the call is over Jill challenges Jack. 'You didn't say much. You don't think anything other than he's a hundred percent wrong, do you?'

'He's totally in the wrong.'

'So why didn't you say something?'

'Probably because of over twenty years of being told off if I speak my mind. I know it's cowardly, you don't have to tell me.'

'What now though?' Jill asks.

'Support for my mother. We should visit her.'

'Good idea, why don't you call to let her know.'

As Jack lifts his phone, Jill's mobile rings. 'It's Mum,' she whispers to Jack, her hand over the mouthpiece. 'Mum, we've got a bit of an emergency here, can I call you back…What's the matter, why are you crying?' Jill slumps down onto the bed and raises her hand to indicate that Jack should delay dialling his own mother. 'How's that happened, is it definite?…You never told me there was a danger…Is he there, can I speak to him?…OK, but please give me a call as soon as he gets back…I'm sure things will work out, but phone the second you hear. Bye.'

'What's that about?' Jack asks.

Jill relays what was said during the brief conversation. Her father's business looks like it's going under and since he's one of the owners, there's a danger he'll be declared bankrupt.

'You've said looks like and a danger. That means nothing's definite.'

'I'm only repeating what Mum told me. It could be because it isn't certain, but knowing her, she might have said that to stop me worrying. She was upset enough though.'

Their lazy Sunday morning is no longer lazy. Jack puts his arm round Jill and pulls her close. 'What do you want to do? Shall we go and see them today?'

'What about your mother?'

'I'll call her then we can decide who gets priority.'

Jack puts the call on speakerphone again. Sabrina informs him that she's staying at home for the time being because Henry has agreed to stay at his Chelsea flat. She'll find a place for herself in London and Henry's going to have to pay the rent. She'll be seeing a divorce lawyer as soon as possible, too.

'What about Seb, where will he live?' Jack asks.

119

'He knows what's going on of course, as by the looks of things does the whole country, but it's too early to make any decisions. It will be up to him. For now, he's here with me.'

'Might you let the dust settle, maybe have a rethink about divorce?'

'Jack, I can tell you now, there's absolutely no chance of that. I'm done with it. This might be the first time it's reached national news, but it's not the first time he's gone astray as well you know.'

'I fully understand why you've made the decision, it's the right one and I respect you for it,' Jack pronounces.

Jill is touched by Jack's supportive words. She takes hold of his hand and gives it a gentle squeeze. 'Me too,' she calls out.

'You're a great pair you two, make sure you look after each other. You know what, I'm not even upset, my only regret is that I've stuck with that man for so long.'

'Mamma, Jill and I have got a further crisis to deal with, do you mind if we catch up with you later?'

'That's fine, Jack, though there is just one more thing.'

'Yes?'

'Could you please stop calling me bloody Mamma?'

'I…'

'Take care both of you.' Sabrina has cut the call, her final words had been spoken in a tone of calm joviality. Jill looks across at Jack and they burst out laughing.

'Now we have your lot to deal with. Let's pop down to see them, maybe we can help.'

'Would you do that for me?'

'Sure, it's doing it for us.'

Half an hour later and they are on their way to London. On arrival they assemble in the kitchen. For the first time Jill sees her parents as ageing, they look haggard.

After niceties and cups of coffee, Paul introduces the topic. 'It's good of you to come, but I'm not sure whether there's much to say that's definite. We've spoken to an insolvency assessor and he's going through our books to see where we stand.'

'What happens if you go bust, can't you just start again?' Jill asks.

'It's not that easy,' her father replies. 'There are bankruptcy laws to contend with.'

'And we might as well be up front, Paul,' Vanessa adds. 'The house is collateral for the business.'

'What does that mean?'

Paul and Vanessa's heads are down, Vanessa is using a teaspoon to stir air in her empty cup. 'It means that if funds are needed to pay creditors, they may recover money from the sale of our house.'

'Sell this house, you're joking,' Jill exclaims.

'Hold on though,' Paul says, 'we're nowhere near that yet, it's more a case of not having enough projects to pay future bills. We can cover current debts.'

'I thought the business was going well. All those awards you've won, Dad.'

'It all started with toilets,' is Vanessa's cryptic contribution.

Paul clarifies the toilet issue before going on to explain that a change of personnel at the planning office has lost them the support when they bid for new work. 'And as far as the private sector goes, there's been an overbuild of

121

offices and what with the forecast of little or no growth next year, that's bad news for all architects.'

'This is terrible,' Jill says.

'Well, it isn't a happy time, to say the least. But as I've said, based on yesterday's meetings I'm sure there's sufficient money to pay current bills. The first problem will be how long can we go on paying staff? Beyond that, although I might be unemployed for a bit, we can cope because your mother earns a good salary and we have savings.'

'Yes, but…' Jill realises she has nothing further to say.

'It's great that you're here and you too, Jack. The weather's glorious so let's enjoy the day.'

They drive out of London to a beauty spot that Jill had loved as a child; she hasn't been back there for years. They trek through woodland, escaping when it seemed the dense cover would never end, and they reach a ridge admiring stunning views across London.

Jack points to the tall buildings in the distance. 'That's Canary Wharf, isn't it? My father sometimes works there.'

There has been lots of chatting, now there is an uncomfortable silence before Vanessa speaks. 'Jack, I hope you don't mind me asking, but was that your father in the newspapers?'

'Mum!'

'No, it's fine to ask, and yes, I'm afraid it was. I'm deeply ashamed of him.'

Clouds have appeared, it seems from nowhere, and there is a light drizzle. 'Let's head off,' Vanessa suggests as she pats Jack on the shoulder. 'I'm sorry, it must be awful for you.'

By the time they've walked back through the woods and reached open ground the shower is over, the sky is again blue and it's as stiflingly hot as before. They have lunch at a pub near the car park. Jack insists on paying and following a good-natured argument, gets his way. They sit on a bench overlooking a green, Jill with happy childhood memories of Frisbee, cricket and handstands.

11

It's been a trying few weeks what with parent concerns and working flat out at university – the end of year examinations count towards the final degree. Jill is a worrier but there's little need because she's racing towards first-class honours.

Jack is summonsed by the Head of History. The walls of the room he enters are filled with books from floor to ceiling. Still more books, files and papers are stacked in piles on the floor and he has to proceed with care to reach a chair.

'You know, Jack, when I first interviewed you I didn't think you'd last. You've surprised me and the rest of the department, you deserve congratulations, I think you're now a 2.1 student or perhaps even better.'

Being addressed as Jack rather than Mr Ashley-Lovett is tied in with his growing reputation. 'Thank you, Professor Dawson, I appreciate that.'

'Have you thought about what use you might make of your degree?'

He's always assumed a City job is his destination but decides to feign indecision. 'No, not yet. I suppose I should start thinking about careers.'

'You're very personable. I think you could be a success as a lecturer or school teacher. Perhaps do a Masters first?'

'Interesting, I'll certainly consider that.' This is a lie, Jack is sure he will have had enough of study by the end of the following year and he has no interest in teaching. He knows he's part fraud; even though he's working harder than ever, his strategy remains to minimise the effort needed to be successful in his studies. Perusing history texts is tolerable, but it's a case of accessing the best sources as quickly as possible, then skim reading to find the arguments and quotes he needs. He's good at this.

The polite chat with the professor continues for a short while, Jack keeping his tutor happy with a discussion about whether the outcome of the War of the Roses was of benefit to the nation.

He's desperate to terminate the conversation because he wants to finalise plans for the forthcoming holiday with Jill. The flights to Nice are booked, next he needs to organise hiring a car at the airport. Jack has been to the South of France several times and he's keen to explore the region with Jill who's always wanted to visit but has never got round to it.

'If you don't mind, Professor Dawson. I'm most intrigued by our discussion, but I'd better finish packing. May I thank you for all the help you've given me, and that includes your willingness to take me on when I was in such a state of turmoil.'

He's said the right thing, the professor is beaming. Jack knows full well that whoever you're talking to, however renowned they are, people love a compliment.

'You will think about a Masters?' Dawson probes.

'Most certainly, thank you for the advice.'

They shake hands, another brownie point for Jack because he's noticed how few people his age shake hands these days and the older generation value it. At school they'd learnt the importance of firm hand-shaking.

~

A couple of weeks later and Jack and Jill are in France, taking in scenery, lying on beaches, visiting historic sites, and drinking and eating far too much. They both speak French and laugh and laugh as they play a game of mixing the two languages in daft statements.

Jill's on the beach across the road from their hotel, novel in hand, when Jack joins her.

'Mon ami, tu dois utiliser le Factor 30 otherwise you'll burn to le frazzle,' she reminds him.

'Je sais. C'est dangeresux, à cause de le global warming, n'est pas?'

'Bien sûr.'

'Mais deux conditions.'

'Quelle conditions, matey?'

'Numéro Un. You smear it on me and I smear it on you. Partout!' Jill is topless.

'Pas de problem.'

'Numéro Deux. Back in the hotel we share a shower to wash it off then le sex, le sex, le sex.'

'Aussi pas de problem.'

The holiday flies by and, well before they'd like it to end, they're back in England, saying their farewells at the airport before heading off to their families. Jack's decided initially to stay with his father and Seb rather than at the small flat that his mother has rented in London.

On Jill's first day home Dan arrives. They sit down with their parents to discuss what's going on. Paul's company is being wound down, fortunately with all debts covered so there's no bankruptcy to contend with. The partners are going their separate ways with six staff made redundant.

'What will you do?' Jill asks her father.

'Well, something's come up and it's rather exciting.'

'What?'

'There's a builder, Greg, who we've used a lot, someone I trust with a good team working for him. He's done some thinking recently.'

'That's useful.'

'No need for sarcasm, Jill, this is a big decision for us,' Vanessa says.

'He's fed up bidding for the diving number of new builds,' Paul continues. 'Everything left is being snapped up by the biggest companies, they can ride low margins for much longer than he can. Greg's convinced the money's in renovating old houses and he wants to specialise. Some of the properties he's working on need to be completely gutted and refurbished, and that needs an architect.'

Vanessa takes up the story. 'You know how much Dad and I love period properties, well this is the opportunity to restore them. It was the fashion in the sixties and seventies to hide anything considered fussy – door panels, fireplaces, cornices – now the fashion is to put them back.'

'So would you be employed by this person?' Dan asks.

'No,' Paul answers. 'And that's where the risk comes in because he wants to form a new company with me as his partner. It makes sense to have a builder and an architect working together because then a customer would know how

127

much it'll cost right from the outset. Without him, I'd have to get quotes from different builders. Without me, he wouldn't be able to cost anything until he had an architect to draw up plans.'

'What would the partnership mean in terms of outlay?' Dan asks.

'Not a fortune. Thousands, possibly reaching a five-figure sum, but not a high one.'

'And this house?' Jill asks. 'You said you might have to sell it.'

'We'll be keeping it, after all, it's our family home.'

While the Cross family conversation is taking place, Jack is sitting in his bedroom staring out the window. With Sabrina absent it no longer feels like home, he's a stranger in his own house what with Seb having a girlfriend staying, a pompous girl who's rude to the servants, and Henry having a new woman in residence. The four of them seem the best of friends, he's the outsider. He's tried to get the men together to discuss Sabrina's situation, but they don't want to know.

'She left us, Jack, remember that,' Seb says in a rare moment when Antoinette and Candice aren't glued to their men.

'Yes, but there was rather a good reason,' Jack replies.

'That's neither here nor there. This is the Ashley-Lovett home and it will remain so for generations to come,' Henry declares. 'Enough of this, I think it's time to adjourn to the library, the girls will be waiting for us.'

Jack is disturbed by the strong alliance between Seb and his father. He doesn't trust either of them but sees little point in any further challenge.

128

After an uncomfortable week he departs and spends a couple of days with Sabrina, sleeping on the well-worn and lumpy couch in her living room. Despite his efforts, he can't get her off the subject of Henry's treachery and how he's intent on preventing her from accessing any money. Jack is genuinely sympathetic and promises to see what he can do to put forward her case, but deep down he's pessimistic about his chances of having any influence. His father is powerful, has never been interested in taking on board his son's opinions, and most importantly, he's the one who controls the family wealth.

He wants to be with Jill, but it's evident from their telephone conversations that she's busy having a whale of a time dashing around London meeting up with friends.

'I can't face a return home, I might as well head back to our uni house,' Jack declares at the end of one call.

There are a couple of weeks to go before the start of the new term and he hopes this comment will generate an invite to stay at Jill's. It isn't forthcoming so he decides to do what he's told her.

He's surprised to discover that Charlotte is already there, she can't take any more family boredom, she tells him. They've always got on well and the obvious thing is to do stuff together. They take it in turns to cook, go out a couple of times for a bite to eat, work their way through Charlotte's stash of dope, go to the pub, and a few days before Jill's return, go to the cinema to see the new release *Exorcist: The Beginning*.

'I warn you,' Charlotte says as they sit down, 'I get terrified by horror.'

'Then why are we seeing this?'

'I like the panic rush.'

It is scary, frightening enough for Charlotte to gasp and scream every so often and to grab hold of Jack. He plays the part of the brave knight shielding a defenceless damsel in distress via a reassuring squeeze of her hand. He rather likes the role, if he were with Jill she'd be laughing at the stupidity of the film and he'd be secretly cowering.

'Fuck, I need a drink,' Charlotte says as they leave the cinema.

'What do you want?' Jack asks as they enter the pub.

'Something short and extraordinarily strong, a double if you don't mind.'

They each drink a double vodka, then another, then another, and possibly one after that. The conversation turns away from a semi-academic critique of the film, agreement reached that it was rubbish, to more base topics.

Later, when Jack is going over what happened, he's unsure whether he was the one who started the conversation about sex or whether it was Charlotte. His question had been fair enough. 'Are you still with that girl, the one who stayed with us the weekend before the end of term?'

'Alex? No, we split. We're still on good terms though.'

'Anyone new?'

'No, but I think the next lover will be male. I'm not that particular about gender, I enjoy sex with either. Do you think that's weird?'

'No, not at all, though I've never been with a bloke.'

'Have you never thought maybe?' Charlotte's face is all but touching his, it's an attractive face and the way she's looking at him is making him wonder as much as it's possible to wonder in such a highly drunken state, whether her ambiguous question implies to him with her.

'Absolutely absolutely not,' Jack replies, hoping this covers both possible interpretations of the question.

Charlotte manages to stand. 'Let's get a couple more drinks.'

'I think I've had enough, thanks.'

'Come on, last two, for the road.'

She's off to the bar before he can reply. He doesn't drink any because as Charlotte slumps back down onto her chair and hands him his drink, she spills it. It runs from the table edge onto his trousers.

'I'm sorry, let me…' Charlotte tries to stand, stumbles and ends up perched on Jack's knee. She undertakes the pointless task of wiping up the liquid with her hand, moving closer and closer to a part of Jack's body that can't help responding to the stimulus.

'I'm turning you on,' she shrieks, at which point Jack lifts her off him and stands, aware that he's as unstably drunk as she is.

They stagger home, leaning on each other. As soon as the front door is shut, Charlotte is kissing Jack. Somewhere at the back of his mind he knows he shouldn't be responding, but he's unclear why not. He remembers Charlotte yanking down his trousers because, she says, she's worried he'll get a chill as they're still wet. His boxers are next off even though they're dry. He has a recollection of other items being tugged and yanked and then of helping to remove hers. He remembers her explaining that taking her clothes off is merely an act of solidarity. That's about as much as Jack can recall when they wake up in bed the next morning.

He springs up, his head pounding, his movement enough to wake Charlotte. He is devastated. She kisses him on the cheek. 'That was fun.'

'Fun! Bloody hell, Charlotte, this is awful. I don't know what to do, I'm going to have to tell Jill and beg for forgiveness.'

'Don't be silly. I'll never tell a soul. We were smashed. It was a one off. I like you, but nothing more. I like Jill lots, too, and I'd hate to upset her.'

Jack says he'll think about what to do, Charlotte reiterates that she'll never tell anyone. He goes for a long walk, he's as guilty as hell.

When he returns there's a note from Charlotte. She's gone home for a couple of days to collect stuff ahead of the start of term. He feels like a criminal as he tears up the piece of paper, with its kiss kiss kiss symbols after her name, into tiny fragments. He takes the shreds outside and drops them into a neighbour's bin.

Jill arrives two days after the betrayal. The bedlinen is fresh, the incriminating sheets washed and hanging on the line to dry. He's decided not to tell her, the lie making him feel as treacherous as the act itself. There's an immediate test of his story. 'Why have you washed the sheets, didn't we put new ones on before we left?' Jill asks.

He now needs to extend the lie, each word adding to the guilt. 'I spilt a whole mug of tea on them.'

'You're so domestic. I love you. I've missed you.'

Jack's guilt has reached a new level.

Later that afternoon when Charlotte walks through the front door, his heart starts pounding. She kisses everyone and asks if they've had a good holiday, Jack is just one of the gang during this conversation. For ages afterwards he's suspicious of every look that Morag or Priya give him in case Charlotte's told them. He hates his disloyalty because being with Jill is the most wonderful experience he's ever known and no one could ever replace her.

~

The final year is racing by.

Morag can sing. She's joined her boyfriend's heavy metal band, practises several evenings a week and gigs about once a fortnight. She hopes this will turn into a career, but full commitment is on hold until she gets her degree.

A module in Charlotte's Psychology course has led to some cross fertilisation with the Forensics Department. This opens up the opportunity to interact with a new contingent of boys, seemingly desperate for live flesh having spent so much time with dead bodies. The other housemates are confronted by a wide variety of guests and there are some fun conversations about gruesome murders. Charlotte seems to have got over her horror phobia.

Priya is less and less engaged socially as she travels back and forth to her fiancé and their two families every Friday, returning Monday mornings.

'Why don't you invite him here for the weekend?' Morag suggests.

'I have asked, but he's not keen.' Priya says. Jill wonders whether she's detected a sadness in her friend's expression.

Jill's father has made a good start with his new company, the success fuelled by a staggering upsurge in London house prices.

'The young might go for minimalist apartments overlooking the Thames, but oldies prefer Victorian and Edwardian charm,' Paul tells Jill and Jack during one of their regular visits. 'Of course, they still want their swimming pools, Jacuzzis, saunas, gyms and home cinemas, so there's plenty for us to do.'

Jill refuses to join Jack on visits to his own home, she can't bear the thought of being with his father, Seb and the two girlfriends. Her loyalty is firmly with Sabrina. Jack journeys home every few weeks and returns full of scorn for the pair of them.

'You should see more of your mother,' she often reminds him.

'I can't stand the incessant moaning.'

'Perhaps she needs to see that you're on her side,' Jill suggests.

'I am, but going on and on about it switches me off.'

'That won't last, as soon as the divorce is finalised she'll feel better. Actually when Mum and I see her she's great fun.'

That's true. The three women socialise often, the two mothers having taken to each other so much that they even meet when Jill can't join them. Sabrina is intent on catching up with all she's missed out on over the years. Top of the list is being in a buzzing city rather than stuck in the middle of nowhere with nothing to do. She's the one who does the organising, emailing Jill and Vanessa about a new play or film she'd like to see, a new exhibition she wants to visit, or a restaurant that's been getting rave reviews.

For Jill these occasions are a welcome break from student life. She spends the night at her parents or takes one of the late trains back to university. If the latter, however late, Jack insists on collecting her from the station.

As they reach the final term, the examinations term, the outings to London come to a temporary end – it's work, work, work.

12

They are celebrating their degree success at a restaurant with a large group of friends from the English and History faculties. Jack leans across to Jill and whispers.

'What surprise?' she mouths.

'Wait and see,' he replies. 'After this.'

Jack is good at surprises, weekends away, ridiculously long-distance treks to see their favourite bands, jewellery that is of perfect taste.

This meal is going on and on, one toast after another, and now the students are making drunken pledges to stay in touch, tears are being shed, boasts made about the start of glamorous careers with tons of money.

'Let's get the bill and head off,' Jill pleads, not so much in impatient anticipation of the surprise, it's more a case of exhaustion. It's been one hell of a day. Getting their results at nine o'clock. Opening a bottle of champagne by ten o'clock. Texting, calling, meeting, hugging, commiserating throughout the afternoon. And then this never-ending meal. She's had enough.

Jack has had his fill, too, so they seize the opportunity as the plans for clubbing begin.

'Come on you two, you've got to join us,' shouts Morag from the other end of the table as she sees them stand up.

'Too tired!' Jill shouts back.

'Middle aged!' is Morag's retort, somewhat overused over the years.

'And the surprise is…?' Jill asks as they head back to their house. She discovers she's drunk, she can barely walk and her speech is slurred. 'Let's get a taxi back.'

'Taxi? We're only a couple of streets away from home.'

Yes, very drunk, she doesn't even know where they are. By the time they reach their house she's forgotten about the surprise. 'I want to fuck you big time,' she declares as she starts to yank off clothes in the hallway. Her shoes are off, her dress is over her head and she has unclipped her bra when Priya steps out the lounge, a mug of coffee in her hand.

'Honestly, Jill, can't you wait?' she asks as a topless Jill rushes towards her.

'Priya, I'm going to so miss you!' she cries out, knocking the drink over her friend as she squeezes her.

'Careful, it's hot.'

Jack pulls Jill away. 'Sorry Priya, she's been celebrating a bit too much. What have you been doing this evening, I thought you would have joined us?'

'On the phone to my fiancé most of the time, I'm heading home tomorrow.'

'Brilliant you getting a first. Hands off, Jill! I think I'd better take her to bed.'

Jill all but drags Jack to the staircase and Priya watches as they struggle up the stairs.

Once in the bedroom, Jill sets upon Jack with unusual ferocity. She gets her shot of sex and is soon fast asleep. Jack smiles as he thinks back to their first night together, three long years ago. Their night outdoors, both pissed out of their minds. He looks at the woman he loves, splayed out across the bed, the surprise ignored. He grabs the pen on the bedside table and writes on her arm. *Remember the surprise!*

The next morning Jack wakes early and heads downstairs. He's groggy, hung over. He makes a cup of tea and watches a chat show on television. Finally, mid-morning, Jill joins him, holding up the arm with the message.

'Ready,' she grins.

'The surprise is, you'll need your passport and clothes for a warm but not baking hot place, and you'll have to be ready at half-past nine on Friday morning.' Despite being pestered, he refuses to give further information.

The following days are strange ones, Jack and Jill not alone in describing their feeling of emptiness. Everyone had been so busy revising and sitting exams and now that there's a huge amount of free time, they don't know how to fill it. Friends are heading home for good; there are promises to stay in touch, but who knows when they'll next meet up.

Friday morning arrives. As they drive to the airport Jill interrogates, but to no avail. They park and walk to the terminal, still no answers are given. They get in a queue and only then does Jill see.

Venice.

She screams and two security guards approach.

138

'Is anything wrong, miss?'

'I've been kidnapped, but I don't mind,' she informs them. 'You can run along boys.'

They don't respond well to her flippancy and order Jack and Jill to accompany them.

They're led into a small windowless room, empty bar two pairs of chairs separated by a table. They're instructed to sit down and to hand over their passports and tickets.

Jack looks at his watch, conscious of moving uncomfortably close to flight time. 'I hope this isn't going to take long.'

'It will take as long as need be, sir,' the older of the two men replies. Thin strands of dyed black hair are stretched over his balding crown. Jack grins at the sight. 'I don't advise laughter, sir.'

The guard turns to face Jill. 'Is this man taking you away under duress?'

'What!'

'I said is this man –'

'– You don't need to repeat it. My 'what' was a response to your ridiculous question. Of course he isn't, I screamed because I was excited.'

'Do your parents know where you're travelling to and that you're with this man?'

'I'm not a child, I can do what I want.'

'So they don't know?'

'They know who this man is, but how can they know where I'm going if I've only just found out myself?'

'I'd like you to call them.'

'Why?'

'I've told you to.'

'That's stupid, I'm not a child.'

'Maybe it's best to just do it,' Jack advises.

Jill does so. It's Vanessa who answers the phone and she's excited to hear the news. The man doing all the talking insists on having a word to double-check that it really is a parent Jill's speaking to. He asks Vanessa to confirm her child's date of birth and the name of the man by her side. This does the trick, their passports and tickets are returned and they're allowed to dash to the check-in desk.

~

Venice is wonderful. They arrive at their hotel by boat, to a building more like a palace than a hotel. The floors are marble, the walls are adorned with frescos, and the furniture is over-the-top Louis XIV if it's ever possible to be over the top in that style. Their bedroom overlooks the Grand Canal, a vast room even by comparison to those in Jack's house. Their bed is positioned slap bang in the centre away from all walls. It has a canopy, the bedlinen is silk, the dressing gowns are silk, and they've been provided with slippers upturned at the toes, just like a gondola.

Without stopping to unpack, they head off to St Mark's Square. Piazza San Marco, Jack informs her. He's taken a module on Italian History at university and it's like having a personal guide as he describes when buildings were constructed and the lives of those who lived and worked in them. When they head back she discovers that their hotel really was a palace before conversion, inhabited from the sixteenth century onwards by a family of wealthy tradesmen. She teases him when the detail resembles a tutorial at university rather than the more general chat fitting for a tourist. But his enthusiasm is ever so sweet.

140

'Another thing though, Jill. Did you know that the first ever paperback was produced here in Venice?'

That first evening they take a gondola to their restaurant, tucked away at the side of one of the eerily beautiful canals. The head waiter greets them as they step off the boat. The food is scrumptious, reinforcing Jill's opinion that anything Italians cook is delicious.

After the meal they stroll back to their hotel, weaving their way over tiny bridges, little lights illuminating the canals, gondolas swishing by. Jill has never been won over by the soppiness of Romance with a capital R, but that evening she believes that Venice has to be the most romantic place in the world.

The next day they take a train to Verona and drink coffee, incredibly expensive, overlooking the Roman arena. Jill runs her hand across one of the giant blocks of stone, this being her way of taking in the magnitude of what Jack is telling her about the two thousand year old building.

'Let's move on,' he orders in true guide fashion.

They watch groups of fifty or so tourists being led around the arena by guides with brightly coloured umbrellas held aloft. Jill reflects on her good fortune, her tour is for one person and her guide is her lover. 'I need a kiss. Now!'

'The next stop is the best place for that, possibly the best in the world.'

Jack is striding off and she chases after him.

They are soon standing under Juliet's balcony, aware that the Capulet family never lived here and Shakespeare never visited Verona, but it's fun to go along with the myth for a while. Jill enters the house and reaches the balcony

141

which they both know is a twentieth century add-on to the fourteenth century house. She waves to Jack down below and recites the speech, offering condescending smiles to those by her side guilty of misquoting.

'Now the kiss,' she orders when she's back with Jack in the mobbed courtyard below the balcony.

He pecks her on the cheek and takes her hand. 'I can't here, it's too corny. There's a better place.'

They take another short walk to Piazza Dante, a wonderful medieval square that is near-deserted. Jack's knowledge of history and Jill's of literature come to life as they visit the palaces off the square, Jill reciting lines from Dante's *Inferno* as they stroll. Here they kiss and kiss some more, sharing the happiness of love intensified by the optimism of youth. University is over and their new lives are about to begin. Whatever challenges this might bring, they will be facing them together.

Back in Venice they spend their time exploring the city on foot, twisting and turning along the canals with their narrow pathways. On the penultimate day they take a boat to the island of Murano, watching glass-making before popping into near-identical shops. Jack leads her off the beaten track to a small shop that he's marked on his map. It's an ancient building with crumbling walls. He pulls a brass knob on the side of the door towards him and they hear the high-pitched tinkle of a bell. The door is opened by a white-haired man who greets them warmly with firm handshakes. Jill senses they are expected. He offers a glass of wine and they chat about the beauty of Venice for quite some time without any reference to buying and selling.

'What you see in many big shops,' he says, 'it is not from our island.'

'It's made in other parts of Italy?' Jill asks.

'No, this is not allowed. But China yes, it is made in China.' The man laughs, the falsetto giggle at odds with his large frame. 'Chinese tourists visit, buy this so-called Murano glass and take it back to where it has been produced. Funny is it not? In this here shop everything Italian, everything Murano.'

'What do you like best?' Jack asks Jill as they look round. Each piece is a beautiful work of art, but she's particularly drawn to a tall vase with a modern design of bold blues and purples. She glances at the price and turns to find something cheaper, smaller. Jack knows her well enough to have noticed her interest and her reason for looking elsewhere. 'This one's amazing,' he says, pointing to her first choice and nodding to the shop owner.

'Look at the price, Jack,' she whispers.

'It's the one you're having – a gift for getting a first. Bitch!'

'Ha-ha. A 2.1 degree isn't bad for a public school thicko.'

'I'm happy with that. And I've got you to thank for making me carry on, I was all set to quit.'

'You've become quite the academic, you should have investigated doing a masters like the professor suggested.'

'Enough is enough. Working in the City might not end up the right choice but I'm willing to give it a go. I can always quit and do something else.'

This conversation takes place while the vase is being packed in miles of bubble wrap and then carefully placed inside a small wooden crate.

'There, it is ready to be shipped. It will take a week or two to reach you.'

Jack pays by credit card, Jill notices that the transit adds several hundred euro to the cost. With the transaction concluded they shake hands and make their way back to the small harbour to catch the boat to the centre of Venice. There is a considerable queue and it's evident that a substantial proportion of the tourists are indeed Chinese. Each one of them is carrying several plastic bags and Jill wonders how many of the products are being taken back to where they were made.

The next day, their last, starts with a late breakfast then packing. They have three or so hours to go before setting off to the airport. Jack insists they take a final look at Piazza San Marco, an odd choice since they'd agreed that their favourite part of Venice were the humped bridges over the small canals.

'Why don't we go for another random walk instead?' Jill suggests.

'No, I think the piazza.'

'But it'll be jam-packed full of tourists this time of day.'

'Exactly.'

They hop onto a boat and make their way down to the square. When they've alighted Jack takes hold of Jill's hand and pushes through the hordes as he marches her to slap bang in the centre of St Mark's.

'This is fine,' he says. 'Let's stop here for a minute.'

Jill glances up to the hundreds of pigeons circling the square in search of leftover fast food then returns her gaze to where Jack should be. He isn't, he's on one knee in front of her.

'Jack, what are you…?' She realises what the answer is and waits for him to speak, surprised by the wave of dizzy nervousness that has hit her.

It's all so dramatic, Jack down on his right knee with his left arm outstretched in this vast square, surrounded by the crowds and the postcard palaces, he clutching a small navy velvet box. Time stands still for a short while before he speaks, she is aware of incessant chatter around her. 'Jill, from the first time I saw you I knew you were special and the only one for me. We've shared so much during our time at university and I want us to carry on sharing for ever. Will you marry me?'

It's as if everyone around her has stopped their shouting, she can only hear Jack's words. There's a short silence before she replies. 'Yes, I would love to.'

The silence isn't imagined because now there is a large cheer from the deep circle of people surrounding them. Jack stands up and they kiss, which brings on a second cheer. They proceed to shake hands with what seems like half the visitors to Venice and a fair number of locals too. In the end, Jack has to announce they have a plane to catch and he steers Jill towards the exit from the square closest to the jetty.

Back at the hotel Jack takes the blue box from his pocket.

'I was worried it might get pinched with all those people around, but here, this is yours.'

'I was wondering why you didn't hand it over, I thought you'd forgotten in all the excitement. Or changed your mind!'

He takes out the silver ring with its row of small diamonds. He knows her so well, this is beautiful, delicate, she wouldn't want a giant stone. He places it on her finger, it fits perfectly.

'How did you know my size?' the ever practical Jill asks.

'I borrowed one of yours and got the jeweller to measure it.'

'The obsidian?'

'Is that a black stone?'

'Yes.'

'That's the one then.'

'I was wondering where that got to, then it suddenly reappeared where I was sure I'd left it in the first place.'

'Do you like this?' he asks, lifting up her hand.

'Love it.'

'Love me?'

'Not as much as the ring, but I suppose you'll do!'

Part 2

13

The start of post-university life is marked by good fortune though with something equivalent to selling their souls to the devil. They have their own property, a lovely mews house in Central London close to Regents Park. Jack's father has found it, vacated by a friend retiring from the City and moving to his countryside home. It costs a small fortune and Henry has agreed to contribute the massive deposit. Jack has been quick to accept the offer but Jill has strong reservations about taking from a man she so despises. Her upbringing has taught her not to use privilege to get on in life; they should have to strive like everyone else out there.

She expresses her concerns to Jack.

'I don't understand. Don't you like the place?'

'Like it? I absolutely love it.'

'So what's the problem?'

Jill tries to articulate her feelings, but she's cut short by Jack. 'With our salaries there's no way we could afford anything like this without help. What's the alternative? A flat in some awful suburb with an hour journey on the Underground to get to work?'

Jill recognises Jack is right and agrees to accept Henry's charity. Even with his contribution, that still leaves a sizeable mortgage, one they can just about cover thanks to Jack's good starting salary and Jill's imminent contribution. She bites the bullet and writes Henry an obsequious thank you letter.

Henry's friend has given permission for them to fill the vacant property with their possessions ahead of the sale being completed, allowing them to jump directly from their student house to the London one. This makes for a busy but enjoyable June as they get everything ready for the move.

Jill has strong opinions about what she wants. 'Retro,' she tells Jack.

'You mean antiques?' he asks, surprised by her choice.

'Ugh, no, I don't want a mini Ashley-Lovett estate. I mean '60s retro.'

She takes him round what Jack perceives as junk shops, but he has to admit she's got a great eye for style and bargains. The combined living and dining room is filled with a walnut table, six purple plastic chairs, a lavender Biba sofa, bold flower power cushions with matching curtains and two Lichtenstein posters.

On their first evening after the move they saunter along neighbourhood streets. Despite the city centre location it has a village feel with its small independent shops and an abundance of trees and green spaces. The area exudes affluence, the cost of their meal in the small bistro alone is evidence of that wealth.

To any fellow diner who cares to observe them, their mutual love is beyond dispute – the smiles and laughter, the holding and squeezing of hands as they plan their future together.

As they stroll home in late evening twilight, the sky an inky blue, they peek into interiors fit for designer magazines. By comparison, their own furnishings do seem rather modest, though they're proud of what they've done so far with their limited resources.

They open a bottle of champagne and drink a toast to the end of an era and the dawn of a new one, the beginning of many happy years together. Lying in bed on top of the orange and red striped quilt, drunk, satiated and happy, Jill tells Jack that she loves him.

'And I love you too,' he replies.

~

It's the first Monday in July, the start of Jack's new job in the City. He's struggled to explain to Jill exactly what he'll be doing, something connected with trading, investment banking, futures and derivatives. She's of the opinion that he doesn't quite know himself but is confident he'll pick it up as he goes along. She'd like to ask him once again if this really is how he wants to make use of his history degree or whether the career choice is a result of family pressure. But of course she doesn't ask, it would be highly inappropriate. She's proud looking across at her man in his suit, crisp white shirt and bold tie.

'More coffee?'

'No, I'd better get going.'

It's approaching seven o'clock. She wishes him good luck and kisses him as they stand at the front door. She's fortunate, there are six more weeks of holiday before she starts her teaching job, although three of them will be taken up on the Teach First residential training course.

151

It's immediately evident that long hours will be the norm for him. On the first Monday, Tuesday and Wednesday he's out the house at the crack of dawn and not back until gone eight at night. During these days Jill's the perfect housewife, each evening there's a meal waiting for him, a glass of wine already poured, and there are even slippers in the hallway. By the Wednesday an in-joke has already set in. Jack calls out "Honey, I'm home" as he steps through the door and Jill comes running out to greet him, re-enacting a 1950s suburban American scene as depicted on television soaps. Her accent is perfect Deep South.

These three days are lovely as Jill makes the most of it ahead of what she knows will be a busy start at work as a new teacher. Each morning she listens to Radio 4 as she sorts their possessions, following Jack's instructions not to touch his personal belongings, his obsession with order remaining. During the afternoons she reads the newspaper from cover to cover, takes a stroll to the local deli to buy ingredients for the evening meal, and finally chills out with Jack in front of the telly.

There's no reason to suppose that the Thursday will be any different. Relaxing in the kitchen with an espresso and a bowl of muesli, Jill switches on the radio. The news is grim, there have been terrorist attacks on the London Underground. For an instant, she forgets she lives in London, so calm and sheltered is their environment.

The words "Liverpool Street" jolt her back to reality.

Liverpool Street is at the heart of the City.

Jack works in the City.

She has no idea which Underground line he takes.

She calls but his phone isn't on.

She switches on the television and watches horrific scenes.

She calls him again and still can't get connected.

A newscaster informs that mobile networks are down because of capacity issues.

She sits down and sobs, helpless.

Her mother calls. 'Have you heard from Jack?'

'No, I can't get through.'

Sabrina calls. 'Have you heard anything, I've been trying to call him but he's not answering?'

'I think the networks are down.'

Jill has to do something.

She walks to the station to double-check her knowledge that theirs is on the Jubilee Line. It is.

It's closed, the whole Underground is closed.

She dashes home to look at the tube map, only a double-check because she's from London and knows the lines inside out. He would have changed at Baker Street and taken the City and Hammersmith or Circle Line to Liverpool Street. It was on the Circle Line that one of the bombs exploded.

The timing is wrong though, or does she mean right as far as Jack is concerned. He left at his usual time that morning and the attack didn't happen until 8.50 am. He'd be at work by then.

Surely.

Jill calls Jack. Still no connection.

She texts a daft message. *Worried. Call as son as poss.* Her hand is shaking so much, she doesn't try to correct her typo.

She knows it has to be OK for Jack, so now, as she watches television, she grieves for those at the wrong place at the wrong time.

Jack calls mid-afternoon. She cries when she hears his voice, he assures her he's fine though shocked, and of course sympathetic for those who have suffered. 'I'm not sure how I'm going to get home. I might as well walk, that's what most people here are thinking of doing. We've been standing around watching the news all day, but now everyone's drifting off.'

Jack is back before seven, ironically earlier than previously that week. They've both watched the extensive news coverage and there is little left to say. Jill holds onto him, reluctant to let go. Jack breaks the silence, describing the camaraderie of people chatting away to strangers as they walked along. 'It must have been like that in the Blitz,' he says, making light of the day's events for Jill's sake.

In bed they cling to each other and Jill can't stop crying. Their house, money, status, it's all insignificant if you lose the one you love. Hold on tightly as you never know what's round the corner.

~

Jill wonders whether Jack will go to work the next day, but he's up, dressed and having breakfast by the time she comes downstairs.

Life goes on, back to normal for those not affected by the events of that terrible day. She carries on unpacking, reading, going for walks, preparing dinner for the later and later arrival of her husband.

The days race by and it's time to set off for her Teach First training.

The course reminds her of the early days at university, the promiscuity around her immense with seemingly everyone scrambling around in search of a mate. Despite wearing her engagement ring she gets offers which she rejects with polite firmness. She phones Jack every evening, ending the conversation with a declaration of love. Her immature, hungover colleagues manage daily to transform into intelligent and conscientious beings who sail through the challenging work, everyone recognising the daunting list of things that will be needed to be a successful teacher.

Jill gets home early evening on the final day of the course, Jack has yet to return from work. She texts to let him know she's back and will get dinner ready. There's a shock in store in the kitchen when she seeks the items she needs for cooking. During her three-week absence Jack's obsession with sorting has run riot. Nothing is in the same place, the changes are nonsensical and she can't find anything.

She hears the key in the door and the brisk footsteps as Jack rushes into the kitchen to greet her. Breaking from their embrace, she gently pulls him back to make eye contact.

'Jack …' she starts.

'I know. I know what you're going to say,' the topic of conversation obvious because every kitchen cupboard is open.

'I'm looking for these things,' she says, handing him a list of eleven items.

'That's easy,' he declares with fake bravado as he takes hold of the piece of paper. Ten minutes later he's still searching, having found five so far. Jill's sitting at the kitchen table, her smile turns to laughter.

'Wine?' Jack asks. 'I know where that is.'

'Good idea.'

Jack extracts a bottle from the wine rack. He's always sorted into reds and whites which is reasonable enough, but now, he announces, he's arranged each row by date of production.

'Sauternes 2001,' he declares. 'This will be good.'

He sets the bottle down on the work surface and Jill watches in disbelief as he starts to lift the whites to the right of the bottle he's taken, moving them one place to the left.

'Jack,' Jill begins. 'That's bonkers. What happens if you buy a 2001 replacement tomorrow?'

'I suppose I'd take them out and re-sort. It doesn't take long.' His expression implies a challenge to her sanity for asking such a daft question.

She bursts out laughing. 'You said you might go to the doctor to discuss OCD. Maybe now's the time.'

'Actually I went when you were away.'

'And?'

'He wasn't at all concerned, at least not until the full examination.'

'Examination? Why?'

'He thought it would be a good idea to check me over.'

'For OCD?'

'Yes. And when I took my trousers off he asked me to refold them because the creases weren't straight.'

'What!'

'Then he insisted I put one sock in each shoe.'

'The man's an utter …'

Jack's broad boyish grin is evident, Jill's been duped. They can still share amusement of silly pranks.

'Did you go though?'

'No, there really is no point. I know I'm a bit fussy, but it's nothing more than that.'

Jill isn't convinced and when they go into the lounge after dinner it's clearly gone beyond fussiness. The bookcase, Jill's bookcase, is empty, her extensive collection of fiction stacked high on the floor.

'What on earth have you done?'

'I'm going to arrange them in alphabetical order by author. They'll be easier to find.'

'No you're not. I'm putting them back right now and I want you to promise you won't interfere with my books again,' Jill says as she grabs a pile and drops them back onto a shelf.

'But…'

'No but.' She plonks another pile onto the shelf.

'What about height order then?'

'Tell me you're not serious, Jack.'

He isn't sure whether he's serious or not. What he does know is that his obsession with the need to sort things has got worse since he's started work. When he's feeling anxious after a hard day the sorting reduces tension, although he frets when thinking about what an idiot he is for doing it. It's an unresolved dilemma – is he more stressed sorting or not sorting?

~

Jill starts teaching at the beginning of September and their world changes dramatically. She's overwhelmed. During weekdays there's little time to do anything together

157

other than a quick early morning conversation about what to eat that evening and who's going to cook it. With his ever-increasing hours of work, Jill misses having Jack at home evenings, but at least it gives her the time to do her marking and lesson preparation in peace. Jack's keen to do things at weekends, but Jill's even occupied then.

'It's because it's my first term,' Jill had said early on, 'everyone says the first term is hell.' Being a bright hardworking Teach Firster, she's expected to do more than others to prove her worth and all sorts of time-consuming responsibilities are dumped on her.

Despite the need to cut down on socialising, Jill sticks with the girls' nights out with Sabrina and her mother every fortnight or so. Usually they combine dinner with cinema, theatre or an art gallery. The two older women have struck up a good friendship.

Poor Sabrina has had a dreadful year of argument with Henry. His solicitor put forward the claim that his client's vast wealth was the family inheritance and therefore his soon to be ex-wife had no entitlement. This proposition was finally overruled in court and the divorce settlement is through after twelve months of conflict. Sabrina has acquired enough money to purchase outright a mansion flat just off the Marylebone Road, not far from Jack and Jill's house. She plans to move before Christmas.

'Don't worry,' she tells Jill during a get-together. 'I won't be visiting you night and day. Mind you, it'll be useful when you have children.'

'That won't be for quite a while, I've got my career to think about.'

'Women keep putting it off these days then wonder why they're so exhausted when they finally get to raise them,' Vanessa says.

'Career women. They work and work and, in the end, have money but nothing else, no family to cherish,' Sabrina adds.

'Modern society, you wonder where it's leading.'

'Common sense has gone out the window. Please don't leave it too long, Jill.'

'Stop it you two, you're being ridiculous. I'm only twenty-two.'

'I agree with Sabrina, you can always develop your career when the children start school.'

'What children? End of conversation, I'll let you know when I'm pregnant, but don't hold your breath.'

Jill assumes the conversation has been tongue in cheek, particularly the words spoken by her so-called progressive, anything goes mother.

The next morning she's all set to moan to Jack about what was said, but he's the first to speak, telling her about the conversation he had with Seb when she was out the previous evening. 'He's keen to discuss the family situation now that the divorce is out of the way. He's been nagging to see our place, too, so I've suggested we meet here.'

'Oh.'

'Is that a problem?'

'No, I suppose not. When?'

'This weekend, he's planning on getting here by lunchtime on Saturday.'

The last thing Jill wants is to play hostess to Jack's brother, she hasn't seen him for over a year.

Seb arrives, full of smiles and bonhomie. He hands Jill a huge bouquet of flowers and Jack gets not a single bottle, but a whole case of red wine. He's filled out, Jill notes, muscular rather than stocky, with a mop of hair swept across his forehead that he remorselessly flicks with the back of his hand.

Jill sits in the corner oozing distaste while the brothers talk.

'I'll be going to Pater's college,' he informs Jack, his posh and booming voice surely perfect for what is considered the most privileged of the Oxford colleges.

'You're not guaranteed a place, you have to make the grades first,' Jack states, his own disappointing results on his mind.

'A mere formality,' Seb assures him. 'They loved me at interview.'

Jill wishes she had religion so she could pray that he fails to get in.

Seb raises the Sabrina situation. He is of the belief that she has robbed their father. 'It's our family's money, it's been with us for generations. Why should it go to an outsider?'

'You can hardly call our mother an outsider,' Jack counters.

Jill notes the potential parallel to herself and leaves the room to let them get on with it while she prepares the meal. Over dinner Seb talks of the girls at school as if they're objects on display in a shop window.

'Dumb blond with great tits.'

'That one can't get enough of it.'

She's never told Jack about his brother's behaviour, including when he was sending her lewd texts six or so months back. She'd deleted them on receipt and assumes his interest in her will have burnt out now that he apparently has the pick of the sixth form girls.

The brothers set to work on the red wine after dinner and Jill retires early.

Jack has a Sunday morning game of tennis, leaving Jill alone with Seb. She's in the kitchen getting lunch ready, a traditional roast out of the kindness of her heart bearing in mind she's more or less given up meat.

'Good morning, Jill.' Seb is in his pyjamas, bringing back memories of their last encounter. He's standing by the kitchen door. 'I still want you, you know,' he tells her, his voice deep, commanding to the point of insistence.

'I would have thought you've got over it,' she says as she wraps the beef in foil and places it in the oven.

'Well you're wrong, I haven't.'

She moves to the sink and begins to peel potatoes. 'I'm afraid that's too bad.'

'We could do it now. See this, it puts Jack's to shame.'

If she'd thought it through she would have recognised his meaning, but she hadn't and turns to face him out of curiosity. His thing is poking out of his pyjama bottoms, erect. He takes hold of it and points in her direction.

She lifts the knife. 'And see this. If you don't get out of this room now, I'll use it on you.'

He smiles. 'I like a filly with fighting spirit.'

His comment angers her more than the dick in his hand – the arrogant posho. Who the fuck at age eighteen calls a woman a fucking filly? She lifts the bowl out the sink, potatoes, peelings, water and all, and hurls it across the room. It strikes him on the shins, dropping onto his bare feet and smashing. There's a small amount of blood amidst the heap of the contents.

'Would you like me to help clear it up?' he asks with a smile, his cool arrogance is intolerable. She's inclined to throw something else at him, but apart from the scope to lob a Brussels sprout or two, there's nothing else.

She opts for words. 'I see it's shrunk rather, maybe you should put it away before I start laughing. You know what, Seb, you're so much like your father. Isn't that something to be proud of?'

He leaves the room and not another word is uttered between them that morning or when Jack returns and they have lunch. After coffee Jill speaks. 'A pity you have to leave now, Seb, but I appreciate how important it is for you to get back to school to revise. I hope you get what you deserve in the exams.'

She goes upstairs into the bedroom and doesn't come down until the front door closes.

'What was that about,' Jack asks.

'He's an absolute shit, that's all, and I'm glad you're so different.'

14

It's New Year's Eve. Jack and Jill are using the time off work to restore energy levels after such a busy few months in their new jobs. There's no indication that the future will be any less stressful. Jill recognises that her promise that the high workload would only be during her first term at school isn't true – she has masses to prepare during the holiday. Jack has discovered the implications of working in a global market – he's expected to be on call any time day or night.

They've rejected all offers of joining festivities, including a tempting one from Morag, their university friend, who's now living in London and is hosting a reunion party. Instead, they decide to flop out in front of the telly, bottle of champagne ready to open, bottle of white already consumed. They receive two early bird texts, one from Sabrina and one from Vanessa, both in reaction to the publicised threat of networks getting jammed on the stroke of midnight. As the clock strikes twelve, other texts flood in, the girls and others from university, people from work, old school friends.

Their plan to start the year with lovemaking on the dot of midnight is abandoned, Jill happy to go along with Jack's suggestion that they wait until the morning and crash out now. He's drunk considerably more than Jill and his crashing out is instant. He's alive enough the next morning though, waking her with divine caresses.

Jack dashes downstairs to prepare a special New Year breakfast of scrambled eggs, smoked salmon, fresh orange juice and champagne. By the time Jill comes down, the table is immaculately set with colour coordinated mats and napkins perfectly positioned next to plates, cups and saucers and champagne flutes.

'I've been thinking,' Jack begins as they sit down. 'An idea to make sure we guarantee quality time together now that we're so busy at work. Let's plan our holidays for the year on each New Year's Day. They'll be fixed in our diaries and we'd have something to look forward to.'

'Perhaps no need to commit to doing it every New Year's Day, but it's a great idea for today.'

'After all, we've got the money. They'd be my treat, you wouldn't have to spend a penny.'

'I earn too.'

'That's beside the point, it's my thank you for being you.'

It turns into a fun day despite the outside gloom. They investigate options online, looking at photos and videos, reading reviews and scrutinising details. By mid-afternoon they've decided, skiing in Switzerland over Easter (Jack's been skiing once or twice a year throughout his youth, for Jill it will be a first), a summer fortnight in the Seychelles, and a Christmas break to the sunshine of the West Indies. Jack intends to book everything after they've had a couple of days to reflect.

They're at Jill's parents for dinner and are all set to tell them about their holiday plans, but ahead of being able to do so, receive an unexpected first shock of the year.

'There's a possibility we'll be moving,' Vanessa announces when the three of them are in the kitchen, she pouring glasses of wine.

'Moving where? Out of London?'

'Maybe out of England. To France for a while, though nothing's certain yet.'

'How nice of you to tell me, Mum.'

'It's only just cropped up and as I said, nothing's at all certain.'

Paul joins them and explains. 'The London market's saturated with architects. I thought renovation was our great opportunity, but that's not turning out to be the case. I'm finding it hard to make ends meet.'

Recently her mother's been less enthusiastic about the meals out and theatre trips with Sabrina. Now Jill understands why.

'It's not fair,' Vanessa asserts like a petulant child.

'Didn't you like a song about life not being fair, Jill?' Paul asks.

'*Life is unfair. Kill yourself or get over it*. Black Box Recorder.'

'Yes, that's it. Well we think we've found a way to do just that, get over it, not kill ourselves! Greg's getting more and more jobs renovating properties for English buyers in France and he's moving out there. Some of the places he's working on are massive projects compared to the London properties. There's loads for an architect to do.'

'But what about you Mum, your job?'

165

Vanessa has been nodding away, only now does she contribute to the conversation. 'Actually I'm delighted. You appreciate what teaching is like now, Jill, I really do think it's for the young. This opportunity's exciting for Paul and there's a chance I can be involved too, dealing with the subcontractors and maybe even on the estate agency side. You know what Dad's French is like and by all accounts Greg can just about muster a *bonjour*. At least I speak the lingo.'

'Is this definite? When will it happen? And this house?'

Her father takes up the explanation. 'No, not definite, but we're a long way down the line and it's likely, probably in spring or early summer. It's a risk, we might not make any money and we might not like it, so we won't be selling the house. We'll let it and rent something out there, probably for considerably less.'

'There are negatives,' Vanessa adds. 'You two and Dan and his wife and baby, we'll miss being able to see you quite as much as we'd like. Mind you, there are cheap flights to all over France so we can visit each other loads.'

Jill is hit by a sense of loss, the end of childhood, of the comfort of having parents to look after her. At least she's fortunate to have Jack.

'Do what you think is right. Go for it,' she tells them and their gratitude is evident.

'Did you mean what you said?' Jack asks in the taxi on the way home.

'They have their lives to lead just as we have ours. I've had the expectation that a parent's sole role is to serve their children and it's suddenly hit me that that's ridiculous.'

'Very wise.' Jack takes hold of Jill's hand. 'Let's book those holidays tomorrow, that'll take your mind off your parents' difficulties.'

So, on the Saturday morning before Monday's return to work, they book a summer holiday to the Seychelles.

'What about skiing?' Jill asks.

'I think we should put that on hold until we know about your parents. They might be moving around Easter and if that's the case we could help.'

'But you love skiing.'

'We can always book a last-minute trip,' Jack suggests. 'For now, you and your family come first. You wouldn't want to be away during their last few days in England.'

'Thank you, Jack. From the bottom of my heart I love you. God, what an old fashioned phrase, but I mean it.'

~

Term starts and Jill is inundated with work. Jack's long hours get still longer if that's possible. His company block book rooms at a nearby hotel and he begins to make use of this facility, staying overnight at least once a week.

It's hard, all the more so during such a severe winter – early mornings, leaving home when it's still dark, bitter winds, the stream of cold air in the Underground passageways, stifling heat on jam-packed trains, back home in the dark. They always try to have a catch up over dinner, sometimes this isn't until gone ten o'clock, then bed and far too quickly it's time to get up the next morning.

On a particularly miserable Friday morning in late January, Jack tells her his week has been disastrous. She struggles to understand what he's on about, all but losing the plot when he refers to European Constant Maturity

167

Swap-linked Tier One products. She perseveres to get the general picture – he'd advised investors to buy the things, they'd dived in price, and the purchasers had made huge losses. Jack admits he doesn't fully understand the product either and has merely followed the herd. Jill wonders how it's possible to spend billions of pounds of other people's money without knowing what you're doing.

He leaves home fearing a considerable reprimand, or worse.

Jill departs forty minutes later, head down against a freezing mist that's reaching down to touch the pavement. At school the kids are particularly restless and Jill's lessons are uninspiring. She's exhausted and worried about Jack. At the end of classes she slumps down in the staff room with a cup of coffee.

As she lifts up the mug for the first caffeine boost she receives a text from Jack. Dreading bad news about his work, she reads an incomprehensible message: *meet london bridge soon as poss for whale see news.*

Other teachers are talking about what's going on. A whale has lost its way and is swimming up the River Thames. Jill visualises a giant blue whale and wonders how it could possibly swim in a river. A biology teacher assures her and the other ignorants that there are eighty-six species of whales and dolphins and they come in different sizes.

Jill texts *on my way* then catches a bus to London Bridge from her workplace in Hackney. It takes a while to find Jack because a large crowd are lining the river. They join the spectators for a couple of hours, the whale nowhere to be seen.

'What about the work crisis?' she asks.

'Sorted. More than sorted, I've made a killing.'

Jill expects additional detail but doesn't get any and their conversation switches to the whale's whereabouts. They abandon waiting and leave the riverside in search of a restaurant before heading home to watch the story unfold on television that evening. Like millions of others they're glued to the screen the following day to see the rescue attempt. When it fails and the whale dies, they sit in their lounge and sob.

'This is ridiculous,' Jack says. 'Murders, earthquakes, wars, and we're crying about a fucking whale.'

'Deep down you're a softie, Mr Ashley-Lovett. That's one of the reasons why I love you.'

They kiss, they make love that evening, the whale forgotten. Or maybe not, because in the morning Jack is in a philosophical mood.

'No one knows what's round the corner,' he says.

'In what way?'

'We take all the good things for granted but we should savour them because for all we know everything could come tumbling down at any time. For instance if I'd got on a later train that day last summer I could have died.'

'But you didn't. Come on, let's get up, I'm starving. I'll pop round to the shop to get our Sunday treat.'

'I didn't die, but plenty of others did. People like us, young, with good jobs and families.'

Jill is up getting dressed. 'Yes, it was awful.'

'I don't think I've told you this. There's a bloke at work, a really nice guy. He lost his wife to cancer last week, she was only thirty.'

169

'Also awful, but I'm not sure where this is leading. Why are you so morbid this morning?'

Jack doesn't answer so Jill gives him a peck on the cheek and heads out.

When she gets back he's in the kitchen making coffee. The table is meticulously laid out with plates, knives, cups and saucers, butter and jam. She puts the rolls and croissants onto a plate and watches as Jack rearranges them in some order, the logic of which is only known to him.

They start to eat.

'Jill, I think it's time we got married. After all, we've been living together for years and we know we get on well.'

'That's hardly the most romantic proposal I've had, not that I've had any other offers. Why is it tagged to thoughts about death?'

'Agreed – silly. But I still think it's time, don't you?'

'I've never doubted that's what I want so I accept, Mr Ashley-Lovett, although I suppose it's only a reaffirmation of that wonderful proposal in Venice. He knelt on one knee amidst the cheering crowds in St. Mark's Square to propose.   Having covered terrorist attacks, murders, earthquakes, wars, cancer and dead whales he proposed. I think I preferred version one!'

Jill is eager to tell anyone and everyone, starting with her parents, but Jack suggests they put this on hold until they've thought through the logistics. 'There are some big considerations, like my parents.'

Jill agrees. Plan then announce rather than announce and be cajoled into a marriage the way others would like it to be. She's particularly thinking of a certain forceful family member on Jack's side. No doubt Henry is on Jack's mind, too.

A few days later during an evening out with her mother and Sabrina, Jill keeps quiet about her news as Vanessa takes centre stage, talking about the move to France. An agent has been round to assess how much rent Jill's parents could charge for their London house and they're soon off to France to view a couple of properties. Jill is irritated that this information is conveyed during a meeting with Sabrina, she would have liked to have been the first to know.

Two weeks on at their next get-together, dinner at Carluccio's, Jill again holds back from revealing her wedding as Sabrina makes a seismic announcement. She'd joined an internet dating service over the Christmas holidays and been contacted by an actor who she'd been extremely fond of all those years ago.

'He's a film critic now, he does reviews for a national newspaper.'

'And? Have you met up?'

'Yes, actually five times.'

'That's a lot in such a short while.'

'We watch the films he's reviewing. You know how much I love films so I'm happy to go along.'

'That explains it,' Vanessa says.

'Explains what?'

'You hardly said a word after *Brokeback Mountain*. You had nothing to add because you'd already discussed it. I'm right, aren't I?'

'Yes, Miss Marples.'

'Why didn't you tell us, we could have seen something else?'

'I knew you both fancied it and I was happy to go a second time.'

Jill changes the subject. 'Anyone fancy a dessert?'

Vanessa and Sabrina go through their usual double act, agreeing to look at the menu even though they couldn't possibly eat another thing, and ending up choosing the gooiest pudding on offer. In this case it's the Dolce di Ciocolato. Jill opts for Sorbeti.

Vanessa's inquisition of Sabrina continues. 'So what's the score now?'

'Meaning?'

'With you and him?'

'Well, we're an item. I think that's how people describe it these days.'

'Sex and all?' Vanessa asks, her mouth full of chocolate and her lips brown.

'Mum!'

'I don't mind saying. We're a couple, sex included.'

'You are a dark horse, we had no idea you were on the lookout for a man did we, Jill?'

'Why should I be alone for the rest of my life?'

'Agreed,' Jill and Vanessa say in unison.

Sabrina asks Jill if she can bring her friend along to their next meal out, one that will be without Vanessa because she has a parents evening.

They arrange to meet at a small bistro, one of their favourite haunts. Sabrina and her man are already at the table when Jill enters. Anthony stands and greets her with a handshake. He's tall, thin and snazzily dressed in jeans, an open-necked white shirt with pastel coloured buttons and a brown woollen jacket with a playful weave. He looks great and Jill soon discovers he's articulate and interesting. The three of them race through listing favourite eighteenth to twenty-first century literature from England, the rest of Europe and America. Jill's delighted, at last Sabrina can cultivate her passion for the arts.

'You must visit us soon, I'm sure Jack would like to meet you,' Jill says as they are about to go their separate ways.

On the way home she texts Sabrina. *He's great!*

Jill's dying to break the news to Jack. She stays up until he gets home late then finds out he already knows, his father had called him at work a few days beforehand.

'Why didn't you tell me?'

'I was meaning to, I forgot. I had loads on my mind when I spoke to him.'

'What did he say?'

'He's fuming, he thinks she lied in court by saying she was alone to increase the size of the financial settlement.'

'That's ridiculous, she only met the man a few weeks ago.'

'I told him she deserved every penny having raised his children for over twenty years. He went berserk. He accused me of always taking sides with my mother and never giving the time of day for his side of the story. I reminded him that the divorce was his fault which made him even angrier. We were shouting by then, he said he regretted giving me money for the house and that was it as far as his support went, at which point I cut the call.'

'Good for you, but why didn't you tell me?'

'Because we're making plans for our marriage and this puts a rather large spanner in the works. For a start, how on earth are we going to get my parents in the same room?'

173

'I'm sure it'll blow over.'

'You don't know my father.'

'Unfortunately I do.'

The following Saturday their mid-morning coffee is interrupted by the gentle thud of letters against the wooden floor in the hall. Ever since childhood Jill has got excited by the arrival of mail, it makes her think of great fiction. At university she'd done her extended research on the importance of the letter in Victorian novels. Within them, dark tidings of departures and deaths were often at the heart of the plot. She still has that rush of anticipation even though the majority of their letters are bills. Today's post has potential. She carries three letters back to the kitchen, two with typed name and address in cellophane windows, it's the third that's intriguing. It's addressed to Jack in a script that isn't quite copperplate, but close to it.

'I think I know this handwriting,' he says as he tears it open.

He reads it then passes the sheet over to Jill. It is from Henry, cold and detached, the sort of letter a lawyer might write to a client. Aghast, she picks out sentences to read back to Jack.

You are my heir, you surely recognise the importance of retaining the full value of the estate in the hands of the Ashley-Lovett family.

Your unbridled support for your mother is not only a great sadness, it is a treachery.

My regret is to have provided a substantial sum of money for you and that woman of yours for the purchase of a property that I found.

I see no reason for further contact and intend to pass on the estate to Sebastian who has been loyal throughout.

Jill's first thought is that the Victorian novel lives on, but this flippancy is immediately replaced by sympathy for Jack. She's already feeling a sense of loss due to her parents' move to France, and now this from Jack's father.

'Fuck him,' Jack declares. 'We've got his money for the house, he can't take that back, and we're earning plenty enough to pay the mortgage. My earnings are going up and up and up – we don't need him.'

This is the weekend they'd set aside for planning their wedding but events have thrown everything into disarray.

'My parents aren't able to help us and clearly your father's not going to contribute. Weddings cost a fortune, should we postpone?' Jill asks.

'It doesn't have to be expensive.'

'Aren't you compelled to have a lord of the manor do?'

'It is the tradition, but so what? We wouldn't get my parents in the same room and anyway, I don't want a grand affair.'

'Well, I don't either.'

With this principle established, the planning commences.

'A small wedding it is then, all paid for by us. Let's think what we mean by small.'

'Yes, but I'm starving, I'll get lunch together first.'

'What have we got?'

'Bearing in mind we have a wedding to pay for, I reckon we might be able to stretch to some crackers, a morsel of cheese, half a bruised apple each and a glass of water.'

'No, seriously, what is there?'

'We've got an olive ciabatta, Manchego cheese, Parma ham, a Cantaloupe melon and some fresh figs.'

They feast as they plan their wedding.

'What about the Marylebone registry office?'

'Is there one?'

'Not sure. There should be.'

'Then a pint and a pie at the local.'

'Just you and me, no guests allowed.'

It takes a while for them to have had enough of frivolity and to start thinking about realistic options. They soon agree on what works best.

With everything decided, Jill is intent on announcing her news at the next get-together with her mother and Sabrina. They see *Rumor Has It* and she allows the post-film discussion about marriage and infidelity to run on for a while.

'Marriage was so different in our day. Even if it didn't always end up so, at least you set out with the expectation of a lifelong commitment.' Sabrina declares.

Vanessa nods in agreement. 'Yes, none of these absurd prenuptial contracts, starting a marriage assuming it'll fail. What do you think about prenuptials, Jill?'

She grabs this opportunity. 'We're getting married.'

There is a silence, rare when the two older women are together, before Vanessa jumps to a conclusion. 'Are you expecting?'

'No, what makes you think that?'

'Why marriage now?'

'I think because of a whale,' Jill says, skipping the obvious "because we love each other" line. She refrains from providing any explanation. Some will be needed as the

176

conversation progresses. 'There isn't going to be a big wedding, no Ashley-Lovett extravaganza.'

Sabrina and Vanessa can understand that.

'It'll be in a registry office, not in a church.'

Vanessa is happy about this, Sabrina less so, but accepts their decision.

'In fact outdoors probably.'

'That's risky in England.'

'Actually, it's not going to be a UK wedding.'

The women are confused.

'I'm sorry but we've made up our minds. The family situation is too complicated, we're getting married in the Seychelles.'

The women are devastated.

15

Wonderful, wonderful Seychelles. A tropical paradise with golden sands and turquoise seas. The ideal place to flop out in after an exhausting first year at work. But the ideal place to get married?

Jack does everything to make it the trip of a lifetime, right down to booking the best suite in the best of several five-star hotels, one with giant French windows and a breathtaking sea view. There's champagne, a bouquet of flowers and strawberries dipped in chocolate in their room on arrival. They make love to the sound of swishing sea and the sight of the sky turning purple as twilight descends.

'I thought this holiday shouldn't only involve lazing around,' he tells her the next morning as he lifts her bikini and a towel off the bed, folding and refolding until some criterion is satisfied and he can put them in her backpack.

'Meaning?'

'You'll see.'

He marches Jill to a scuba diving centre. He's enrolled her on a beginners' class while he goes deep-sea diving having got past beginner level when still a child. By mid-afternoon on the second day Jill is swimming amidst stunning fluorescent coral reefs and she loves it.

Their wedding ceremony is a couple of days later, outdoors with a backdrop of vibrant flowering plants, palm trees and distant mountains. Led by a local marriage commissioner, it's a simple, low-key affair with two of the official's colleagues called in as witnesses.

Back in their room Jill admits to regretting that no family or friends were with them. Jack reminds her of the reasons. 'I'm not speaking to my father, my mother wouldn't be seen dead in the same room as him anyway, and your two are busy in France.'

'Then what about friends?'

'We'll have a party when we get home. Look, we are where we are. Being here is special, let's make the most of it.'

Jill forgets her misgivings during their mini honeymoon, a trip to the Vallee de Mai Nature Reserve, a dense palm forest full of the most colourful, oddest birds imaginable.

'I wonder when we should try for our first little Lovett,' Jill says as she swallows her contraceptive pill with a wine chaser on their penultimate evening.

They're sitting on the veranda watching the sun set, the burning orange sky turning deep purple and the indigo blue sea turning navy, until it's impossible to tell where one ends and the other begins.

'Let's practise how to manufacture a baby,' Jack suggests.

As they do so, the imminent return to London and work, rather than babies or even the joy of sex, is at the forefront of their thoughts.

They're greeted by grey skies and an unseasonal chill, London is having a dreadful summer with record rainfall.

179

The relentless gloom is in sharp contrast to the fierce light of the Seychelles and with Jack back at work after a weekend at home, their dream holiday seems like a lifetime ago.

Their relationship takes a back seat as they work, eat, sleep then work, eat and sleep some more. Life is all about planning who does what – the food shopping, putting out the dustbins, arranging to service the boiler. Their jobs could hardly be more different but one thing they share is long, long hours of work.

~

A full two years have passed and it hasn't always been easy. They've stuck to their resolution to plan their holidays on New Year's Day and in that period have been to St Moritz, Aspen, Maldives, Dubai and Zanzibar, increasingly luxurious destinations, affordable because Jack's earning a fortune.

Jill cherishes these breaks, the fun and passion of their university years is recaptured with Jack unrecognisable from the worryingly detached London husband. They embark on marathon walks, risk daring ski slopes, relax for lazy hours on tropical beaches. Jill loves it when Jack re-engages with history, guidebook in hand, as they explore the resorts. And then there's bed, bed and more bed, their lust rekindled.

But forty-eight weeks a year remain outside of holidays, during which time they struggle to stay in touch with each other's feelings and needs. It's not that London life is unpleasant for either of them, but satisfaction can often exclude their partner. Jill's getting a real buzz from teaching, she's popular with colleagues and pupils and her results are excellent. Jack has developed the reputation as a trader worth following, he's influential enough to make markets move.

The success at work is part of the problem, the associated lifestyles are pulling them apart.

One evening, a short while after their second wedding anniversary, Jill broaches the subject, it's been on her mind for some while. 'I've been thinking, let's consider how we could put more effort into our relationship,' she declares.

'What do you mean?'

'Well, for a start, we should communicate more.'

'OK, communicate now, explain what you mean.'

The comment annoys Jill, it's become typical of Jack to want an instant solution so he can move on to something else.

'It's not that simple, Jack, it's not a case of identifying a problem then that's it, everything will be better.'

'But I don't understand what you want, what you think is wrong.'

'Oh, never mind.'

Still annoyed, Jill realises that what with her own long hours preparing lessons and marking, blame for the distancing is shared. Over an after-school drink with a work colleague, she admits that the responsibility for what she now describes as her marriage problems is partly her fault.

'However, I don't think that the responsibility is equal. Sometimes Jack is unrecognisable from the man I love. He doesn't finish work 'til late which can't be helped, but I do mind when, several times a week, he remains behind on a drinking session. And then I get a text that he's staying over, I don't even get a call.'

181

'Isn't that lifestyle par for the course in the City?' the friend suggests.

'I don't see why it has to be like that.'

'Haven't you got one of your super holidays coming up? That'll make you both feel better.'

'I suppose you're right.'

'Suppose. Jesus, if I went to some of the places you get to, I'd be feeling brilliant for the next decade. Didn't you chat with Harrison Ford when you were in Santa Monica?'

'No, he was next door having his hair cut. It was Morgan Freeman we spoke to.'

'See?'

See what, Jill thinks, what has speaking to Morgan Freeman got to do with her relationship with Jack?

At times like this she'd have talked things through with her mother in the past, but that's no longer possible except by telephone which isn't the same. She misses her parents. They live in a remote part of France that's far more than the short hop on a plane she'd been led to believe. Since their move two years ago she's visited three times, once with Jack and twice alone. She hates the place and can't understand how these city lovers could be so at ease in a tiny, boring village. It's a parody of all the telly programmes the family used to mock, shows like *A Year in Provence* and *The Good Life*. When Jill was last there, Vanessa had seemed perfectly happy joining the locals in the daily early morning plod to the boulangerie to buy a baguette. Jill doesn't see much of her brother either now that he's moved to Newcastle – she could make the effort, but doesn't. She's sad, wishing her family were back in London.

She remains close to Sabrina, her surrogate mother, though she's wary of discussing Jack with her. Sabrina is a true star though, bursting with enthusiasm about anything and everything, cramming in all those things she missed out on during her years with Henry. She knows so much about what's going on in London she could put herself forward as editor of *Time Out.*

Jill enjoys their hours together, often with Anthony in tow, though she wishes Jack would join them. It's only via Sabrina that she gets updates about Henry because there's still no contact between father and son, not a word since Jack received the letter accusing him of treachery.

She finds out that Henry's remarried to a young woman from well-bred old stock, another family with a double-barrelled name.

Sabrina and Jill laugh away as they mock Henry.

'I believe she's one of the Winchester stock,' Jill suggests, replicating the accent heard when at the theatre for a revival of *Lady Windermere's Fan.* 'Thereby providing a fine match of the Lovett-Ashleys with the Ashley-Lovetts,'

'I think not, that particular girl was betrothed to one of the Liquorish-Allsorts. Henry's filly is an Abbott-Rowley.'

'I do believe they are away in Scotland grouse shooting at present.'

'Yes, indeed, both are passionate about all forms of hunting. If it moves, kill it.'

'And on the subject of passion, does Henry's passion for threesomes remain?'

'Why of course, that goes without saying.'

When Jill tells Jack that his father has remarried he shows little interest and barely smiles at the three in a bed jibe. He rarely smiles at all now, though had in a mocking way when she'd informed him that she was going vegetarian, to be exact, a vegetarian who eats fish.

'You're not a vegetarian then, you're a pescatarian,' he'd told her.

'I do know that word, but I don't like it, it makes me sound like a shellfish. I'm going to stick with vegetarian, if you don't mind.'

Some sniping arises as a result of Jill's vegetarian-who-eats-fishism.

'What's the difference between killing a fish and killing a chicken?' Jack asks.

She doesn't answer, why should she? She simply does what feels right for her.

'It's not as if it affects you, I'm happy to cook chicken or any other assassinated animal for your dinner.'

As his digs about her diet grow, her willingness to cook meat for him diminishes. After all, he can get enough meat intake when he's at restaurants with his City chums.

Absurdly, petty teasing about food becomes a trigger for hostility.

Jill: 'Maybe you should be worried about the high fat content in chunks of dead animal.'

Jack: 'And you should worry about the lack of protein in a fucking cucumber.'

Jill: 'I'm going to cook more of the things I used to eat when I was at home.'

Jack: 'This is your home. Remember?'

Jack: 'What sort of bread is this?'

184

Jill: 'Sourdough. Like it?'

Jack: 'No, it's a solid lump of half-cooked flour.'

Jill: 'I think it's tasty, it's good for you, too.'

Jack: 'Think of the name, Jill. Sour plus dough, that hardly suggests a gourmet delight.'

Jill: 'You mean unlike the elegant sound of Pate de Foie Gras?'

Jack: 'Well it has a nicer ring to it than sourdough.'

Jill: 'Not to the poor force-fed fucking geese. It's cruel.'

Jack: 'How do you know, have you ever spoken to a goose?'

Jill: 'Don't be stupid.'

As Jack walks off, Jill wonders how they could have got so angry about food. They're moving from a growing indifference towards meanness. She wonders whether something to counter their fast-paced lives might help the relationship.

On the Underground the next day, as if by fate, she spots an article in the free paper about tai chi. Apparently it does wonders for balance, strength and the mind. There's an evening class in the nearby primary school and she decides to give it a go.

'Please, please, please come with me,' she urges Jack and he relents.

He's an utter embarrassment. As they learn the first slow motion moves he parodies the experience, waving his arms around like a madman, stamping his foot onto the floor with a thud having been told to softly place it.

'I'm not sure it's quite the thing for me,' he states with sarcasm as they walk home, he's twitching with hyperactivity. 'Maybe when I'm over sixty-five like everyone else there I might give it a go, but for now I'll stick with exercise that makes my heartbeat. And I don't mean beat faster, I mean beat.'

Jill is too embarrassed to return to the class following Jack's behaviour, though she hadn't been enamoured either.

Next on the list is yoga and this time Jack isn't invited. She's always been supple and is able to make good progress, going to class once a week and practising most afternoons after school. Weekends she practises early morning before Jack's up.

One Saturday he's by the door watching.

'It's called yoga.' She tells him.

'Very funny. But I am impressed how well you can bend.'

'It doesn't come straight away, I've built up to it. At first I couldn't get half this far.'

'How on earth do you twist your legs like that?' Jack sits on the floor beside her, trying it out.

'Go easy, slowly, gently the first time.'

Over the next three and a bit weeks, in order, Jack uses ice packs, takes ibuprofen, sees an osteopath, visits a chiropractor, and gives acupuncture a go. Improvement is slow, from the starting point of not being able to stand up on that fateful Saturday. He has to take a taxi to work the following two weeks. Jill struggles not to laugh as her hunchback husband hobbles round the house.

Several in her yoga class do meditation and based on their comments, Jill decides to give it a go. She's told it brings true happiness and she could do with some of that. Before long, she's somehow putting aside time each day for both yoga and meditation. The seemingly simple task of not letting her mind wander during the exercises is a struggle, her attention drawn to the need to put on a whites wash, plan dinners for the week, and consider how to get Zoe, her brightest student, to improve her essay writing if she's to have any chance of getting into Oxford.

Jack has kept well away from Jill's mini studio since his yoga injury, but one Saturday morning he's by the door.

'Jill?'

She knows he knows she's not meant to speak while meditating.

'Jill?'

She's reached a count of thirty-two breaths.

'Jill!'

There's no way she's going to open her eyes and turn round, he can wait.

'For fuck's sake, Jill, answer me will you!'

She can sense Jack's right in front of her, there's no point continuing. Relaxing her pose, she takes a deep breath and opens her eyes.

'I only wanted to ask if you'd like a coffee.'

'Yes but you could see I was busy.'

'Busy? No you weren't, you weren't doing anything.'

'Don't be an idiot, you know what meditation is about. It *is* doing something, it's clearing my mind of all the shit that's clogging it up.'

'How is doing nothing going to make that happen?'

'I'm not entirely sure, I'm new to it. It's mindfulness.'

'Why call it mindfulness if you're trying to empty your mind of everything?'

'I don't know!'

'Mindlessness would be a better name for it. So do you want a cup of coffee or not?'

Jill's lost interest in meditation. She looks across and laughs. 'I think what I most want is to go back to bed. Fancy?'

Jack beams like he used to and occasionally still does. 'You bet.'

That's what it's like. There can be great times together when they laugh so much it hurts, when they snuggle up on the couch to watch a movie, when bedtime isn't for sleeping. Increasingly often it's less great though, the teasing is cutting, or worse still, the lack of interest absolute.

Jack knows he's at fault and in danger of losing the one thing he loves in the world and he also knows that Jill's trying harder than him to put things right. It's to no avail, he's increasingly being sucked into the City lifestyle.

He agrees to one of her requests, to meet Sabrina's man.

They go to Anthony's house for Sunday lunch. He lives in Notting Hill on a street of attractive Victorian properties with large pots with olive, bay leaf and palm trees flanking Farrow & Ball painted front doors. They park adjacent to Volvos, BMWs and SUVs.

However, Anthony's house wouldn't win a prize for affluence. The mud brown paint on the door is flaking, there are no pots to its side, the front garden is untidily pebbled with weeds pushing through bar a single spindly rose bush.

'These houses were built for the working classes, but now they're full of the wealthy arty set,' Jack informs Jill in a tone suggesting the start of a history documentary.

'People just like me,' Anthony says having opened the door and caught the comment.

'It wasn't a criticism, just a fact.'

'No harm even if it is a criticism though my conscience is clear, I moved in well before the price hike. And as you can see, I hardly match my neighbours' elegance. Come on in.'

They step inside a house with décor and contents that could diplomatically be defined as eclectic. If bypassing diplomacy, it would be fair to say that the place was a shambles with patterns, colours, eras, shapes and sizes at odds with each other. In the lounge Jill sits on a modern armchair with a Nordic feel, Jack on an ornate and uncomfortable Victorian chair, and Sabrina and Anthony are sprawled out on a Laura Ashley lookalike couch that has seen far better days. The haphazard artwork battles for attention. Opposite Jill is a countryside scene with cows grazing, next to it an abstract with diagonal red lines piercing a grey block. She nudges Jack and nods towards the first painting.

Sabrina catches them looking. 'Yes, that's from the Ashley-Lovett home, I got permission to take a couple of paintings as part of the settlement. The family portraits were excluded of course, not that I'd want them! I took the ones I thought had the highest value. If you're wondering why this one's here, it's on loan because Anthony was born in the village next to the farm in it.'

'Quite true, I remember buying eggs there when I was a kid.'

'Mind you, he only knows that because it's named on the back.'

The conversation flows between history and literature. Jack is engaging with enthusiasm and Jill should be in her element, but she's saddened that this is such a rare show of interest from him. She wants more like this.

They adjourn to the dining room for lunch. Anthony has made a vegetarian dish for Jill and a roast for the rest of them. Hers is possibly delicious but she picks at it, her appetite gone. She watches the new Jack drink as if there's no tomorrow while the old Jack considers whether the literature of the time sparked the French Revolution.

'What do you reckon, Jill?' he asks.

She loves this man, she holds back tears. 'I don't know.'

After lunch they sit in the garden drinking tea, relishing the spring warmth. Converting a novel into a screenplay is now the theme, it's Anthony's specialism and Jack is fascinated to discover how much his favourite books have been savaged when making films. Jill's heard it all before from Anthony. She savours this glimpse of Jack's passion for knowledge.

'Jill, could you help carry things in, please?' Sabrina asks.

'Sure.'

The two women load the crockery, teapot and a plate of uneaten biscuits onto two trays. 'Is everything alright?' Sabrina asks as they make their way to the kitchen.

'Fine.'

'You're unusually quiet.'

'Sorry. Time of the month. I've enjoyed today masses, I think so has Jack.'

~

'I like him. A lot,' Jack declares when they're in the car.

'I knew you would.'

'He's perfect for my mother.'

190

'He's perfect for you too, Jack. There's nothing to stop you getting to know him more.'

There's a hesitancy before he replies, centuries of Ashley-Lovett tradition, loyalty and sticking together at all costs weighing down upon him. 'Maybe,' is his lame reply.

'You were quiet,' he says as they edge round the North Circular Road. He looks across. 'What's the matter? Why are you crying?'

She has to say something. 'I loved hearing you chat away about history and the cinema. It's so rare to hear you being so enthusiastic and it made me sad.'

'That's ridiculous.'

Jill wants her old Jack back.

16

The following weekend is the opportunity to get her old Jack back because their university friend Charlotte is in town and has asked if she can visit. There'd been so many resolutions and promises before they went their separate ways, but until now the only contact with their old housemates had been through Facebook and emails. Now there's a chance to reminisce and happy memories might instigate a happy present.

Charlotte arrives mid-morning on the Saturday, carrying a huge bunch of flowers in one hand and a bottle of champagne in the other. Jill gets the flowers, Jack the alcohol and then there are hugs all round.

'Tea or coffee,' Jill asks when they're in the lounge, Jill sitting on one sofa, Jack and Charlotte on the other.

'Let's open this,' Charlotte says, looking across at the bottle which is now on the coffee table.

'It's a bit early, isn't it? I thought we'd leave that until later.' Charlotte and Jack's grins intensify Jill's feeling that she's sounded like a parent. 'Oh what the hell, come on then,' she adds.

Jack is up in a shot, all but sprinting to the kitchen to fetch three flutes. On his return he drops down onto the couch, this vigorous action not wise when about to uncork champagne. As he opens the bottle the liquid shoots out and lands on his trousers. He pours what's left as Charlotte extracts a tissue from her girlie backpack. She proceeds to dab his trouser leg, starting at his right knee and moving up his thigh.

The wiper and the wiped one's eyes meet. *Don't say anything*, Jack attempts to convey without words, but to no avail because Charlotte declares 'Remember the last time I did this?'

'What do you mean?' Jill asks.

'You must have been out,' Charlotte continues as calmly as can be. 'We were at home and when Jack spilt wine I had to do the mopping up.'

Jill looks across at Jack, she knows him well enough to recognise discomfort even though Charlotte's countenance is giving nothing away.

'You never told me about that, Jack. When was it?'

'Everyone has their secrets,' Charlotte says, Jill considers patronisingly as if speaking to a child.

Jack stands and hands out the drinks. 'Let's toast. To times gone by.'

'Times gone by,' Charlotte and Jill chorus.

'I've got something else if you'd like,' Charlotte says and attention switches to the possessions she's tipped onto the sofa. She lifts a skimpy pair of knickers. 'I don't mean these,' she jokes as she returns them to the backpack. 'I mean this.' She has a stash of marijuana. 'Who fancies a smoke?'

193

'We don't anymore and actually it's best not to have dope in the house what with me being a teacher. That'd be it for me if we were caught.'

'The police are hardly going to burst through the door. I'd love a smoke,' Jack says. 'Come on, Jill.'

'No, I don't fancy. You two go ahead, I'll get things ready for lunch.'

She leaves them to it, feeling uncomfortable in her own house. Charlotte had been *her* friend at uni but today she feels like the outsider. The Smiths are playing, that's one of the special bands she shares with Jack. Charlotte looks gorgeous in her designer clothes. Jill feels frumpy and conservative. By the time she re-joins them, the joint is finished. A pity, she fancies a smoke after all.

Charlotte talks about her job at an advertising agency, one well known for its daring promotions. She claims that the forensics part of her psychology degree has been of value because torture and death are a feature of several of her projects. 'So you can see I've got over my fear of horror, Jack. Do you remember what I was like when we saw that movie?'

'What movie?' Jill asks.

'We went to see something in town, you weren't back from holidays yet.'

Jill refrains from a second *you never told me that* statement, there's no reason why she should know absolutely everything Jack did when she wasn't around, but a sixth sense is kicking in as she glances across to Jack.

After lunch they go for a walk in Regent's Park. Jill has to go back indoors to get a fleece for the lightly clad

Charlotte because the weather has suddenly turned and they've stepped out to face a bitter wind.

As they walk Jack chats about his job, Jill finding out more than she's ever been told. She starts to blame herself for not showing sufficient interest to ask about what he does, then recognises it's not Charlotte asking, it's Jack telling. When the conversation turns to her own teaching it all seems so boring. Preparing, delivering, disciplining, marking, then more preparing, delivering, disciplining and marking.

That evening they go to a pub and Jill makes a half-hearted attempt to match the alcohol consumption of the other two. Back at home they watch a late-night movie before bed. Jill wonders whether she should interrogate Jack because she has this feeling that he's slept with Charlotte. He falls asleep while she's planning what to say. Possibly just as well, she concludes.

She's dozing off when there's a sudden buzzing followed by groaning from the guest room, the volume enough to wake even the comatose Jack.

'What's that?' he asks.

'It's more a case of who's that. It's Charlotte.'

'Is she alright?'

'Didn't you see that silver contraption she tipped out her bag? I think she's using it.'

'Oh, you mean a…'

'Yes, I do.'

'I didn't think she got noisy during sex.'

Jill springs up. 'How do you know that?'

She grasps Jack's pyjama top and yanks him up.

'What are you doing?'

'I said how do you know that?'

'Because we never heard anything when we lived with her.'

'Her bedroom was on the opposite side of the house, we'd hardly be able to hear anything.'

'Well, maybe it was because it was always quiet when I was going to the bathroom. Anyway, what does it matter?'

It does matter to Jill, but what's the point of an inquisition?

'At any rate, it's the same old Charlotte, she hasn't changed,' Jack states.

If he's on about her frequently declared interest in sex, Jill would like to remind her husband that she hasn't changed either, she loves sex. For an instant she struggles to speak then dismisses her pride. 'Nor have I. Or you.'

She takes hold of him but doesn't enjoy their lovemaking, not with the nagging feeling about Jack's possible deceit.

Jack doesn't notice the detachment, he's thankful Jill isn't pursuing the questioning. Having the one-night stand with Charlotte had been reckless, he could have lost Jill, the love of his life.

The next morning both Jack and Jill are nervy, Jill wondering what new revelations will emerge and Jack fearing what else Charlotte might say. It turns out to be a relaxed atmosphere, Jill even questioning her previous suspicion as Jack sits by her side oozing affection.

Their guest leaves soon after lunch and Jack and Jill bitch about their university friend. Surely it's time, they agree, for her to move on from her incessant talk about drink, drugs, partying and men.

'She's so superficial,' Jack concludes, though a minute or so later is unable to disguise his disappointment when Jill tells him she's going to have to spend the rest of the day and evening planning how to get her lowest set through their English Literature exam. But she can't concentrate, her mind on how carefree Jack was in the company of Charlotte. She envies Charlotte for her superficiality, it's a good state to be in. What Charlotte and Jack did at university hardly matters, it's *her* and Jack *now* that's on her mind. The current role-playing sucks, she the authoritarian mum and he the truculent schoolboy.

It doesn't take long for the petty bickering to start up again, the theme of the week being green issues because Jill's started to recycle meticulously and to use biodegradable cleaning products. She piles up the plastic containers, cans and cartons on the work surface next to the sink. For Jack, obsessively tidy, this is an abomination.

For a while he's compliant, though with a mission to get things out the kitchen and into the dustbins as soon as possible, but one evening he challenges the whole concept of recycling.

'Look,' he declares as he's clearing up after dinner. 'Even if it says biodegradable, they still dump it in a sea somewhere. They're only playing a game to conform to European law.'

'How do you know that?'

'I read it,' he says as he discards cartons, food waste and containers into a single plastic bag.

'Jack! Will you please separate that stuff?'

'Too late. And I've had enough of sorting.'

'What you said about Europe can't be true. If the press found out, all hell would break loose.'

'Look Jill, even if it is processed, there's still no point. How are a few middle-class Europeans going to have an impact when billions of Asians dump everything?'

'If everyone said that, nothing would improve.'

'Most people do say that,' he utters as he heads outside with the plastic bag.

Jill goes to the sink, squirts eco washing-up liquid into a bowl and adds hot water.

Jack, now back indoors, watches. 'And that stuff doesn't do the job.'

'Yes it does.'

'No, it doesn't.'

A Punch and Judy scene is averted by Jack leaving the room.

When he gets home the next evening he takes a non-recyclable plastic bottle of perfumed mainstream washing-up liquid out his briefcase and places it on the draining board.

'Why have you got that?' she asks.

'I want something that works, your stuff doesn't.'

So they start using different products when it's their turn to do the washing up.

Once upon a time teasing and sarcasm had been good natured, a pleasant feature of their relationship. Now it can get nasty, with Jill giving as good as she takes. Her counter to Jack's ridicule of green issues, meditation and "hippy" yoga, as he insists on calling them, is an attack on his obsession with tidiness. Sometimes she deliberately messes up his ordered possessions and takes pleasure in watching him re-sort.

Another opportunity to goad develops because of his wish to purchase the latest high-priced gadgets. He's hardly a techi wizard, even compared to Jill, possessing little understanding of how to use his new toys.

The day after the washing-up liquid dispute, he comes into the kitchen holding up his new mobile phone. 'The latest and it's brilliant,' he declares ahead of seeing her crouch down and sink her hands into the bin. 'What are you doing?'

'I'm extracting the organic waste to add to one of these recycling bags I've bought. Now we won't have to leave anything on the counter.'

Jack doesn't comment, his mind on something else. 'Take a look at this.'

'I can't yet, my hands are covered in the remains of your meat.'

'Please rinse them, you must see this.'

She concedes and takes hold of his phone. 'What is it?' She's looking at *42n8ly* on the screen.

'Can't you see?' he asks, excited like a little boy.

'No.'

'It's text speak for *fortunately.* I made it up, what do you reckon?'

'I don't think I reckon anything. What's the point?'

'It's quicker.'

'No, it isn't, not if you use predictive text.'

'What's that?'

'I've shown you before.'

'Anyway, this is pretty cool, isn't it?'

'Only if you're a fifteen year old geek.'

He grabs the phone and exits without saying another word, without looking at her, and Jill wonders why she's been cutting about such a harmless thing.

~

Jack is disturbed by Jill's unpleasantness though fully aware that his own behaviour contributes to the negative atmosphere. It's got to the point of preferring the times when she's not around to those when they're together. The bickering is shifting to drawn out arguments, from tiffs about a one-off issue to generalised denunciations.

Where once Jill might have said of his cooking, 'I think there's a bit too much salt in this,' she's now declaring 'will you never learn, you always add too much salt.' There's a broader criticism, too. 'I'm fed up doing nearly all the cooking. I'm as busy as you so you should do half.'

His response is to go home for dinner less and less, he'd rather stay out with work mates than come back to be told off. He is drinking more and more, too much he knows, but it helps him cope with the fast-paced work.

Jill confronts him about his alcohol consumption, this out of genuine concern, but it turns into another topic to argue about.

'I've told you a million times, there's nothing to worry about. I'm able to decide what to drink, I'm not a kid.'

'It's only your health I'm thinking of.'

'When did I last have to go to the doctor?'

'A few weeks ago, to discuss the OCD.'

'That doesn't count, I only went because you insisted. When apart from that?'

'It's not as simple as needing a doctor, it's the longer term effects that…'

'Look Jill,' he snaps, 'let me do what I want, will you.'

Jack all but leaps off the sofa and stomps to the kitchen. He returns with a glass of wine in one hand, no glass for Jill, the bottle in the other. It's an act of defiance, he knows he's already had enough to drink for one evening.

~

Jill is convinced alcohol has become a problem, Jack's shifted from liking to needing it. The first thing he does when he comes in is to open a bottle of wine and that's after having been drinking before heading home. But any drink problem is dwarfed by a new discovery. One Saturday morning she's about to load one of his shirts into the washing machine when powder falls out of the breast pocket onto the floor. She sweeps it up without consideration, it's a few days later when realisation dawns. She rummages through his suits and sure enough, there are plastic bags of the stuff in two jacket pockets. Cocaine.

She confronts him that evening and he's open and unapologetic. It's no big deal, he tells her, everyone at work does it and no one's addicted. It's recreational, something to help get through hectic days.

'Are you telling me you take it while you're at work? That's not recreational.'

'Only occasionally at work, hardly ever.'

Jill is exasperated, all the more so when he asks if she'd like to try some. She declines, but her mind is in turmoil. She could, she knows some teachers at school do, let alone whatever the kids get up to. But she's back in the role of disciplinarian mother, reprimanding Jack for late nights, alcohol and drugs.

They're eating different foods; washing up with different liquids; have conflicting standpoints on recycling; are respectively a drug taker and an abstainer; hardly see each other during the week; increasingly avoid each other at weekends; and sex has become a rare event.

On a restless night when all these thoughts are on Jill's mind, she smells perfume on Jack as he joins her in bed after a late night home. It's not one she uses. It might be the result of close proximity to a female work colleague, but it might be more.

~

It takes many months before Jill has the courage to have a heart-to-heart with Sabrina about her relationship with Jack. A miserable winter and spring have passed, their holidays together seemingly abandoned since there had been no New Year's Day planning. Jack's been skiing with work colleagues and Jill has visited her parents in France. Neither recounts their experiences when back home, Jack to avoid deceit and Jill unwilling to admit how boring it had been.

Jill has asked Sabrina if they can meet without Anthony present. They sit in a wine bar, noisy with the buzz of happy young couples flirting. Jill dives in, able to articulate what it's like but not the reasons why. 'That's about it,' she concludes, 'and I have no idea what I can do to change things. I'm not even sure I want to change things rather than end it.'

Her head has been down, now she looks up to Sabrina who has barely spoken a word all evening. There's a sadness in her eyes as she speaks. 'I did a lot of analysing about Henry and me. At first I thought it was largely my fault. But I changed my mind, I now realise it's the Ashley-Lovetts and all men like them. Their upper-class upbringing supersedes any good qualities they might possess. Jack's kind-hearted enough, I'm sure he wouldn't hurt a fly. But he's stuck with his genes.'

'That's true, he's never touched me, he doesn't even shout. His words can be harsh though, as are mine.'

'At home and every bit as much at school, he's been trained to believe he's always right so he can do whatever he likes. I love Jack, but in the end he's his father's son and I see too much of Henry in him. I wish I had an idea for you but I'm not sure what to say that might help.'

'In that case I might as well pack it in now.' Jill knocks back a near full glass of wine. 'How on earth could things have changed from being so wonderful to so fucking awful?'

'You're lucky. With Henry, I skipped the wonderful and jumped straight to the fucking awful. I'm desperately upset though because I've always thought that if anyone could make a success of it with an Ashley-Lovett, it would be you. But look, there have been good times, you know what it can be like, so there must be a possibility of resolution. Keep your distance for a while, do more of your own thing, and who knows, you may come through the other side.'

'More of my own thing? That's pretty well the case already.'

'Yes, but for you it all seems about work. Do something social you can get your teeth into.'

'There's something I haven't told you. I think Jack's an alcoholic or close to it.'

'Well, that's following in his father's footsteps.'

'And he does cocaine.'

'I don't think even Henry does that unless his adolescent wife has got him started. It's still illegal isn't it?'

'Yes.'

'Well, he's on dangerous ground if he's caught.'

'He reckons everyone at work does it.'

'He's a silly boy, and boy is the right word. Ashley-Lovett men and their ilk don't seem to grow up.'

Jill and Sabrina depart with an embrace and a promise, whatever happens, to stay friends.

17

Sitting on the Underground on her way home, the carriage pleasantly devoid of the twice a day rush-hour crush she has to endure on her way to and from school, Jill decides to take Sabrina's advice: she'll ride the storm. She makes a resolution to accept the invitations to socialise with fellow teachers, until now by and large turned down.

If only she could adopt a more philosophical outlook on life, something other than through meditation which doesn't seem to be working for her. But what?

Her carriage is littered with free newspapers. She picks up a tattered copy of the *Evening Standard* from the ledge behind her. Tucked away in the what's on section, she spots an advert for a festival at the Hare Krishna Centre the following Saturday. She's seen small groups of followers parading through Central London chanting and has never had the slightest interest in finding out more, her indifference seemingly shared by every other onlooker. She has to start her search for a meaning to life somewhere, so why not with this? Maybe the problem with meditation has been that it's a solo activity when what she needs is to be part of a group. But hang on a minute, Hare Krishna? Aren't they a cult?

She's home well past eleven and is surprised Jack isn't back because that morning he'd indicated he wouldn't be late. 'I'm shattered, an early night will do me good,' he'd said.

This had been Jack's intention right up to the end of his working day. As he was about to leave he got a text and seven male colleagues were waiting for him in the lobby. Their plan was to start at a pub then go on to a recently opened lap-dancing club.

'Not for me guys, I'm off home,' Jack informs them.

'Got to get back or else it's big trouble with wifey?' one of his so-called friends teases.

'Just the pub then,' he concedes.

By the time he's had a few drinks tagging on with his mates seems the obvious thing to do. The room they enter at the club is stuffy and loud. The audience is largely made up of City traders, men with the power to manipulate the world's money markets and to make or break economies. Here any workplace civility they might possess is cast away as they wolf whistle and cheer as the dancers strip.

Jack's not enjoying it, he's having one of his regular feelings of remorse as he thinks about Jill. For a start, her body knocks these women for six, though defining Jill by her body intensifies his self-loathing. What about all the wonderful qualities, her wisdom, humour and compassion.

He and his friends are sitting at a table with near-naked dancers. He shuns the bidding war going on for who will be pairing up with the girls. Three winners emerge leaving Jack and his remaining colleagues to stagger back to the hotel the company uses. Once there he texts Jill: *busy evening staying over*, a hopelessly late message sent at two in the morning. On waking, the guilt still with him, he calls her. She doesn't answer.

That evening he returns early with a big bouquet of yellow roses, intent on making amends. Jill's angry and unforgiving, her resolution to ride the storm well and truly threatened.

Silence prevails during dinner. Afterwards, in the lounge, while watching Jack re-sort his CDs, she introduces a topic that she's sure will bring ridicule.

'By the way, have I told you I'm out all day Saturday at a Hare Krishna festival? Hopefully I'll find something to put some purpose back into my life. Who knows, I might even rediscover happiness.'

Jill observes Jack as he clenches his fists, but he doesn't look up or reply, he returns to lining up his CDs on the carpet. They had been sorted alphabetically by artist and she wonders what new criterion is to be adopted.

'Did you hear, Jack? I'm off to a Hare Krishna festival on Saturday, I'm really excited.'

'I heard you loud and clear and I was left speechless.'

'Why?'

'Why? We've seen those weirdos walking round London hitting teeny-weeny bells and you've taken the piss every bit as much as I have. Why on earth would you want to join them?'

'They're not doing any harm.'

'Actually they are. They're harming rather a lot of my senses – sight, smell and hearing for starters. For fuck's sake, Jill, you're a middle-class woman living in London on a high income in the twenty-first century. Why pretend you're an Indian peasant from hundreds of years ago?'

'That *is* the reason. It's because I'm those things that I want to find something other than fast-paced mass consumption to give life some meaning.'

Jack musters a fake yawn. 'Yeah, right. So wearing an orange robe and tinkling a bell provides meaning, does it?'

Jack starts to hum Monty Python's *The Meaning of Life* as he sorts.

'If for some demented OCD reason you feel the need to rearrange CDs, make sure you keep mine separate. I want them left as they are.'

She leaves the room, the separation of their CD collection adding to a growing list – eating different foods, washing up with different products, incompatible standpoints on recycling to name but a few.

In the spare bedroom. unable to sleep, she tosses and turns all night, dismayed that her plan to be tolerant has failed before it's started.

~

The rest of the week is more civil. Jack's aware that the mocking of anything Jill wants to do that's out of the ordinary doesn't help matters. After all, what constitutes ordinary? Getting blasted, stoned and visiting lap-dancing clubs? He tries to make amends. He replaces the flowers that had been left on the table without water with a larger bouquet which he puts in a vase. He's home early each evening. He takes her out to dinner on the Thursday and cooks the meal on the Friday; that evening they're back to sharing the double bed. An improvement, Jill notes.

Early Saturday morning she's getting ready to go to the Hare Krishna festival. Who knows, maybe the improvement can be prolonged? 'Would you like to come with me?'

Unthinkingly, Jack strikes with the first barb. 'I'm struggling to think of anything worse I could do today.'

Jill hits back. 'Perhaps snorting coke might be perceived as being worse.'

Jack retaliates. 'Not by me.'

'Remember, you better not have any in this house, I don't want to lose my job.'

'You won't.'

'I doubt whether I'll be back for dinner, get something for yourself.'

'Great, I can eat meat without being made to feel guilty.'

'I never do that.'

'What about the lectures on the danger of fat, cholesterol, sugar and whatever?'

They aren't even in sight of each other, the conversation is taking place between kitchen and hall with the front door open. Jill glares at a neighbour who's stopped to listen. He moves on and she leaves with a slam of the door, setting off on her journey across north London. By the time she reaches the end of the road she reckons she's wasting her time and is tempted to go back, but there's too much pride for that.

Jack takes a cup of coffee into the lounge and slumps into an armchair. Some of the liquid spills, specks of brown marking the beige fabric. He can't be bothered to wash them out, he can't be bothered to do anything. He's feeling guilty because there's no harm in what Jill has chosen to do. Maybe they'll have a good laugh about it when she gets home. But will they? In the past, yes, but now? A feeling of utter isolation hits hard, making him gasp for breath. His father and brother are lost for good, he wasn't even invited to their weddings. Conversations with his mother are stilted, she's preoccupied with her new man and would rather hang out with Jill than him. He's lost touch with schoolmates and university friends. His social life centres on cold, ruthless and competitive work colleagues who he doesn't even like. Most are male, the few females possess traits every bit as disagreeable as the men. Casual sex is rampant and he's been a guilty party. Twice.

He wants things back like they used to be with Jill. He has no idea how their relationship has got to this point other than it's all his fault. He's clueless about how to revive it.

It's approaching eleven. Jack downs the last dregs of coffee and pours his first alcohol of the day, a large glass of Merlot. He puts on the new *Beach House* CD which, together with the sorting he's started, calms him. He's pulled out all the CDs again. Arranging by album name didn't work, it's impossible to remember hundreds of titles. He restores the previous arrangement by name of artist, adding Jill's in with the hope that she'll be happy now that they're back as before. It's an enjoyable task, taking almost two hours and three-quarters of the bottle of wine. He looks across to the DVDs, currently arranged by title. It would be a triumph if he could sort by date of release. The first he pulls out is *The Lust of the Slave Girl.* He fancies physical release so inserts the disk and presses play.

~

Jill's Hare Krishna day is an absolute waste of time. She gets caught up in traffic, queues for parking, and by the time she arrives the place is mobbed. A fair number of the crowd are wearing the orange robes seen in Oxford Street. Visitors are an odd mix of new age, hippies, punks and eco warriors. She feels old and conservative in her jeans, blouse and sensible shoes.

She tries to give it a chance – *all we are saying is give peace a chance* she can't get out of her head as she walks around – but it doesn't help. Within ninety minutes of sitting in on sessions she knows it's not for her, but she can't go home too quickly as this would admit defeat to Jack.

Jill picks up an information leaflet and takes a seat in the pleasant grounds, more than pleasant, the centre is lavish to the point of opulence. She opens the booklet at a random page and reads. *O Lord Krishna, You are the supreme primal objective; You are inexhaustible, You are the eternal Personality of God.* Fundamentally, she concludes, little different to the religion she's rejected. She closes the leaflet, closes her eyes and thinks about Jack. The good times – their first night at university, the second one, the next, their house together, holidays, the proposal, the wedding.

At that precise moment, Jack is watching the slave girl give her well-endowed master a blowjob.

Jill stays for lunch, maybe she should sign up after all because the food is great. She opts for a quinoa crumble with chickpeas and cranberry relish. Having enjoyed her meal, she returns to the grounds to sit in the sunshine along with the others who have abandoned lectures and discussions. She texts Jack: *will be back for dinner.* On the way home she pops into Waitrose and buys the best steak on offer as a peace offering. Into her basket she adds passion fruit mousse, a bottle of sparkling and a piece of salmon for herself.

When she gets home Jack's in the kitchen cooking the sea bass, mash and veg he's got from Marks & Spencer. Profiteroles and sparkling wine are in the fridge.

As she takes what she's bought out of her bag they laugh at both having used food to say sorry. The morning's unpleasantness has blown away.

'Think back to what we used to eat at uni. God knows how we survived,' Jill says, having had her first mouthful of sea bass garnished with rosemary and herb butter.

'It was pretty awful. That food hall, they should have called it Carbohydrate Castle.'

'Or Saturated Fatland. Mind you, if I remember rightly you were a carbo king, I did fine with salads.'

'I don't think I've ever told you, but when we first met, you were eating so little I was worried about anorexia. No chance of that now!'

'What do you mean? Are you suggesting I'm fat?'

'No, not fat. I'd call you pleasantly plump.'

Jill's all set to retaliate with a comment about his emerging pot belly before spotting Jack's giveaway beam. 'We didn't eat any better when we were in the student house. It was a nice treat when we went to restaurants though.'

'And I loved our hotel breaks. We should do that sometimes now, even midweek.' Jack takes his last forkful of mashed potato. 'More sparkling?'

'Yeah, why not.'

He tops up the two glasses before asking what he's wanted to discover since Jill returned home. 'How was it today?'

He's dismayed, she's gushing with enthusiasm. 'Incredible, it was so interesting. I really do believe that the Hare Krishna movement is the best antidote to today's capitalist, consumer-driven society you could possibly imagine.'

Jack struggles to be polite. 'That's a big claim. In what way?'

'It provides a pathway to peace, love and goodwill that's inspirational but also practical.'

'So what are you going to do next?'

'Well, actually nothing because I thought it was a complete load of bollocks.'

There's the wonderful sound of shared laughter. Jill admits to walking out of all the sessions before they'd finished. 'Shall I get the other bottle?' she asks, noting the first is empty.

'Why not? We can have a Waitrose versus Marks & Spencer competition.'

Jill opens the wine and pours before continuing her take on the day's proceedings. 'One nice thing though, the colour was staggering – their clothes, the buildings, the flowers. They love flowers, they were everywhere.'

'Krishnanthemums?'

'What?'

'Krishnanthemums.'

Jill gets it second time round and laughs.

'Was everyone rushing around?' Jack asks.

'Why?'

'Hurry Krishna.'

'Enough schoolboy humour. Let's go to bed.'

Jack hesitates, the slave girl has worn him out. 'What about dessert?'

'We can have that later. No, I've got a better idea, let's take the profiteroles up with us. Then I can smear chocolate and cream all over you and lick it off.'

There had been no profiteroles in *The Lust of the Slave Girl,* not surprising since there was no Marks & Spencer in first-century Rome. As they head upstairs, Arescusa and her daughter Cherusa cease to be on his mind. Jack is fully focused on his wonderful wife.

18

It had been a great weekend, but unusually so because unpleasantness has become the norm. Jill is largely to blame, her hostility being the response to the suspicion that Jack is having sex with other women. There's the scent of perfume on his clothes when he returns home late evenings, and she spots, cliché of all clichés, lipstick that isn't her colour on his shirt collar.

She puts further effort into taking the advice offered by Sabrina, to do more of her own thing. She gives jogging a go, a half hour or so run after school a couple of times a week. It's enjoyable, but company is what she needs so she joins the young and cool set of work colleagues for evenings out.

They're a nice bunch. None are married and if the frequency of casual coupling is anything to go by, no one has the slightest interest in monogamy. Everyone knows she's married but that doesn't stop advances and Jill is flattered rather than offended.

Dressing up for nights out is the done thing and Jill takes as much care as the other women, though there are limits. She doesn't participate in the how-short-can-my-skirt-be competition. Should she be shocked when they're out bowling and you can see Karen's knickers as she bends low to lift a ball? Or when Robert whispers something that makes Abbie laugh as he places his hand on her bum. Or when Emily exposes a thong above low rise trousers and Dave displays a luminous Calvin Klein band above jeans that must be in danger of falling down. It looks like Emily and Dave will be a couple that night, and if that's the case, removal of clothes will be a doddle.

Jill embraces the flirtatious atmosphere, at first demurely, but soon more openly. The looks and the touches seem genuinely affectionate even if they are lecherous.

An insatiable round of bowling, cinema, restaurants, bars and nightclubs are on the agenda for the group. Before long exhausted and with work suffering, Jill opts out of most of the mid-week activities. Friday is her Big Night Out, fitting in well with Jack who ends the working week with his City mates.

A new art teacher has joined the school mid-year, his name is Ryan Shaw. His rugged good looks, quite possibly enhanced by a single earring and a tattoo visible on the back of his neck (where does it end?), have made him an instant hit with the young female teachers, in fact also the older female teachers and the sixth form girls. You can hear the gasp as he comes into assembly and sense the frisson as he enters the staff room.

He's taken to sitting next to Jill and she's happy to chat with him, endeavouring to convince herself that the attraction is based on his considerable charisma and not because he's gorgeous.

One Friday evening he joins the gang at a pub near the school. The flirting and adulation around him are an embarrassment for Jill to observe.

'I think art is as much about the idea as the execution,' Jill hears Ryan tell one of her colleagues.

'You are so right,' says Female Teacher Number One. She's crammed her body into a dress with astonishing cleavage. 'If only everyone saw things the way you do, art would be in a much better place, wouldn't it?'

To give him credit, Ryan refrains from mocking this meaningless drivel. 'Do you visit galleries a lot?'

'Yes, I absolutely love going.'

'What was the last thing you saw?'

'Pardon?'

'What have you seen lately?'

'There's Jill. I'll be back in a sec, I need to catch her for something. Don't go away.' Female Teacher Number One, a maths specialist who until that point had never shown the slightest interest in anything other than maths, grabs hold of Jill and leads her some distance away from Ryan.

'Quick Jill, you know all about art. What can I say to impress him?'

Jill decides to play devil's advocate. 'Tell him you loved the Rodin.'

Female Teacher Number One rushes back to Ryan. 'Sorry about that. Now what did you say?'

'I asked if you've seen any good exhibitions lately.'

'I saw the Rodin a while back.'

'Yeah, me too.' Ryan glances across at Jill and smiles. 'Did you have a favourite piece?' he continues.

'All his paintings are equally wonderful. Such vibrant colours.'

Jill looks on in anticipation of Ryan informing the flirting fraud that Rodin is a sculptor. He goes up in her estimation when he takes the polite route. 'I like his stuff a lot.'

Jill does wonder whether his politeness has an ulterior motive bearing in mind this maths teacher and her cleavage are attractive.

It's like an interview evening. As soon as one woman has moved on, another presents herself.

'Are you new to London, Ryan?' asks Female Teacher Number Four.

'No, I've lived here a couple of years.'

'You'll absolutely love London, there's so much to do.'

'I know, I have lived here for two years.'

'Maybe we can see the sites together.'

Ryan looks across at Jill again. It's as if they're sharing a conspiracy, then it crosses her mind that his smiles could well be mocking ones because of her undue interest in his conversations with other women.

If this is the case, he's a good actor because after Female Teacher Number Four has been politely discharged, Ryan approaches Jill and rests a hand on her shoulder which instigates a shock wave of desire. 'Drink?' he asks.

'Thanks, a white wine please. Anything except Chardonnay.'

'I was thinking of going somewhere else. This place is awful and some of the women, present company excluded, are driving me up the wall.'

Jill, usually decisive, is unsure how to respond. If they left together, everyone would notice and draw conclusions. Incorrect ones because all they'd be doing is heading off for a drink and a chat, but that wouldn't stop the gossip.

Ryan makes up her mind for her. 'Come on,' he says taking hold of her hand. This second touch is as electric as the first.

They leave a bar bursting at the seams, with music blaring and people shouting to be heard. It has become *the* place to be in Hackney, having supplanted what used to be "the place" which is where they are now sitting. Fashion is so fickle, Jill observes, there are no more than thirty customers in the cavernous room.

She watches Ryan as he stands by the bar, chatting away to the barman and generating laughter. He's ever so good looking – and she's married. When he returns, in an action to maximise dramatic effect, she raises her left hand and rotates her engagement and wedding rings before taking hold of the glass.

Ryan is all smiles again and she really can't tell whether it's fondness or teasing. 'Cheers,' he says and they clink glasses.

Foreigner's *I Want to Know What Love Is* strikes up and Jill takes another gulp as 'I want you to show me' is sung.

'I used to love this,' Ryan tells her. 'It was released when I met the love of my life.'

Phew, he's taken.

'We played it over and over again.'

He must love her so much, is that a tear of joy?

'We were all set to get married.'

219

No ring visible, so did they decide to skip matrimony? Why bother these days, just remaining partners is fine.

'Then she upped and left. Said she needed financial security and couldn't see how an artist would ever be able to provide it. She transformed from free-spirited socialist to arch capitalist overnight.'

'Didn't you try to keep her?'

'Yes I did, but soon realised it was pointless. Once someone's shifted ground so much it's impossible to turn back.'

'I suppose so,' Jill says, thoughts about her and Jack avalanching.

Roxy Music's *Love is a Drug* is playing. 'This is also a great, they must know my favourites.'

It's also one of Jill's picks, it had been one of Jack's too; she has little idea what he listens to now. This avalanche is forceful, frightening.

'I like you loads, Jill. I know it sounds like a chat-up line from an arty fart, but I do mean it.'

Jill is swivelling her rings again, thinking of Jack's proposal in Venice as she examines the tastefully unostentatious row of small diamonds on her engagement band. 'I am married, you know.'

'Yes, I can see that.'

Now Bad Company's *Feel Like Makin' Love* is playing. Who's choosing this music?

Jill stands up, she needs time to gather her thoughts even if only for a moment. 'I fancy another drink, hand me your glass.'

Ryan does as ordered. Any lightness has gone as he looks up at her.

Jill's hands are shaking as she carries the glasses to the bar and sets them down. Where is this going? Does she even like Ryan or is this no more than revenge for Jack's infidelities?

'That's £11.50, please.'

She scans her card and remains at the bar. She can't go back yet because nothing's been resolved.

The barman looks on inquisitively. 'Anything else?'

'Nuts. Do you sell nuts?'

'Yeah, we got cashews, salted or dry roasted peanuts.'

This simple decision is beyond her. 'I'll have one of each, please.'

She looks across to Ryan who should be laughing at her clumsy attempt to pick up the glass of wine, pint of beer, three packets of nuts and her bag, but his smiles have evaporated. She points to the items resting on the bar and shrugs her shoulders. He gets the message and comes across to help.

They sit down, Ryan sipping and Jill gulping in silence.

'Let's ease up on the intensity, shall we?' Ryan suggests. 'I do like you, Jill, but first and foremost you're a great colleague and hopefully a friend, too.'

Jill doesn't reply, she can't because this could be moving towards the most sensible conclusion and she's unhappy with it.

'What's wrong, you look so sad? I'm a good listener, tell me.'

Jill starts by stating just how much she loves Jack, but before long all the difficulties pour out. Ryan's the first person she's opened up to with such force about her relationship, somehow it's easier with a near-stranger than

221

anyone close. As she speaks she realises that everything she's saying about her husband is critical: the drinking, the drug taking, the staying out, how he's changed since working in the City.

'It's not surprising he doesn't want anything to do with me the way I have a go at him all the time. I'm like a controlling mother.'

'Hold on. Bearing in mind what you've told me, you're being too hard on yourself.'

'No I'm not. I deliberately do things to annoy him. All the recycling for instance, I do care, but I'm not the obsessive I make out to be. Now that I'm thinking it through, it's all my fault. Since I started teaching I've got boring.'

'Jill, let me tell you now, you are not boring.'

Jill only realises she's crying when a tear lands on the table. She spreads it with her index finger. Ryan takes hold and she gazes at their hands locked together, she doesn't want to look up into his eyes.

'What should I do because I can't go on the way things are?' she asks as R.E.M.'s *Every Day is Yours to Win* strikes up. Her tears turn to laughter.

'What is it?'

'The music. It's like we're in some cheesy film and the director's chosen appropriate songs.'

Ryan laughs too. 'It's Dolly Parton next then.'

'What d'you mean?'

'D-I-V-O-R-C-E.'

'God, who knows. Another drink?'

'No, I'm done for the night.'

'I've probably had enough, too. Let's go.'

'How are you getting home?' Ryan asks when they're outside.

'Underground, I suppose.'

A group of noisy teenagers push past them. 'That's probably not the safest way to travel this time of night, let's share a taxi.'

They're fortunate, at that moment one approaches. They signal, it stops and they jump in. Since Ryan's house is on the way to Jill's, he instructs the driver to make his place the first stop. They sit quietly, Jill leaning on his shoulder.

'Next right and I'm the third house down,' Ryan directs. He takes out his wallet and offers Jill two twenty-pound notes. 'This'll cover it.'

Jill looks down at the money then back to Ryan. The taxi has stopped. 'I'd like to stay with you tonight,' she murmurs.

Ryan nods and they leave the cab together. Inside the house, Jill follows Ryan up a flight of stairs to the entrance to his flat. Only then does he speak as he fumbles with keys, mundane words. 'I'd like somewhere bigger to live, but you know how high rents are in London.'

'It's in a nice area.'

'I suppose so. I'd like to buy, but I'm light years away from having a big enough deposit.'

'Do you want to live in London permanently?'

'Who's to say? Here we are.'

He opens the front door.

As soon as it's closed, the chit chat ends and lust takes over. Any indecisiveness or remorse dissolves as they tear at each other's clothes, literally, and there's a pause for laughter as a button on Ryan's shirt flies off. Power, shared power, surpasses tenderness in their first lovemaking.

Later, in Ryan's bedroom, Jill texts Jack. *staying out at friends tonight.*

When Jill wakes she expects a rush of guilt, but it doesn't arrive. She's content.

Ryan looks across. 'Good morning. I'm glad you're here, but what now?'

'God knows. I suppose the immediate short term is that I go home. Do you want an affair with a married woman?'

'As long as the married woman is you.'

'If you're alright with it, I suppose that's where we're at for now.'

'And what about beyond now?'

'Who knows? I don't care if Jack catches me out, but we do live together so we'll have to plan carefully when to meet. Sometimes I might even have to cancel at short notice.'

'You make it sound like a business proposition. Whenever you're available I'll be happy, very happy.'

'Sorry, I've gone into organising mode and you're quite right. Being with you is bliss.'

They kiss, they make love.

~

By the time the taxi pulls up outside her house, Jill has weighed up the situation rationally. Her initial feeling is that she likes the man a lot but she has to keep her feet firmly on the ground, getting to know Ryan with no strings attached is the way forward. And they are going to have to keep a distance at school to avoid gossip.

What about Jack? She'll stay put until it becomes obvious what to do next. It might be out of her control, her husband might make the decision for her.

Jack isn't home. She checks her phone and reads his message. *Fine, I'm also out tonight.*

19

Jill loves being with Ryan. There's no problem keeping the affair from Jack because he has so little interest in her he wouldn't notice if Ryan was a lodger.

After less than four years her marriage has reached a state of indifference. There are rarely huge arguments, it's usually perfectly civil, so politely English, their time together veering between tolerance, at times even comfort, and irritability.

But how long can a marriage go on like this?

No longer is the answer because events over the past few days have pushed their relationship to the limits.

It had started on the Sunday morning with Jack and Jill sitting in the lounge together after a late breakfast, reading the newspapers.

'Is it OK to open a window, Jack? I'm baking hot.'

'No, go on. Funnily enough I'm reading something that's linked. It's a record temperature for March, it looks like global warming's finally arrived.'

'That's why you need to take recycling more seriously.' As she speaks Jill regrets sermonising.

'You know my view, the tiny bit us Europeans can do has absolutely no impact.'

Jill avoids repeating her usual "if everybody said that" statement. They carry on reading for a while.

'This looks good,' Jack says, holding up the arts supplement. 'The new Penelope Cruz film. Fancy seeing it this afternoon?'

This poses a problem. Jill has arranged to see it with Ryan that same afternoon. 'Sorry, can't. I'm popping round to a colleague to work on the new syllabus.'

Jack nods and leaves the room. Nodding and walking out has become his reaction of choice when he's fed up. She hates lying, even though she knows Jack fobs her off with deceitful excuses many a time.

He's back a couple of minutes later carrying his kit bag. 'I'm off to the gym,' he tells her and promptly leaves.

Jill's lost enthusiasm to go to the cinema and calls Ryan to cancel before settling down to work on the new syllabus. Alone. She wastes time, she can't concentrate.

It's approaching half past six when Jack gets back. Without a greeting he heads for the kitchen, Jill knows this is to get hold of his first evening intake of wine. There's the sound of clinking and clanking as he rearranges the crockery, cutlery, glasses and saucepans that she maliciously dumped in the dishwasher after lunch.

Rearranging the dishwasher is a common activity when Jack is tense, Jill once suggested he should add it to his CV. He repositions the untidily stacked mugs on the top shelf then adds his wine glass, watching as the red dregs trickle down onto a plate underneath. Jill has placed four of them diagonally so they're taking up far more space than needed in the lower compartment. He lifts them out, gives them a quick rinse and returns them. His irritation about Jill's lack of care when loading is tempered by the pleasure he derives from re-sorting. It feels good, very good. The mix of wine, he's downed a second glass, and the clandestine snort of cocaine (in the car because Jill's banned it from home), have lightened his mood. He addresses the chaos in the orange cutlery container. He's told her a thousand times, if a spoon's put face down it won't get clean, it's as simple as that. He wonders whether Jill's deliberately placed a single spoon in each of the eight sections. He lifts them up, spins them round and relocates into a single compartment, his right hand now coated in the sticky remains of Jill's porridge.

As he washes his hands the *EastEnders* signature tune belts out from the lounge, it's the omnibus show. Does he hate the tune because he hates the programme or does the jolly jingle merit contempt in its own right? Jill claims she shares Jack's dislike of the soap but needs to watch to stay in touch with what the schoolkids view.

She's ironing. It's hotting up for Dawn and Garry on Albert Square, it looks like they're about to give it a go. Everyone at school will be talking about it tomorrow. She smoothes out a pair of her socks before dropping them in the basket. Jack irons his socks! He says unironed socks are uncomfortable and abrasive; he wants his to be smooth and soft.

Jack pours a third glass of Merlot. He takes a clean glass for each drink, he believes the dregs in a used one interferes with taste. Probably all in the mind, he concedes. He knows Jill thinks he's mad because she's told him so. He's twitchy now that he's thinking of all the things Jill does wrong. Take toothpaste for instance. A hardened ball can build up on the top of the tube but there's a simple way to prevent it – run the plastic end of the container over the toothbrush when dispensing. He's explained this, even demonstrated, and she hasn't taken a blind bit of notice. He knocks back the rest of his wine, places the glass in the dishwasher, takes a new one from the cupboard and pours another generous amount. His head, he recognises, is fucked, petty things to do with toothpaste and spoons now of monumental importance.

EastEnders is over, the telly is switched off. Jill hasn't got as far as she would have liked with her pile of clothes but she must stop because there's marking to do. As she's about to start, books piled high on the floor, Jack calls out.

'Jill, I need to show you something.'

'I'm busy, can't it wait?'

'Not really, it's important.' He leads her up to the bathroom. 'Watch me.' His demonstration of how to dispense toothpaste properly is a failure because his hand is shaking; a line of gel plops onto the surface of the cabinet.

'Oh, I see what I'm meant to do,' Jill jibes. 'Very impressive. You know, you have shown me how to do this several times before.'

'Then if I've shown you, why aren't you doing it properly?'

'Like you? Honestly, you're pathetic,' she mutters as she goes out, leaving him to clear up his mess.

A few minutes later Jack enters the lounge and glances at the pile of books. From day one he's disliked her bringing work home. 'If it were me, I'd organise things to get everything finished during lessons,' he says, sticking to a well-used script. 'That's what my teachers used to do.'

She provides her stock answer. 'They must have been bloody lazy then. Let's face it, public schools are only after money, the teachers don't give a toss about educating. They don't have to, it's not exactly hard to get selected kids with pushy parents through exams.'

'That's not true,' he states. Now it's his turn to leave a room.

Maybe not true, Jill thinks, but it has to be easier than her job, what with all the discipline problems and the administration that drives her up the wall.

Jack turns on the computer and grimaces in the face of the untidy array of icons that fill the screen. He really must get his own machine, if his head wasn't so fuzzy he'd order one online now. He accesses the internet and clicks into 'Favorites', cursoring through the endless websites Jill has saved before reaching the folder entitled *Jack*. Inside this are his own favourites, neatly sorted into sub-folders with the exception of *YouTube* which is a stand-alone. He turns on the speakers and selects from the most popular hits of the day.

He laughs, maybe genuine, maybe fake, he's not even sure himself. He used to laugh loads for real, but now? 'This can't be true. Jill, come and look at this, a scientist's dipping cheeseburgers into acid. Quick, look what happens to the food. Jill!'

'I'm working, Jack.'

'It'd be nice if you could spend a minute of your precious time with me.'

'And it'd be nice if you could spend an evening or two of your precious time at home. Anyway, watching *YouTube* is hardly an enticing offer.'

230

'Sod off,' he mumbles as he turns up the speaker volume. He types in "heavy metal" and selects Savage Circus playing *Between the Devil and the Seas*, this solely based on the title and the look of the Neanderthal-like men in the photo. He lets it blast, a good choice as a piercing shriek precedes thumping guitar chords and pounding drums.

'Jack! Turn it down!'

He does, he's made his point. It was crap anyway. He types in "latest films" and watches trailers.

Half an hour or so later, Jill emerges from the lounge. Not a word is spoken as she passes him on the way to the kitchen. She checks on the vegetarian lasagne in the oven. Of course, Jack won't like it because it's meatless. Too bad. He'll cut into the lasagne and discover roasted veg instead of meat which will piss him off if he's still sober enough to know what's what. Ryan's a vegetarian.

She's about to inspect how Jack has addressed her deliberate mayhem in the dishwasher when he comes into the kitchen carrying a parcel tidily wrapped in candy striped pink and pistachio paper with a gold bow on the top. 'For you, your birthday. I've got to leave early tomorrow morning and I'm not sure what time I'll be home, so it's best to give it now.'

He's remembered, Jill wasn't sure he would because he's been forgetting things lately. He's smiling and a touch of affection surfaces. She opens her present – it's a Wii Fit.

'This'll help you get rid of some of that flabby stomach of yours,' he says, patting her belly. He's still smiling, it reminds her of the way he used to, but now she can't gauge whether this smile is cheeky or spiteful. 'Like it?' he asks.

She doesn't, but avoids explicit negativity and opts for sarcasm. 'Yes thanks, it's just what I need.'

He's by her side now, stroking her arm. Touching is such a rarity. 'The food can wait, let's go upstairs,' he suggests.

There remains too much between them for her not to feel a physical attraction, though her thoughts are chaotic because so much has gone on with Ryan recently.

'Sure. I'll just turn down the oven.'

~

'Sophie!' Jack calls out as he ejaculates.

And again when she thought he was asleep. 'Sophie,' he sighs.

Jill puts on her dressing gown and goes downstairs to prepare their meal. She calls out to get him down when it's on the table.

'Who's Sophie?' she asks as she watches Jack extract the parsnips and carrots from the vegetable lasagne. Parsnips and carrots are the main ingredients in the Parsnip and Carrot Lasagne recipe she found online.

He seems intent on killing a carrot with a ferocious attack using his fork. 'Sophie? Not sure, I do have a P.A. called Sophie. Why?'

'It's just that you called out her name when we were in bed.'

The carrot, now surely deceased, is ushered onto his side plate. 'There's so much stuff going on at work, I must have been thinking of what I've got to give her to do tomorrow. More wine?'

'No thanks.'

'Sure? It is your birthday in a few hours' time,' Jack says as he pours himself a generous glass.

'I'm fine. Anyway, you're drinking for the two of us.'

'Here you go again. Don't spoil it.'

There's nothing left to spoil she feels like informing him as she takes hold of the plates and tips Jack's leftovers into the recycling bin. She hears his tut as she untidily stacks the plates in the dishwasher.

'I'm off to bed,' she announces. 'Since you're leaving early I think I'll sleep in the spare room. It's half term so I'll be able to have a lie in.'

Jack lifts his glass and downs the remains before giving her a kiss on the cheek. 'Happy birthday, Darling.'

Upstairs, Jill can hear him rearranging the dishwasher.

The following morning she decides to investigate something she's never bothered about before. The task is surprisingly easy. There are photos of key staff on his company's website and she locates a Sophie who is Marketing Director. She looks attractive in a *Hello* magazine sort of way, older than Jack, perhaps by ten years or so.

That afternoon Jill heads to the office and waits across the road to see if she can catch a glimpse of Sophie. Silly really, why bother? Just curiosity. It's a long wait but at 6.42 pm out she comes. It's summer, the best season to show off a beautiful body, and hers is beautiful. She's tall, possibly as tall as Jack, and catwalk slim. She has stopped at the foot of the stairway that leads up to the impressively grand glass doors of the office block. Jill sees Jack come bounding down, all smiles. He reaches Sophie and puts his arms round her waist. They kiss. The sort of kiss Jill only gets and gives with Ryan nowadays.

Jack lifts his mobile and dials. Her own phone rings.

'Hi Jill. Happy birthday! Look, I'm ever so sorry but I'm stuck in the office with an emergency. I've no idea what time I can get away, but no need to wait up.'

'That's a pity, but thanks for letting me know, and for remembering my birthday when you're so busy. Might you want something to eat when you get back, I'm making vegetable moussaka.'

'No, I'll grab a sandwich or something here. Thanks for the offer though.'

'All right, but look, you make sure you don't work too hard. Bye.'

Jill terminates the call and watches as Jack and Sophie walk off, holding hands just as she had done in what seems like a very distant past.

She dials. 'Hey Ryan, good news, Jack's out for a few hours, can you make it over?…Great, I'll be home in about half an hour…Love you too.'

~

Ryan arrives a little before eight with a bunch of pink carnations and a bottle of pink Cava.

'Happy birthday, Jill,' he says as he opens the bottle. He takes two glasses out the cupboard, he knows his way round, pours and hands one to Jill. 'Cheers,' he says as they clink glasses.

Jill serves up the moussaka.

After dinner, they go upstairs and start to undress.

'Now let me see that flabby belly of yours,' he mocks as he lifts off her T-shirt and kneels down to kiss it. 'Yep, the good news is the Wii Fit's already working.'

'I haven't used it yet.'

'Must be psychosomatic then. And it's also helping here,' he adds as he pulls down her knickers and moves his tongue downwards. She laughs, Ryan makes her laugh and he does a lot more for her, too.

'You're beautiful, Jill,' Ryan says as they lie side by side, naked and fulfilled.

'Yeah, I know I am,' she teases. 'Come on, let's do it. Bathroom first.'

'Sure thing.'

They dress quickly, keen to partake in an activity that has grown in scale to reach near obsession in recent weeks.

In the bathroom Ryan repositions the shower gels and shampoos in the rack, placing one of the bottles on its side. He lifts up the plastic lid and squeezes some of the thick green liquid onto the floor of the shower basin.

'Look at this,' Jill calls out, holding up the toothpaste dispenser. There's a thick blob of already hardening gel blocking the nozzle. 'Jack's worst nightmare.'

In the kitchen Jill sets to work rearranging the dishwasher while Ryan opens one of the food cupboards. With post-modern artistic finesse, he dismantles the neat stacks to create chaos, hiding the smallest spice jars behind the largest cans of vegetables.

Jill watches as he completes the task. 'Actually *that's* probably his worst nightmare, or maybe this is,' she calls out as she reaches the computer. She knocks off the Auto Arrange that Jack had reset the previous evening and sets about moving icons randomly across the screen.

Ryan joins her. 'You can fill the screen with loads more,' he suggests, 'by making shortcuts for all the programs.' Jill knows this but is happy not to dampen Ryan's playful enthusiasm and she lets him get on with it.

'One last thing,' Jill announces as she knocks *YouTube* off Jack's 'My Favorites' list. 'But that's enough for tonight, in fact maybe you should go, just in case.'

As soon as Ryan has left, Jill dashes upstairs to change the sheets and take a quick shower. She's sitting downstairs planning a lesson when Jack arrives. She can never understand why he doesn't say anything about the chaos he returns to. Perhaps it's because he's so enthusiastic about re-sorting things, but she thinks it might be because his mind is permanently dulled by the high intake of alcohol and cocaine.

She looks up and fakes a welcoming smile. 'Hello, you're back earlier than you thought.'

'Yeah, the meeting didn't drag on,' he slurs.

'All go well?'

'As good as an evening meeting can go. What have you been doing?'

'Preparing, I've got loads on.'

A nod and exit follow. Jill hears the clink, clink, clink of glasses and china being rearranged in the dishwasher.

There's an almighty crash.

'Fuck!' she hears.

'Everything alright in there?' she calls out.

'I've dropped two fucking plates.'

She leaves him to it. Six, maybe even three months ago she would have rushed in to help. There's the sound of fragments being swept into a pan. Jack returns to the lounge carrying the empty bottle of pink Cava. Usually Jill is meticulous in clearing away evidence of her visitor, tonight she's failed.

'What's this? It was in the kitchen bin.'

'It's an empty bottle of wine.'

'We never buy this pink rubbish.'

Jill's mind races, considering in a flash every feasible response. She could tell Jack that a work colleague or two made a surprise visit to celebrate her birthday and brought along a bottle of wine.

But no, enough is enough, the corniest of all options stands out.

'Jack, it's time we talked.'

20

The conversation that night is short and incoherent.

'It's not working,' is Jill's first statement.

'What isn't? What do you mean?'

'I mean us.'

'Why are you saying that?'

'Jack don't be silly. We hardly see each other, hardly speak when we do. And I know about Sophie.'

'What are you talking about? I need a drink.' Jack leaves the room, returning a couple of minutes later with a bottle and single glass. He pours, drinks, pours, drinks, then speaks. 'I'd like to know what you mean about Sophie.'

'Don't pretend. What's the point?'

'There's nothing going on.'

'That's not true. I was outside your office today, I saw you together.'

One thing about Jack, there's never an ounce of malice in him, there's no "How dare you follow me" or similar statement. His head is down and when he looks up there are tears. 'I'm sorry. It's because Sophie understands me.'

'That's an absurd cliché. *My wife doesn't understand me*. Honestly, even if it's true that someone understands you more than I do, you're not compelled to have sex with them. Just be truthful, for God's sake.'

'But it's true, she gets it how I feel about things.'

'She's your bit on the side!'

'She understands me,' he repeats.

This hurts Jill, she used to think no one could ever know Jack more than her. 'There's not much to understand, you're see-through.'

'I'm sorry you think that.'

'Still not good enough. You can't expect me to say never mind and I forgive you for having an affair, because I'm not going to.' The irony of her statement hits hard bearing in mind her relationship with Ryan. Once respected as kind and sensitive, Jill now considers herself to be two-faced and malicious. Jack needs help, she should be offering support. The sad thing is, she doesn't think she can.

'And what about this?' Jack asks, holding up the empty Cava bottle.

Jill owns up about her affair. 'Two can play at that game, Jack.'

Jack lifts a plastic bag from his jacket pocket, at which point Jill stands up. 'You promised you wouldn't bring that stuff home. I don't want the police turning up.'

Jack ignores her and prepares to snort. He's looking older, weak, she notes before storming out and marching upstairs to shift more of her possessions into the spare room.

It's impossible to sleep. She hears Jack coming upstairs, tripping and cursing as he ascends. In equal doses she wants to and doesn't want to see if he's all right. She hates him, she loves him, and she wonders what will be. She cries.

When she wakes late morning, Jack has left for work. There's a note on the kitchen table, a piece of paper folded in half as if it were a secret message that others mustn't see. Her name is on the front. His boyish handwriting, she loved it, she loves it.

Jill, I've no idea what happens next, do you? It seems as if we've lost it even though I still love you. I've no idea what happens next. Sorry, already written that. I can't think clearly. Can we talk tonight? Jack.

Not thinking clearly is part of your problem, she wants to tell him, maybe will tell him that evening.

Jill wanders around Regent's Park for hours. She visits the zoo even though she hates zoos. It starts raining, she hasn't brought an umbrella. She carries on walking, getting drenched seems like a fitting penance. She doesn't know whether she wants the marriage to end. It's not as simple as a quick swap from Jack to Ryan, that would be ridiculous. On the way home she picks up a fillet steak for Jack and some Dover sole for her. There should at least be civility.

She's in the kitchen preparing the meal when Jack texts. *Very busy, either home late or will stay over.*

Jill is furious. Tonight of all nights when there's so much to discuss. She calls him. 'Hello, Jack's phone,' a woman answers.

'Who are you?'

'Sophie. Who are you?'

Sophie must know, her own name would be displayed on screen. 'Is Jack there?'

'He's a bit out of action, I'm afraid.'

Jill hears chat and then Jack speaks, mumbles. 'Is that you?'

'Of course it's fucking me.'

'I'm not sure I can make it home tonight, I'll see you tomorrow, love.'

Jill ends the call. "Love", he's never called her that. Is it a Sophie endearment? Or some other woman. She's seething, her husband is too smashed to remember the importance of what he'd suggested that morning.

Jill calls Ryan. 'I need to see you.'

'Now? Can it wait until tomorrow, I'm tied up painting?'

'It's important, please can we meet?'

'Alright, that café, I can be there in about twenty minutes.'

~

A Street Café Named Desire is a rather pretentious arts café close to where he lives. They've been there a couple of times, once for the opening of Ryan's exhibition, the second to see a 1930s Russian propaganda film about how wonderful Stalin was.

Jill gets there first and half listens to squeaky random-notes-every-few-seconds jazz as she waits. Ryan arrives and puts his arm round her. 'Hi. You all right?' Jill is sensitive to it being a cursory question because he is continuing without giving her time to reply. 'I'll grab some drinks. What do you want?' he says.

'A coffee would be nice. No, make that wine. White. Large.'

As soon as Ryan's back she launches into an account of what had happened the previous evening.

'You're usually careful clearing up when I leave.'

'That's hardly the point. My marriage is over because of Jack, not because of you and me,' she snaps, hating herself

241

for being abrasive. 'Sorry, I didn't mean that, of course it's about us, too.'

Jill relays what she regards as the final straw, Sophie answering Jack's phone.

'What now?' Ryan asks.

'Well, it's over. A separation I suppose.' The finality of this statement sends a shiver down her back. She qualifies it. 'It's too early to think of divorce though.'

'What does Jack think?'

'That's what I was hoping to find out this evening. Anyway, it hardly matters because it's my decision. I can't live with him anymore.'

'Yeah, but does he think the same about you?'

'Based on the way he's acting, yes. Actually, he's so stoned most of the time, he probably doesn't do much thinking.'

'Have you suggested doing something to address his addiction if that's what it is?'

Jill is perturbed. Ryan is acting as the peacemaker, the problem solver. There's no indication of delight with this opportunity to further their relationship. Suddenly she is feeling extremely lonely.

A middle-aged man walks onto the tiny stage, microphone in hand. 'Ladies and gentlemen, we're honoured to welcome as our guest poet the one and only Eliza Cobham. Some of you will have seen him here a few months ago and by popular demand he's back.'

Jill looks around, there are a dozen customers at most, popular demand seems a bit of an exaggeration.

'So, ladies and gentlemen, please put your hands together to welcome Eliza.'

A few join the announcer in applauding, others carry on with their conversations. Jill claps out of politeness, Ryan doesn't, he's deep in thought. There's piercing feedback as the announcer walks past the loudspeaker. A woman grabs the mike, moves to the centre of the stage and hands it to Eliza.

'The first one I want to recite is, I suppose, the one you all know best. *Love is so bloody fragile.*

> *Tender hearts are bound together*
> *Together by this love that is youth*
> *Until shards of glass pierce the hearts*
> *And lifeblood drips to the floor…'*

'Ryan, we must escape before I laugh or kill him.'

'It's not great, is it? Come on.'

Ryan takes hold of Jill's hand and they leave. He stops as soon as they're outside the café. 'So what now?'

'You've already asked me that and I don't know. Can I stay with you tonight? Or maybe I should book into a hotel.'

'Don't be silly, tonight's fine.'

Only for one night? Jill tries to gauge what Ryan is thinking because what he's saying gives little indication. Is the offer based on love or is it an act of charity – she really can't tell. She's not stayed overnight at Ryan's often, maybe he likes it that way.

They saunter back to his place, hand in hand, Jill thinking of Jack and Sophie holding hands. When they make love, Jill fights to dismiss memories of when she and Jack had made equally tender love. Ryan pulls her close as she sobs.

The next morning Jill is still unsure about Ryan's feelings. He's woken her with a giant mug of tea and a good morning kiss, all smiles, and now sits on the edge of the bed.

'What are your plans today?' he asks. This is a tumultuous day for Jill, the aftermath of life with Jack, so a heart-to-heart about how their relationship might develop would be nice. But Ryan seems oblivious to the need. 'I've got a painting I must finish, the one I was doing yesterday evening when you called.' Is he blaming me for distracting him, Jill wonders? 'Then I'll need to dash to the gallery to show them photos of the pieces they want to display.' Might he invite me to join him, she speculates.

No invitation is forthcoming. 'I suppose I could go for a walk or maybe a run. I'll need to pop home to get some clothes, too. But look, is it OK if I live here for a while?'

There's an uncomfortable pause, but when the reply arrives it seems genuine enough. 'That would be lovely. Would you like me to come with you to your place to get stuff?'

'No, you do your jobs. I can use the car and Jack will be at work.'

Her phone rings. It's Jack.

'I'll leave you to it,' Ryan says as she answers.

'I don't want us to split, we can work things out,' are Jack's first words.

'That wasn't on your agenda yesterday…What I mean is that you wrote about loving me and wanting to talk it over then you texted you wouldn't be back and Sophie answered your bloody phone…It's not good enough blaming it all on drink…But I've heard this before, Jack. I'm taking some time apart to think things through…I'll be staying at a friend's…Yes, he's male.'

The call is terminated.

Jill drives to her house, maybe her ex-house, and packs a couple of suitcases. She wanders round every room reminiscing, looking at the life she's leaving behind. She runs her hand along the smooth glass of the Murano vase that marked their engagement. She lifts it, unsure whether her intention is to take it with her or smash it to smithereens. She places it back on the table.

In the kitchen she leaves a note next to the one Jack had written. *I've collected some stuff. Like you, I've no idea where this will end, we'll see won't we.* Though it might be true, she can't add the 'I still love you' that Jack has written.

Before departing, she calls her parents. As soon as her mother answers she gets straight to the point, coolly announcing she's leaving Jack as if relating someone else's crisis.

'Why not come over? It would be good to get away from everything for a while.'

'I'm working, Mum. I can't do that.'

'Take compassionate leave, even if it's only for a couple of days.'

Two days would mean four because it would use up a day to reach them and another to return. It's not on. And, she realises, being with Ryan is something she prefers.

'Where are you staying?'

'With a friend.'

There's a short pause before Vanessa asks the same question Jack had done.

'A male,' Jill replies.

Unlike in the conversation with Jack, this call isn't terminated though Vanessa's miniscule response of "Oh" sounds judgemental.

Jill considers how to respond. She could outline all the things Jack's done wrong to justify her own behaviour, but she's too drained to do so. 'He's just a friend.'

Vanessa doesn't pursue the interrogation. 'Please keep in touch.'

'I will, but I must go now. I'll call you soon.'

She changes into running gear and jogs to Regent's Park where she runs faster and further than she's ever done. She presses on until dizziness prevents any thought other than where to place the next foot. Finally Jill draws to a halt and collapses onto the ground. A summer cloudburst provides what is turning out to be her daily penitential soaking.

~

The following days and weeks are bizarrely uneventful given the grand scheme of things. She's living with Ryan and her initial uncertainty about whether he wants her there has disappeared. He needs his time alone to paint which is fine with Jill because when they're together all is going well. It's similar to what life was like a couple of years ago – shopping, eating, watching television, having sex – only with a different man. She's surprised how quickly it's become the norm.

There's no communication from Jack. She's planned what to say when he calls, but this remains theoretical because he doesn't phone. She wonders whether she'll see him at the school gates one day, but he doesn't show. Will he discover where she's living and come knocking on Ryan's door full of rage? No.

246

Ryan is lovely. 'Ryan, you are lovely!' she informs him one morning as she watches him paint.

Jill blocks thoughts about what the future might bring, there seems little point. She might end up with Ryan. She might go back to Jack. There might be another man. Perhaps she was once a romantic but she now knows that "the only one for me" doesn't hold water.

Sabrina calls. It's about a month after the separation. They've been in touch since but only through brief telephone calls. 'Let's meet,' she asks after an exchange of pleasantries.

'I don't think I'm ready for that yet.' After all, Sabrina is Jack's mother and Jill is wary and embarrassed despite the good relationship with her mother-in-law.

'Please. I'd just like to chat.'

Jill relents and a couple of days later they meet early evening at Baker Street Station. It's chilly and damp, an early hint of autumn. Sabrina has reserved a table at a small Italian near Oxford Street. They've been there before and it's one of their favourites, only a short walk off the beaten track but serenely devoid of tourists.

'I've had more conversations with Jack over the past month than I've had for years,' Sabrina states.

'Well I haven't heard a word from him.'

'Not that he says much when we're on the phone, only that he's devastated. I decided to pop round last weekend. Uninvited. He looks dreadful and he was knocking back wine like there's no tomorrow, and that was at eleven in the morning.'

'I know all too well about the drinking.'

'I wondered whether he was able to work properly.'

'I hadn't thought of work as a problem, his lifestyle seems pretty much the same as everyone else in the City. He must be coping if the money he makes is anything to go by.'

'Call it mother's intuition, but I sense disaster on the horizon.'

The waiter brings the main courses. They tuck into sea bass stuffed with rosemary and black olives, little cubes of roast potatoes and Mediterranean vegetables. 'This is delicious,' Jill says as she lifts a strip of courgette onto her fork. 'Do Henry and Seb know what's going on?'

'Through me. I tell Seb and he tells Henry. According to Seb there's still no contact between Jack and his father and the brothers haven't spoken for months.'

'That's a pity, Jack misses them even though he's not prepared to admit it.'

They watch as the waiter clears their plates.

'Do you think this is it between you two?'

'I honestly don't know, Sabrina. All I can say is that it's hopeless now, he's changed so much. Probably I have, too, it wouldn't be fair to say it's all one way.'

'I'm not taking sides, but I can see why you've left him. I hope it's retrievable.'

Jill can't voice what she imagines Sabrina probably wants to hear, that she hopes so too. She looks down at the dessert menu.

'This man you're with, is it serious?'

'Who knows?' Jill has to tell Sabrina some home truths. 'Our separation isn't because of my infidelity. Jack's having an affair with a woman from work and it isn't his first.'

'I know, she was there when I visited.'

Jill's first reaction is fury, but it subsides. After all, she's also living with someone. 'I've seen her, she's the marketing director at the company.'

'No, she's a corporate lawyer. They don't work together.'

'You're mistaken. It's Sophie, I've seen them together.'

'It wasn't a Sophie there, it was Felicity.'

They exchange looks, recognising the implication. Nothing more needs to be said about the matter.

Sabrina chats on about other things, life with Anthony, films, books, updates about Jill's parents.

Sabrina's final words are reassuring. 'If it's any comfort, I support what you've done. And look at me, an old lady, resurgent with a new man. You're still young, Jill, there'll be plenty of opportunities to find new happiness.'

21

There's Sophie and there's Felicity, too. There are lap dancers and a prostitute. There's Jack's old school girlfriend, Caroline Curbishly, who has reappeared as a bit player in the drama called Jack's Crumbling Life. Jack would agree with this label. Although a participant, at times he feels like the audience as an Ancient Greek tragedy unfolds.

'Jack, I think you should invite me for a drink after work,' Sophie had commanded a month or so before Jill had seen them together. Sophie was a perfect fit for the role of senior executive at a City corporation. She beat the boys at their own game, a ruthless, hard-nosed, cold-hearted woman, happy to trample on anyone who got in her way, intent on picking up men to satisfy her insatiable appetite for young lovers.

Jack's a rising star and Sophie is particularly attracted to rising stars. He's good looking in a boyish sort of way.

Senior executives are able to make use of the company's account at a nearby prestigious hotel and Jack is the latest of a long line of employees taken to her favourite room, a suite with a circular bed, giant screen TV, Jacuzzi and a fridge that has enough stock to supply a small party. They start their first evening in a bar. She outdrinks him, one up for her, that takes some doing. Together they stagger to the hotel where Sophie strips in the lift then races naked along the corridor to her room. Poor Jack thinks this erotic dare is for him alone when in fact it has been Sophie's routine for all-comers. She's currently dating two men in addition to Jack. Dating is the word she's selected to use with irony, it couldn't be more inappropriate because there is nothing in her short-term relationships beyond sex, drink and cocaine.

Poor, poor Jack is a true gentleman. He wants to find out more about Sophie, what are her family like, where is she from, what are her outside interests, would she like to go for a meal together, the cinema or theatre, when is her birthday because he'd like to get her something? She has no desire to engage, not the slightest interest in him beyond his anatomy.

From the first encounter onwards, Jack has wanted to call it a day, not an easy task because Sophie has almighty influence at the company, offending her could be dangerous. When she'd asked him to meet her after work on that Monday of Jill's birthday, he'd been too cowardly to decline.

When sober his resolve is strong, when drunk it disappears. On the day that Jill sees them together, he's intent on staying clear-headed. He would go to the hotel one last time, then as politely as possible announce that it was over. I have a wife, he would say, and I can't carry on with this deceit.

That evening he goes through with it. Sophie is indifferent to the news bar a casual comment that if he ever changes his mind, he should let her know.

'I won't be doing that, Sophie. I love my wife. I'm going to repair things between us.'

'It's the modern world, Jack. If something's broken you simply get a new one, an upgrade.'

'This is different, I promise.'

'There's no need to promise me. I'm fine, it's a global market out there.'

Jack realises he hates this woman and rushes home with a determination to put things right. Striding back from the station, he's considering how to make things better. As soon as he steps through the door there's the accusation. He's prepared to admit and apologise, but on being attacked with the same old sarcasm, he wavers. And then Jill tells him she's having an affair.

During a restless night he weighs up what he wants to happen. By the time he's at work he knows – to get back to what it used to be like with Jill. He wants this so much, but things, no, not things, *he*, is too far gone to repair the damage. Midday he abandons his desk and spends the afternoon at his favourite bar, now near deserted ahead of the evening rush. He's switched off his mobile so is unaware that major clients are trying to make contact. A financial crisis in the Asian property sector has erupted, his team need him to deal with it, are desperately searching for him, but he's nowhere to be found. When he returns to his desk soon after five, barely able to stand, his P.A. informs him that the head of division wants to see him immediately.

'Don't let him know I'm back. Tell him I've called in unwell.'

As he flees the building, he phones Sophie. She laughs, teasing him about his quick change of mind, but agreeing to meet her at the hotel. By six o'clock they're together in the room with the circular bed, Jacuzzi and party bar, Jack near comatose by the time Sophie takes Jill's call.

Soon afterwards, Sophie receives a text from a colleague. Jack's lied about being ill, staff have seen him leave the office, and he's in big trouble for deserting his desk at time of crisis. There's a growing perception that he's losing the plot, the star boy is no longer on a winning streak. Once a reputation is questioned the outcome is an unglamorous exit.

Sophie can't take the risk of being associated with a loser. 'Out!'

'Pardon?'

'Get dressed and get out.'

'But…'

'This is it for us, Jack. I'm afraid you're a has-been and I don't hang out with has-beens.'

Jack's too drained to respond, either with a plea for her to reconsider or a tirade against her callousness. 'No bother,' he whispers. 'I'll just take a shower then go.'

'Best to skip the shower.'

Outside the hotel he calls Felicity. He's been having an on-off affair with her for a few months, having met in one of the chic City bars. She has a luxury apartment near Canary Wharf, paid for by her super rich father which allows her to spend her huge corporate lawyer's income on luxuries including expensive wine and cocaine.

He takes a taxi to her place, the dog yaps as he approaches the front door. The dog is a poodle with snow-white fur. It shares Felicity's love of luxuries, and today is sporting a diamanté collar and a Burberry waistcoat.

Jack doesn't much like Felicity, she's a snob with seismic arrogance. She'd fit perfectly into a past era, perhaps 1930s Germany where she would be more than comfortable with the concept of the master race. She detests her Russian, Middle Eastern and Chinese neighbours even though they seem exceedingly polite and friendly whenever Jack passes them by.

'It's a big problem, Jack, the plebs and all the foreigners in England are breeding so much more than people like us. They'll swamp the nation.'

Jack is sitting on an armchair in the bedroom as she says this. Felicity is very ordered ahead of cocaine and sex. He watches her lay out tissues, oil and vibrator at the side of the bed before selecting the porn movie they are to watch.

'Right, all set,' she declares as she hits Play on the DVD machine. The cocaine is out, the clothes come off, and as usual, Yapper is allowed to spectate.

The next morning Felicity is first up, slipping on the Versace dressing gown fit for a diva. The brand name is displayed in garish pink across the back of the white silk garment. Jack wishes he was with Jill, they could mock this show of wealth together. He follows her into the kitchen, she's making coffee on a machine large enough for use in a restaurant. The coffee is served with croissants and cocaine. Jack tells her about his problems with Jill and Sophie.

'Great. We can toast the new phase of our relationship,' she announces as she lifts a bottle of champagne out the fridge.

By the time they've showered it's late. Felicity has a meeting at ten thirty and it's already gone ten. 'Drive me there, would you?' she asks Jack.

'Can't you drive?'

'It'd take me ages to find a parking place. You can drop me off at my office then keep the car in your company garage until you come back this evening.'

Jack's worried about work, he's already late and has some explaining to do. He's had a fair bit to drink, and there's the cocaine, too. But Felicity never welcomes opposition to her ideas so he agrees to drive.

~

Two mornings later, before the start of lessons, a colleague hands Jill a newspaper.

Dramatic fall for the king of traders
The secret alcohol, drugs and sex life of a City star

Jack Ashley-Lovett had it all, a fantastic job, a huge salary, a wife, and a future without limits. It's all gone now, a drink-driving offence only the start of his problems. While in this state, he narrowly missed hitting a mother and baby in pram as his out of control Jaguar hurtled into a lamppost. Two police officers were witnesses. It is understood that they found a substantial amount of cocaine in Ashley-Lovett's possession.

The car owner, Felicity Taverner, is a lawyer at Cross, Zukerman and Reid. Ms Taverner has issued a statement indicating that she had implored her boyfriend not to drive that morning due to his intoxicated state. She had no idea that he was taking drugs.

A spokeswoman at International Investors plc maintains that Mr Ashley-Lovett was due to be suspended on the day of the accident ahead of an investigation for irregular trading.

This is one more example of how highly paid young men and women who work in the banking sector lead lifestyles that destroy the reputation of their profession. Only last week we reported a £25,000 bill for alcohol during a night out for seven men who had completed a multi-million deal. During that same week, a hotel chain launched an investigation into the ethics of their bookings policy after details of prostitutes entertaining bankers at their London flagship hotel were uncovered.

Jill skipped the part of the article about others' misdemeanours and read the final paragraph,

Jack Ashley-Lovett is the son of Henry Ashley-Lovett, the prominent banker involved in a sex scandal some years back. Mr Ashley-Lovett's wife is a teacher at a secondary school in a deprived area of London.

Journalists haven't contacted her yet, but Jill reckons it's only a question of time. She calls Jack for an update. There's no answer and she doesn't leave a voicemail.

~

After the accident and time spent at the police station, Jack had gone home, switched off his mobile and disconnected his landline. His worst fears were confirmed when he was featured in all the tabloids. It was time to lay low for a while.

He can't think straight. He drinks. He sleeps.

Switching his mobile back on, he sees the missed call from Jill. She can wait. He phones Felicity, disappointed by her distancing according to the newspaper reports. The accident was minutes after dropping her off at work.

'Yes?'

'What do you mean by yes? You can see it's me.'

'What do you want, Jack?'

'Your comment in the newspapers. Is that really what you told them?'

'I've got a reputation to protect.'

'So have I.'

'For you I think it's more a case of *had* a reputation.'

'Let's meet tonight to think through how to handle this?'

'I've handled it, you need to deal with your own problems.'

'Hang on a minute…'

'Get lost, Jack.'

The call is terminated.

Sophie's gone and now Felicity's gone. And Jill, too. He can't call her because he doesn't know what to say.

He's delayed resolving work difficulties for long enough, for starters questioning the ridiculous statement about irregular trading. He'll take whoever said that to the cleaners. When he calls his line manager's P.A. to make an appointment, he's told there are no slots for a meeting that week. She transfers him to his own P.A. to be informed that she's being reassigned to another member of staff with an instruction not to speak to him.

There's only one thing for it. He travels to the International Investors office, dressed for an ordinary working day. It's around lunchtime when he arrives at reception. Colleagues heading out for a break are ignoring him, the very same colleagues who shared champagne, vodka, drugs and women with him only a few days beforehand. Others, people he's seen but couldn't name, point and whisper as they walk by.

'I don't know who you need to call, but I'm not leaving until I've spoken with someone who can tell me what's going on,' he informs the woman at the front desk with more bravado than he feels.

'Take a seat and I'll see what I can do.' She's pretty, Jack thinks. He offers one of his irresistible smiles to no effect; she points to the chairs and he does as instructed.

Ten minutes later, he's approached by another attractive young woman. The company is full of young and beautiful things; the City is full of young and beautiful things. Where are all the obese people with limp oily hair, severe acne, fashionless clothes?

He stands, trying to charm with his smile; again it is ignored by the stony-faced woman in front of him.

'I'm Sharon, from Human Resource Management.'

'Hi, Sharon. Who will I be seeing today?'

'Me, I've been asked to deal with this.'

'What about someone from my department. This talk of irregular trading is absurd, I…' Jack notices those around him are listening, they could be clients, politicians, the press. 'Can we go somewhere to talk in private?'

Sharon suggests they stay put but keep their voices down.

'Aren't I allowed into the building?' he asks.

The reply is short and to the point. 'No.'

Sharon has a statement to read out. He has disgraced the company by his actions. His absence from his desk without notifying colleagues was a breach of code of behaviour meriting a disciplinary proceeding. Other performance issues have proliferated – Jack smiles, she's struggled to say this word, made it sound like profiterole, and he misses the rest of her sentence.

'Sorry, could you say the last bit. Maybe start from the proliferation.'

'Your behaviour has led to the decision to terminate your contract.'

Jack's feeling of flippancy dissolves. 'I don't accept that. I've always exceeded my targets.'

'Off the record, Mr Ashley-Lovett, refusal to accept our offer of termination would not be a good idea. We can announce you are leaving by mutual consent because of personal issues which you have begun to deal with. The alternative is to develop a case against you based on your irregular trading.'

'What irregular trading? There isn't any.'

'We can develop a case to show there has been.'

'But I've never done anything wrong.'

'We *will* develop a case to show irregular trading that will be of interest to the authorities.'

'Right, I get it.'

International Investors plc don't want him and will do whatever it takes to get rid of him. He could contest for unfair dismissal, but they'd have top lawyers, people like Felicity, to fight their case. Jack is resigned to his fate. His world is falling down and suddenly he's exhausted. 'OK. Let me collect my things from my office.'

'That's been sorted. There's a box at reception. I assume, then, that you accept the situation?'

'I don't seem to have much choice.'

'In which case, here's your letter of resignation. If you wouldn't mind signing it.' Sharon hands Jack one of the expensive envelopes the company uses. He lifts the flap as she continues. 'You will see that we are granting you three month's gardening leave. Although not stated in the letter, I've been assured a reference of sorts would be forthcoming should you require one.'

Jack signs the letter and a duplicate to keep, collects his box of possessions and heads home. Home is such a cosy word, too cosy for what now exists. With life as he knew it well and truly over, a wish that life itself was over crosses his mind.

Out of the box from work he lifts the photo of him and Jill on holiday in the Seychelles. He leans it against the Murano vase. He opens a bottle of wine. The alcohol fails to numb his senses as he dwells on the agony of loneliness. Lifting the vase, he cuddles it as if it were Jill herself.

He calls Caroline Curbishly. 'Are you free tonight?'

'Hi, bad boy. I sure am.'

22

Jill shouldn't care but she does. She's tried calling Jack several times but he hasn't answered. A couple of visits to the house have been futile, too. A rancid carton of milk on the kitchen table, broken glass on the floor, overflowing bins, unmade bed. But no Jack. Having scanned the newspapers daily for further salacious revelations of Jack's demise, she finds only one reference, this in the Financial Times – a notification that he has left his job at International Investors plc by mutual consent. There follows a summary of his successes, the past tense making it read like an obituary.

She's left to concentrate on the blossoming relationship with Ryan, though a nagging feeling of disloyalty to Jack won't go away.

When her mother calls for an update she responds as if talking to a stranger.

'What about you, Jill. Are you OK?'

'Everything's great, Mum. Absolutely great.'

'Care to elaborate?'

'No need really. Work's going well, they're thinking of promoting me to the senior management team which is great. I'm very happy with Ryan, we're getting along fine, more than fine, it's great. I'm doing lots of new things socially, life's great.'

'That's a lot of greats. Have you spoken to Jack?'

'It takes two to have a conversation. I've already told you, I've tried to get in touch but he doesn't respond. Look I must go, there's a party at one of Ryan's arty farty friends and I need to get ready.'

'Maybe we'll see you in France soon. Ryan too.'

'Yes, we must arrange dates.'

Jill is disturbed, she's changed. She'd always confided to her mother and now she can't. She hadn't even asked how they were getting on. Why this lack of concern for others, she hasn't even seen her brother for ages despite the arrival of a new nephew? Has she really tried hard enough to contact Jack? Is she dismissing their seven years together as history to be forgotten?

At the party she drinks far too much and when they're home fucks Ryan with furious detachment. The sweet man is tolerant of her tetchiness, though how long will that last? He's all smiles the next morning when he brings tea up to her in bed. I *am* happy, she tells herself as they lie together chatting.

'You know what I'd like to do,' he says. 'Some sketches of you to use for a painting.'

'What, now? Here in bed? Sure.'

Ryan skips out of the room, returning a moment later with pad and charcoals. He sits across from her and draws, she follows his instruction to lie in a particular way. A week or so later she's preparing lessons in the lounge when Ryan enters carrying a substantial painting.

'Da-da,' he sings as he turns it towards her. It depicts Jill sprawled out on the bed with Ryan lying by her side.

'I don't remember you being there,' Jill says.

'I used a photo for me. Like it?'

'Actually yes. Lots.' It's charged with eroticism, the lifelike pair partly covered with a purple duvet. The crimson wall behind them should clash with the duvet but doesn't. In terms of colour, it doesn't replicate Ryan's bedroom; in terms of mood when they are together, it's perfect.

'I'll hang it on the wall opposite the bed then we can see it when we're making love,' he tells her.

This comment brings to mind the paintings that had hung in her parent's London house. She smiles; there can't be that many bedrooms adorned with nude paintings of the occupants in poses verging on erotic.

This thought of her parents leads to Jill calling her mother later that morning, the first conversation since the dismissive one a little over a week earlier.

'Mum, I'm sorry I was a bit abrupt last time we spoke, it's all rather difficult.'

The chat is friendly enough though there is little for Jill to relate to Vanessa. Still with Ryan. Still no news about Jack. Still meeting up with Sabrina. School going well.

'Enough about me though, what about you two?'

Vanessa's answer makes Jill feel guiltier than ever for not keeping up with their news. There's cause for concern. As ever her mother sets out to prevent distressing Jill with bad tidings, but Jill's well aware of this tactic and can read between the lines. Paul and his builder partner are running out of English clients who have loads of money and the inclination to purchase a wreck of a chateau that requires renovation.

'What will you do?'

'Oh, we're not worried, I'm sure things will work out.'

'But…'

'Honestly Jill, we're fine.'

'Please keep me in the loop.'

'Of course.'

'Mum, you know those paintings that were in your bedroom in London, have you still got them?'

'Yes, we brought them with us though we've never got round to hanging them up.'

'They're of you two, aren't they?'

'Yes, you know they are. Well, sort of but it is art.'

Jill recalls the semi-erect penis and the woman who appears to be stroking herself in one of the paintings.

'Why do you ask?' Vanessa continues.

'Oh, I was just thinking about what our house was like, room by room. Must go, I'll catch up soon.'

In bed that night, Jill looks across at the painting now up on the wall facing them. 'Ryan, did I tell you my parents had pictures of them naked in their bedroom?'

'Like this?'

'As in as erotic? Yes, pretty much. Does my body really look like that?'

'I'll need to check,' he says, pulling back the quilt and taking off Jill's oversized T-shirt. 'Yes in your case it's a carbon copy.'

'Let's see for you.' She pulls down his pyjama bottoms. 'Oh! But this is smaller than the one in the painting.'

'It will grow on you.'

Jill chats on as she helps it to grow. 'I think you've given me too many pubes.'

Ryan slides down the bed. 'Let's check this out.'

'I'm so happy being with you,' she tells him as he plays.

~

An act of madness brings Jill's newly found happiness tumbling down.

It's near the end of term, Christmas is approaching, as yet without a glimpse of winter cold. Jill and Ryan will be going their own separate ways over the holiday, Jill to France to be with her parents, in part a mission to discover the state of play. Ryan will be off to the Yorkshire coast near Scarborough, this his childhood home where his parents, two brothers and sister still live.

It's been a hectic term without any winding down because Ryan is putting the final touches to scenery for the school performance of *Jesus Christ Superstar.* He also has an exhibition to prepare and is staying on late most afternoons to get the larger pieces finished in school where there's more space to work in than at home.

Most days Jill stays on until he's finished, busy developing a proposal for student voice that she will be presenting to the principal. At around six each day she makes her way to the art department to see how Ryan's getting on. She loves his paintings of make-believe boats struggling in stormy seas.

Four days to go then it's the holidays. Tonight's the dress rehearsal for the play, then there are two evening performances plus a matinee during school time for the younger pupils, then the last day of term.

'How's it going?' she asks.

Ryan is washing brushes. 'Brilliant, I'm on schedule and feel quite inspired.'

'Will you include our bedroom picture in the exhibition? I want the whole world to see me naked!'

'What's got into you?'

'Endoftermitis,' she says, putting her arms round Ryan's waist, his back towards her as he wipes the brushes. She's professional, sensible, a risk avoider, but has this sudden compulsion. Lowering her hands, she unzips his trousers, releases his penis from his boxers and starts to rub him.

'Erm, Jill, can you hold on until we get home?'

'But I am holding on, sir!'

'Very funny.'

'Please sir, can I give you a blow job?'

'No, I'm afraid students aren't allowed to do that.'

'Oh please sir, I promise not to tell anyone.' Jill pulls Ryan round, lowers his trousers, and follows the script of the role play.

'Please sir, could we have some…' The question ends abruptly. The voice isn't Jill's.

With as much speed as possible Jill shoves Ryan's penis back inside his boxers and yanks up his trousers. He swivels round to be greeted by two sixth form students, Mary Magdalene and Jesus Christ. In the short period of silence, Ryan and Jill are desperately thinking of excuses that could be made, aware that it's not going to be easy to deceive seventeen-year olds.

Jill is the first to speak, getting straight to the point. 'You're probably aware that Mr Shaw and I are in a relationship so this isn't illicit. We do regret it though, don't we, Mr Shaw? I hope you'll respect our privacy.'

Mary Magdalene, real name Yasmin, has always been a mouthy girl. 'It's hardly privacy if you're giving him a blow job in school.'

'I was just kissing it, nothing more,' Jill declares.

Ryan tries to move the conversation on. 'You were about to say you needed something. What would you like?'

Jesus, aka Gordon, speaks, 'We've finished the dress rehearsal and think an additional side screen would be useful.'

'That's no problem, I'll do it first thing in the morning,' Ryan offers, with a nicer tone than he's ever used with Gordon.

'We can do without it. Let's go, Yasmin.'

'Don't forget what I asked,' Jill calls out, followed by "Shit!" when they're out of earshot.

They spend the evening weighing up the chances of being grassed on. Ryan considers offering a bribe for not telling, Jill thinks that could get them into deeper trouble.

They fear Yasmin most; she has a reputation for spreading gossip.

It turns out that Gordon is the bigger problem. He has a high moral stance, in fact as an ardent Christian his role as Jesus is appropriate, though the real Jesus might have been rather more forgiving.

Gordon gets in well before the start of school the next day and stands outside the principal's office waiting for him to arrive. After describing what he's seen, Yasmin is called in to verify the story. Governors are contacted immediately and by break time Jill and Ryan are in the principal's office.

It's a short meeting. They admit to their wrongdoing and are suspended ahead of dismissal. They're given thirty minutes to collect their possessions before vacating the premises. Jill places her completed policy document on student voice in her bag alongside a letter received the previous week, offering her a position in the senior management team. She helps Ryan load the car with his paintings leaving barely any time to say goodbyes to staff clearly in the know about the situation.

The devastated pair sit in Ryan's lounge, mulling over the certainty that their teaching careers are over. Ryan talks about trying to make a go of it with his art, admitting how tough it would be to make enough money to survive as a full-time artist.

'What about you, Jill?'

'Maybe writing? Journalism?'

Though unspoken, they both know those pathways are no easier than art.

'If you don't mind I'm going to France as soon as possible, fleeing London and England seems like a good idea.'

'And I'll be setting off for bloody Scarborough.'

'Do you think we'll be in the papers?'

'Perhaps not, the school's PR machine will probably swing into action to block the bad publicity.'

Unfortunately, the school's PR machine doesn't have enough influence to avert a headline in the local paper the day after the incident. On the front page is a picture of *'shocked sixth form student Yasmin'*, looking fittingly horrified. Jill reckons it would have been Yasmin who'd broken the story. *'What I saw was awful, I'm just thankful it wasn't a younger student who caught them at it because it was so traumatic it could have ruined their life.'*

Jill's reading the paper in Ryan's flat, he's already departed. The full story is on the second page.

School for Scandal

Below the headline in marginally smaller font is a true enough statement.

Career prospects tumble for two outstanding teachers following act of depravity

Jill thinks what follows is unnecessarily explicit. Sweet little Yasmin describes Miss Cross on her knees sucking Mr Shaw's *"thing"* with his bottom on show. Philosophical little Yasmin, who doesn't have an ounce of religion in her, concludes: *"We were about to perform Jesus Christ Superstar. What an irony that this was going on when in our musical we're celebrating the life and personal sacrifices of the Son of God."*

Well done, Yasmin, you have a career in tabloid journalism ahead of you.

The school principal churns out phrases as expected. A disgrace. Against all the school stands for. Instant dismissal. Parents can be assured that safeguards are being put in place to ensure such a thing never happens again.

There are portrait photos of Jill and Ryan. He looks angelic, Jill reckons she looks devious and wonders where they got the photo from. With Ryan away in Scarborough, she's the one who has to stand by the front door refusing to comment on the story and she's the one filmed when she pops out to purchase milk, some apples and a *Be Good to Yourself* butternut squash cannelloni.

She phones her parents who fortunately don't have access to East London local papers. 'If it's all right with you, I think I'll come over a bit earlier than planned.'

'Lovely, though won't you miss end of term?'

'I'd rather not explain over the phone, I'll tell you all about it when I'm there. I'll email my travel details.'

Jill packs a bag, hops on a bus to St Pancras International, purchases a ticket for the Eurostar, and breathes a sigh of relief as the train enters the Channel Tunnel.

23

Jill travels through French countryside in the state of the art train, arriving at Paris Gare du Nord in little over three hours. That's the easy bit. Next comes the trek across Paris to Gare d'Austerlitz on the crowded metro, her suitcase seemingly gaining in weight as she climbs countless staircases. There follows a three-hour journey on a leisurely train that stops at numerous towns and villages.

Between boarding Eurostar at St Pancras and being met by her father, she has seven hours to take part in a one-person brainstorming session.

Question One: How much do I tell my parents?

Question Two: How quickly do I make contact with Ryan? Part Two of Question Two: Should I invite him over?

Question Three: Should I try to get in touch with Jack again?

Question Four: How much should I keep Sabrina in the loop?

Question Five: Should I write a letter of apology to the school principal? Part Two of Question Five: Might he like to read my report on student voice? Part Three of Question Five: Would he be prepared to write a reference?

Question Six: Based on the belief that I will never be allowed to teach again, what on earth can I do?

Question Seven: How long should I stay in France?

Seven hours of travel, seven questions, ten if you count the supplementary ones, and by the end of the journey not a single one answered. In fact barely considered because Jill has passed the time staring out of windows and observing fellow passengers.

Aboard Eurostar, clone businesspeople tap away on their laptops. The man by her side doesn't even acknowledge her presence as he cursors between four spreadsheets with tiny numbers in a multitude of rows and columns.

The Metro is as cramped, smelly and uninviting as rush-hour Underground.

Finally, there's the slow train with its scattering of rural folk, unfashionably dressed, not a laptop in sight. About an hour or so into her journey, a middle-aged man with considerable belly, bulbous nose and greasy hair swept across his brow, sits next to her even though there are plenty of empty double seats in the carriage.

He addresses Jill, the first person to speak to her since the escape from her London home. Her French is good, but she pretends otherwise. 'Padonner me, I am anglais,' she replies.

'Oh, English, that is formidable. Welcome to France. And where do you travel this day?'

Jill doesn't intend to engage because this man is a cretin. 'No anglais, angolais, from Africa, afrique.'

His look is one of puzzlement, perhaps wary of engaging with anyone from Africa or surprised by the colour of her skin. Whatever his rationale, it does the trick and he turns

272

away disinterested. However, he remains in his seat, alcohol and body odour combining to make Jill feel rather sick and unable to concentrate on her questions.

All in all, by the time she's reached her destination she's had her fill of travelling, this the same feeling every time she journeys to her parents. She rushes up and hugs her father, genuinely glad to see his friendly and reliable face.

'Good trip?'

'The usual.'

As they drive through ten kilometres of innocuous countryside towards the insignificant village where her parents live, they compare the temperature and precipitation levels in London with that in this French wasteland. Clearly, her father has been instructed to avoid big issues until her mother is with them.

Once home, sitting in the sparsely furnished chilly lounge, there seems little point telling anything other than the truth. She dives straight in with the news of the sex in the classroom incident and her and Ryan's instant dismissal. Her liberal parents look downcast though don't pass judgement.

It's her father who first raises the question of her relationship with Jack; she informs that there's been no contact despite her efforts to get in touch.

'How hard have you tried?' Vanessa asks.

'Hard enough,' she replies, not convinced this is the case.

'And Ryan?'

'What about him?'

'How strong is the relationship?'

'We get on well, I really like him.'

'Enough to end it with Jack?'

'The two aren't linked. Jack and I have huge difficulties, the relationship is irredeemable.'

'You're going to need to talk to him, at the very least there's sorting out to do.'

This is true, it's on her mind, but what exactly is needed? A lawyer?

~

A week on from her arrival and her ever so nice parents are driving her mad. Jill is trying to be nice back but it's not easy. She's twenty-six and is being treated like a child half that age. In response, she's acting like the teenager she never was, needy, stroppy and indifferent to their kindness.

'Any clothes need washing, Jill?'

'What would you like to eat tonight, Jill?'

'We're off to the hypermarket, what can we get you, Jill?'

'It's a lovely day, fancy a walk, Jill?'

Such helpful and considerate questions and she's responding harshly, going bananas with frustration. Boredom too, for the first time she realises just how much of her time had been taken up with schoolwork. Now that it's gone there's a massive void to fill. She reads, she walks, and each morning takes on baguette duty, strolling down with a Pied Piper stream of locals to buy the daily loaf. The shop assistant likes her, he chats her up. He's obnoxious, quite possibly an inbred relative of the man on the train. She's friendly and smiles though for her parents' sake.

There are conversations with Ryan most evenings. He's doing a lot of painting, but like her is finding living back with his parents a strain. He declines Jill's offer to come out

274

to France, telling her he has some reflecting to do. Jill takes that as a possible forewarning to being dumped. She likes Ryan, possibly loves him, but if she's to be ditched she wouldn't mind. Yes she would, she must escape her couldn't care less what happens mood.

Money has never been a strong interest, Jack having always managed their finances, but now Jill has to work out how to earn some. A new career is required though somehow career sounds far too grand. It's more a case of finding anything to bring in income and enable her to escape this hibernation in France. Her worry about her parents' situation adds to the stress. With less and less work available they're considering a return to England.

'We'd love to be able to help you out, but that's hard at present. Mind you, it would be different if we sold the house in London and got something for half the price somewhere away from the south east,' her father tells her.

'We've been thinking about moving closer to Dan and his family. I could do some teaching to bring money in,' Vanessa adds.

Jill recognises that these statements aren't spontaneous, a move to near Dan is in the pipeline. She feels abandoned, there's no one left to care for her. She calls Ryan and asks him to meet her in France. He tells her that a journalist has tracked him down so he's planning an escape to a relative in Ireland for a while. His suggestion that Jill could join him there seems half-hearted.

'Let me think about it,' she replies.

She calls Jack.

'Hi there, Jill.'

'Who the hell are *you*?' Jill asks the female who's taken the call.

'I'm Caroline Curbishly. I'll get him for you, hang on a sec.'

Jill's inclined to abandon the conversation. Judging by the jolly, friendly tone, this Caroline is unphased by a call from Jack's wife.

She does hang on as requested, there are issues that need to be resolved as part of the moving on.

~

Jack has been living with Caroline Curbishly since the evening he lost his job. Unlike Sophie and Felicity, both of whom had ruthlessly ousted him when his world turned upside down, Caroline has been good to him, possibly taking pleasure in being associated with a City bad boy who's fallen from grace.

He watches lots of daytime television, broken by a midday walk to the supermarket to buy wine and whatever Caroline has requested on the daily list left on the kitchen table. As he steps beyond the gated security guarded enclosure, he is immediately confronted by a world of poverty. Men, many he notes of around his age, loiter on street corners or outside the betting shop, or are tucked away in sleeping bags in the doorways of derelict shops. He still has a considerable amount of money based on the settlement with work and past savings, but that won't last for ever bearing in mind he's paying the mortgage on the house. He'll have to sell or rent it but should speak to Jill ahead of doing anything.

He's relieved when back inside the gated community unharmed, alleviating the paranoid fear of having his wine

276

stolen. He opens one of his bottles as soon as he's home and carries on drinking until Caroline returns from work.

'I drink too much,' he tells her, not for the first time. They're watching a DVD of *The Untouchables,* and that evening's statement is triggered by Eliot Ness and his team disposing of barrels of illicit booze.

'Yes, you do.'

'I'm going to cut down.'

'Good idea.'

'But how? What am I going to do?' he asks as the credits roll.

'Don't buy any more. If it's not in front of you there'll be nothing to drink.'

'Not only alcohol, bigger than that. I mean what am I going to do with my life?'

'What do you most want?'

'I don't know, except, I hope you don't mind me saying this, I've been such a fool with Jill. Getting back with her is what I most want.'

Caroline had made it clear from the start that her relationship with Jack would be a temporary one and has accepted heart-to-hearts about Jill from the outset. 'Well, then that's your target. You need to put a strategy in place, a timeline that includes a stop to drinking and also coke, reflection on a new career and a plan for engaging with Jill again. Possibly also your family. I can show you how to do a Gantt chart if you like.'

Caroline is full of business speak. Having followed her dream to take an art degree, she finally surrendered to her father's pressure to embark on a "proper" career. Utilising his many corporate contacts she got a job at one of the

277

consultancy giants and is now advising Footsie 250 companies on how to improve efficiency. This is the woman who at school struggled with anything remotely requiring logical thought. She's been bombarding Jack with Magic Bullets, Value Propositions, Game Plans, Ideation, Negatron and a set of acronyms like PAC, F2F and JDI to help him solve his problems.

He listens. He nods. He smiles. Picking up the bottle of wine, he's about to pour another glass but sets it down. That gets an appreciative nod from Caroline who is cutting down herself as an act of solidarity with Jack.

'Good start. Put it in the fridge for tomorrow or even chuck it down the sink,' she tells him.

Caroline had let him stay because, as she put it, 'I'm between boyfriends.' Staying can include sex 'to cheer us up a bit' she informed him when setting the conditions of his residency.

Jack had hoped that there would be a considerable time lapse between boyfriends but it was not to be. It had only taken three weeks to acquire a new lover. Quite a catch, she tells Jack, because he works two floors above her office in the physically hierarchal building – it's a bit like getting promoted.

Jack is allowed a final week at Caroline's, this possible because her new man needs time to gently break the news of separation from his current partner.

It is the penultimate evening when Jill calls. Jack's packed and is set to return to their ex-marital home. Not for long though because it's too expensive to keep. At some stage Jill will need to know that.

He returns from the kitchen having flushed the wine down the sink and Caroline hands him the phone.

'It's Jill.'

24

Hello, Jill.

Hi.

How are you?

I'm OK. You?

I'm OK, too.

Who's Caroline?

An old school friend, I've been staying at hers for a while.

Oh, I never heard you mention a Caroline.

We lost touch after school but then I bumped into her. I'm moving out tomorrow though, back to the house. I didn't want to live there for a while after…look, there's something I must tell you. I lost my job. I was sacked.

I know, everyone in Britain does. I could hardly miss it.

What the newspapers said wasn't true. Once they wanted me out they conjured up the lie about the insider trading.

They can't sack someone without a reason, it's against the law.

I was in a difficult position, I decided I couldn't challenge them.

I tried to get in touch when I heard the news but you never answered.

I'm sorry, things were difficult. I'm off drugs and alcohol.

What you do is up to you, Jack.

I thought maybe you'd like to know. How are things going?

All good. I'm in France with my parents.

Do send them my love.

I will.

It's nice to hear your voice. Jill?

Yes?

Nothing. Well something, I'm sorry for everything.

There's nothing to be sorry about. Stuff happens, doesn't it, I think it's called life. I must go, Mum's calling me for dinner. Bye.

Bye.

~

They'd finished dinner ages ago.

Jill sits in her bedroom, unable to face her parents. The conversation with Jack had the warmth of an arctic blizzard, as much her fault as his. And she should have raised finances. She examines the doodle she'd done during the call. Teardrops raining down onto flowers with giant petals. She screws up the piece of paper and chucks it in the bin.

She calls Ryan again. 'I want to see you. I don't mind whether it's in Scarborough or Ireland.'

'Great. It's Ireland.'

Jill travels to Paris on the slow-so-slow train, then to the airport and across to Dublin. Although the fare and cost of the hotel are reasonable – it had to be a hotel, Ryan's aunt doesn't allow cohabitation – she's well aware her savings are rapidly dwindling.

Ryan meets her at the airport and looks great whereas she feels dowdy and frumpy having spent too long sitting around doing nothing.

Once in Dublin she cheers up. She hasn't realised how much she's missed being with Ryan and she enjoys the vibrancy of the city, too. Ryan stays at her hotel and a couple of days into the visit takes her to his aunt's huge ramshackle house on the outskirts of the city. He's busy setting up a studio there.

'Looks like your plan is for a long stay,' Jill comments.

'I was hounded in Scarborough, I won't be going back until the story is well and truly dead.'

'What about London?'

'If the press can find me in Yorkshire it'll be worse there. I'll need to visit to sell to galleries, but not to live.'

'Never?'

'Never say never, but I can't see it. What about you?'

London is the only place she feels she can call home, but what is there for her there? 'No idea,' she tells him. 'I don't think a glittering career in teaching is on the cards. I can't think of a single thing I want to do, all I have is a list of things I can't or don't want to do.'

Ryan does have compassion. He wraps his arms around her shoulders and pulls her close. She sinks her head into his chest, appreciating his concern and greedy for physical contact.

With Ryan asleep by her side in the hotel room, her mind is in overdrive. She's not going to be able to stay in Dublin for long. Apart from running out of money, the current temporary set-up isn't going to resolve anything. Mind you, does that matter, she could simply let life drift by? But drifting doesn't come easily to Jill and the next morning, as soon as Ryan has set off to work on preparing his studio, she texts old college friends, girls she's had little contact with recently except through Facebook and Christmas cards.

Can you help? I'm stuck for accommodation, any chance of a spare room to rent. By lunchtime three tentative offers have arrived, all indicating the need to supplement their income to pay the huge cost of their London mortgage or rent. Nadia's tone is particularly friendly and welcoming, she was a close friend in the sixth form. Jill arranges to meet her.

That afternoon she lets Ryan know that it's to be her last two days in Dublin. He's accepting, a little too accepting for Jill's liking. They spend a great two days and nights together, parting on good terms with promises to meet as soon as possible once everything is sorted. But there's no match in how they see their futures and Jill senses this is the end of their relationship. Maybe the school incident wrecked any chance of happiness.

Nadia's lovely flat is on the ground floor of an Edwardian mansion located in a leafy suburb of London. The spare room, her room, is attractively decorated and furnished though too small to contain anything but the basics. She thinks about all the stuff in her house and wonders when she and Jack will get together to organise a split of their possessions. She has a key, should she pop in to collect a few books and CDs? But what if Jack's there when she visits?

Nadia works for a marketing agency and is doing well, no surprise because in college she was bright and sparky.

283

When she gets home on Jill's second evening at the flat, she lets her know a temporary post as office administrator has cropped up.

'It's not high level, but if you're looking for something to get you started it might suit.'

'That would be brilliant. I'd happily take office work.'

'Being unemployed is an advantage because we need to fill the vacancy quickly.'

Jill applies online that evening and is invited to interview two days later.

'I could start tomorrow,' she informs them.

The interviewers recognise that this candidate has considerable talent. She tells them she's been living in France for a while so it might be difficult to provide a reference, but since she's been recommended by the trusted Nadia, they are prepared to take her on.

It's a huge relief to have a stop gap while she considers what to do next.

~

It isn't easy for Jack to set foot in the house, there are too many memories. He makes a start cleaning; the place is a tip. Beginning in the kitchen, he glances at the wine rack as he scrubs the table, work surfaces and sink, scouring until his hands are red raw. An old shopping list started by Jill is pinned on the fridge door – skimmed milk, toilet paper, apples. He adds rubber gloves and all-purpose surface cleaner to replace the container that is now empty. For the umpteenth time he looks down at the bottles of wine, twenty or more, red and white, plonk and vintage. He opens them all and pours every drop down the sink.

In the bedroom he hoovers and dusts. Opening Jill's section of the wardrobe he's surprised to find most of her clothes still hanging. The red dress with the white velvet collar and cuffs sparks a vivid memory, she'd dressed up as a Sexy Santa at the first Christmas party at his company. Heads had turned that evening. He searches drawers for further reminders, but these are empty, underwear, tights, socks and nightwear taken. The bed is unmade and under her pillow is a crumpled pair of pyjamas. He smoothes them out and lays them in an empty drawer.

He puts on sports gear and sets off for a run, frustrated when he has to stop, gasping for breath, after such a short while. Adopting the regime for beginners, he runs for a minute followed by a minute of walking. Repeat, but faster. Repeat, but a longer run. Penance because he's exhausted and it's freezing cold. He'll get fit though and stay that way.

Back home what he most fancies is a glass of wine, fortunately there's nothing left. He settles for a cup of tea and opens his laptop for a long overdue look at the financial situation. Within an hour he's wishing he'd kept a bottle of wine to drown his sorrows because unless he finds employment, the mortgage will be impossible to pay beyond three or four months. But who's going to employ him after his high-profile dismissal? The house has to be put on the market and Jill needs to know.

When he calls his mother to tell her he's back at home, she invites him over for dinner and he accepts. He's been promising to catch up since the separation, though he does have a vague memory of Sabrina having visited soon after he lost his job.

He's as open as he's ever been with her, prepared to expose fears and insecurities possibly for the first time since childhood. It doesn't take long for the financial worries to be raised and Sabrina is quick to respond. 'You need to ask your father for support. I wish I could help. I can give you several hundred pounds, but that's nothing like the sort of money you're talking about.'

'I did write to him when I was staying with my friend, in fact she suggested it.'

'And?'

'I got a reply, but not what I'd hoped for.' He pulls his phone out of his jacket inside pocket, touches the screen then hands it across.

She flicks through a message before reading out loud. *Woe is the wicked! Disaster is upon them! They will be paid back for what their hands have done. Isaiah 3:11.* 'What the…? The man is an absolute idiot.'

Anthony has said little all evening, but now chips in. 'A father should be there to help his son at time of crisis, whatever's gone on between them. If the man thinks he's found God, I'm sure we can find a bible quote about kindness and compassion somewhere!'

'Have you been in contact with Seb? Maybe he would be prepared to discuss it with your father,' Sabrina suggests.

'I got a mocking email from him after I lost the job. Before that I discovered that he'd offended Jill big time, telling her she should have chosen him instead of me. Mind you, the way things have turned out, maybe he was right.'

'He's hardly her type. And talking of Jill, what's the state of play with her?'

286

'It's well and truly over. I've been an utter fool. We had a conversation recently and it was clear that she's happy with her new man.'

'I don't think happy is appropriate right now.'

'What do you mean?'

Sabrina relates the news about Jill getting the sack with no opportunity to teach again. Jack doesn't respond, he's weighing things up. OK she's been an absolute idiot, but the offence was based on the intense relationship with her new man.

Sabrina appears to be second guessing what he's thinking. 'There's something deep-seated between the two of you. You must fight if you want her back.'

'I'm afraid it's too late, Mother. It's too late.'

Anthony serves up the steaks, baked potatoes and French beans. He refills Sabrina and his own glass with Rioja. 'Are you sure you're not drinking tonight, Jack.'

'No, thanks.' He looks down at the steak, rare, oozing red, he doesn't much fancy it, he's gone off meat.

'For now you have no job and it looks like there won't be any money coming from Henry. So what's the plan?' Sabrina asks.

'The lottery?' Jack watches Anthony put too much salt on his potato. 'Obviously I'm going to have to sell the house.'

'That's to get some cash in, but what about longer term?'

'Longer term? I have absolutely no idea. I suppose a job, any job that helps pay the bills. There's such a lot to work out. I wish I could get away for a short while ahead of tackling everything that's resulted from my mess up. I think I might, even if it means eating into savings.'

'Where to?'

Jack thinks of a very special day four or more years ago and is close to weeping. 'Italy. Maybe Venice.'

'I think that's a good idea and I'd like to pay for your trip.'

Part 3

25

It is two years to the day since Jill moved to Venice. There had been no plan of what to do once there beyond the need to run away from her past. She couldn't stay in London any longer, couldn't contemplate life with her parents in France, and wasn't enticed by Ryan's half-hearted suggestion that she move to Dublin. She had found a small flat close to the centre, the rent exorbitant, and a job in an upmarket bar frequented by local businessmen. They swarmed around her, testing their pidgin English with cliched chat up lines. She enjoyed the camaraderie and gentle flirting and she realised that there was a career opportunity.

It's the final session of the term for her Venetian businessmen. For two hours a day over the past eight weeks they've been learning conversational English in the stuffy room in a house adjacent to a tiny canal. The building opposite is so close you could almost touch it were you to lean out of the window. The nine men have taken their studies seriously, though with a humour and politeness that has made them a pleasure to teach. This has been true of all the groups Jill has worked with over the past twenty or so months. She's popular, never short of takers.

As usual, she's planned a surprise final session for them, perhaps a special one to mark the anniversary of her arrival in this magical city. 'Something different today,' she announces when they're seated. 'We're escaping this gloomy room and heading for the sunshine of St Mark's Square. You won't be using the English you've learnt to describe the benefits of the products you sell. Today, I want you to talk about the beauty of the Square, about your wonderful city, its history and its customs. After all, as you've so often told me, when an English-speaking client visits, informal chats are as important as any technical details you provide. All set? Let's go!'

They leave the house and walk in single file along the narrow pathway by the side of the canal, their lightweight designer suits, shirts and ties in sharp contrast to the shorts, chinos, jeans and T-shirts worn by the tourists around them.

On reaching the wider promenade alongside the Grand Canal, they stroll in pairs, vying to be by Jill's side.

Roberto is next to her. 'You perhaps remember what I told you during our first class, at university it was history that I studied. So this will be a pleasuresome time for me.'

'I'm glad, though I think pleasurable is the better word to use.'

'Pleasurable. Yes, I like that.'

'Stop!' Alessandro calls out. 'Coffee is surely needed, but please, not in St Mark's. I know a great place near here. It will be my treat for you all.'

Jill accepts the suggestion and they follow Alessandro through an alleyway, soon reaching a small square with a café on the corner. Her intention had been to buy everyone a Bombolone from a stall as they walked along, but café prices are out of reach so she decides to let Alessandro foot the bill. He's an exporter of Parmigiano-Reggiano, he has the money. There's noticeable though unspoken rivalry to sit next to their attractive teacher. Each class has had its ardent though largely unsuccessful suitors.

The men chat away like old friends.

'Excuse me! May I remind you that this is still an English class so I don't want to hear any Italian spoken,' Jill declares with mock reprimand.

Her students take up the challenge to parody.

'This coffee is simply divine. Would you care for a biscotti?'

'How kind of you to offer, but I think I must abstain, I need to watch my line.' Luigi pats his belly, this statement and action coming from the leanest of the men, he's wafer thin.

'What delightful weather we are having,' Roberto exclaims. 'I do believe summer has finally arrived.' It's early July and summer has been well and truly present for over a month with blue skies and blazing sunshine.

'We must worry with climate change,' Luca states.

'Worry *about*, Luca,' Jill says, as ever the conscientious teacher.

'Thank you, Jill. The point is serious though. June was the hottest on record following our wettest ever Spring. There won't be a Venice to enjoy for much longer unless we take action.' Luca is the most serious in the group with an excellent command of English. His warning is no doubt influenced by the fact that he owns three hotels in the city.

'I think you are exaggerating the danger, my friend. We have ways to prevent flooding,' Mario contributes, his statement prejudiced by his job as CEO of a company manufacturing sea defence equipment.

Jill stands. 'We can carry on the debate as we walk, but let's get going.'

They make their way towards St Mark's Square.

~

The Real Italy tour group have travelled from Verona to Venice early morning and are now standing in the centre of the Square along with a thousand or more other tourists. Jack is outlining the local history to the ten holidaymakers, nine women and one man. His company doesn't target a particular customer but he always ends up leading a predominantly female, middle-class, middle-aged group, mostly travelling alone. There's plenty of time to get to know everyone over their two weeks together as they journey from Rome to Verona and finally on to Venice. He's well liked, and being a sympathetic listener, he's often something of an agony aunt, receiving detailed intimate accounts of divorces, deaths of beloved partners, estrangements from children and lots more. 'Things can only get better,' is the stock phrase he uses to console the tearful ones. Do they get better, he wonders? He's as lonely a soul as any of his customers and being young somehow makes it worse.

Jack researches the sites meticulously and shares his knowledge with passion, mixing this with tongue in cheek anecdotes about current Italian culture. As ever the group are in awe as they stand in a semicircle in front of him.

'Perhaps this is the highlight of our trip, Piazza San Marco,' he announces with a perfect Italian accent. His command of the language is impressive, the doting women

294

see it as a further reason to be in love with this handsome man.

'Napoleon called this the drawing room of Europe, *a salon designed for the sky to serve as a canopy*. Rather poetic for a soldier who set out to conquer Europe.' Groups usually laugh when he says this, today they are silent. Edith, approaching three times his age, has drawn so close that her arm is resting against his. He edges away from her and continues with his history lesson as they saunter around the Square, stopping to admire the beauty of the Basilica, Clock Tower and Procuratie Vecchie. He's an expert at bringing it all to life, sparking their imagination about what Venice has been like over the centuries.

However, this is his tenth tour in less than two years and he's struggling not to appear stale. If the truth be told, he's bored, so this is to be his last visit to Italy for a while. This decision is for all the right reasons – the business is booming and he needs to spend more time in the office. Recently he's recruited the perfect person to accompany the groups, a young male graduate fresh out of university with a joint honours degree in History and Italian.

'One final thing I'd like to show you before you have free time to wander round or drink yet another cappuccino,' he tells the group. 'Look at that bell tower, isn't it magnificent? Well, it's not as old as you might think. It was first built in the ninth century and they did some renovation in the sixteenth, but it turned out not particularly well. It collapsed in 1902, so when I say not particularly well I'm being polite. By all accounts the workmanship was…'

'Was what?' Stephanie enquires.

Jack has caught sight of Jill surrounded by a circle of men, all laughing away as they look up to the bell tower. She picks up his gaze and their eyes fix. For both there's a repeat of the chemistry of that first encounter at the university freshers' ball, the drawing together without having spoken a word. They walk towards each other, their groups following, under the impression that their teacher or guide has something else to translate or point out.

'Hello Jill.'

'Hello Jack.'

'What are you doing here?' they ask in unison.

'Did anyone die when the tower collapsed?' Adrienne asks.

Jack ignores the question. 'I'm with this group. I run trips to Italy, that's my job now.'

'Did they?' Adrienne persists.

'That probably depends on whether it fell sideways or just collapsed downwards,' Edith guesses.

'What about you, Jill? How come you're in Venice?'

'I live here. I teach.'

Roberto takes up the challenge posed by Adrienne's question. He's keen to use his historical knowledge and practise speaking English at the same time. The prettiness of the questioner is a further incentive to engage. 'May I tell you, madam? Fortunately no one died though the caretaker's cat was killed. And your friend is on the right railway line when she talks of how it fell. It was downwards so there was little secondary damage, only the loggetta and a corner of the Biblioteca Marciana.'

Adrienne, a young looking and trendy mid-fifties woman, has taken an instant fancy to Roberto. 'Marciana,

296

that's the library, isn't it? But I'm not sure what you mean about the railway line. Did trains run here?'

'No, madam…'

'…Oh, do call me Adrienne.'

'And I am Roberto. A pleasure.' He takes hold of her hand and kisses it. Edith is ignored. She leaves them, moving across to where the rest of the Italian men are talking to the other English ladies.

'No trains have been here,' Roberto continues. 'I have tried to explain in my poor English that your friend is on the right…thematica.'

Adrienne looks puzzled, then gets it. 'Oh, you don't mean railway line, you mean track. Edith was on the right track.'

'But are not track and railway line the same?'

'Not in this case, you see…'

Roberto's English lesson with this pretty and flirty substitute for Jill continues while Jill is explaining to Jack exactly what she's doing in Venice with this group of men.

'I'm usually giving lessons in a stuffy classroom, but today is their special end of term treat.'

A few steps away from them, Luca has discovered that Jacqueline is an interior designer for restaurants and hotels. He's been looking to upgrade his three hotels for some time and is attracted to the idea of engaging an English person to do the work, bearing in mind many of his customers are from England. Though more significant than any business benefit, he's attracted to Jacqueline and it appears to be reciprocated. 'However, Luca,' she points out, 'please take care when saying English and England because I'm Scottish.'

'That is a region in England?'

'No, it is not! We're a separate country and if I had my way, we'd be completely independent.'

'Your country makes whisky. I like it.'

'And I like your wine.'

'Would you care for a glass now? I know an excellent bar a short ramble from here.'

Jacqueline smiles, this man's use of English is all part of his attraction. 'Why not, though I'd better let Jack know.'

She's not the first to approach Jack to tell him she's heading off with one of Jill's men. He nods in agreement, lost in conversation. He usually takes such care to know the whereabouts of his group. Not now.

'Have the good holiday, Jill. And lots of thankyous for learning me English,' Luca says as he takes hold of Jacqueline's arm.

'I miss you so much, I think of you every day,' Jacqueline, Luca and Jill hear Jack pronounce.

'I will leave you two birds in your love nest,' Luca tells the unresponsive pair, but he lingers, curious.

'I think you mean lovebirds in their nest,' Jacqueline corrects Luca, equally keen to stay to see what's going on.

'You never got in touch after we sorted finances,' Jill says, still shaken by this chance encounter. For no obvious reason, she's thought a lot about Jack lately but has no intention to tell him.

'But all animals make love, Jaccolina, so why we say this only for the birds?' Luca asks. 'Why not lovetigers or lovekangaroos?'

'It's their actual name, the birds are called lovebirds. They're a type of parrot; they sit together in pairs for hours,'

298

Jacqueline explains, reddening at the thought of animals making love.

'Ah, I think piccioncini in Italian,' exclaims Luca, equally excited by thoughts of lovemaking. 'Let us go to drink.'

'I tried. I called you a lot. I wanted to see how you were getting on but your phone was always dead,' Jack explains.

This could be true. Jill had bought a new mobile when she moved to Italy and only switches on her English one when she's back home.

'And your emails bounced back.'

Also true, she'd changed her address after receiving disgusting messages about her school misdemeanour.

'And your solicitor refused to pass on details. I had no idea where you were living, I assumed you were still with that man.'

'No, we ended it. He moved to Ireland.'

'I even tried to contact your parents, but that was hopeless, their phone was also dead.' There's an explanation for that, too. Jack wasn't to know they'd returned to England.

'What about Sabrina?' Jill asks, testing how hard Jack's tried. 'We're still in touch so you could have made contact through her.'

'Yes, I could have,' Jack replies, now avoiding her gaze. 'Do you know what though? I was terrified that if we spoke and you said no, then all hope would be lost for ever.'

'Say no to what?'

'To a cup of coffee – in St Mark's Square!' Jack beams, it's the one she remembers from their first days together.

Should she accept? 'Alright. Let me just say goodbye to my class.'

'I'd better do the same with my group, I'll arrange to meet them back at the hotel.'

They turn to discover there's no one left to inform except the single man from Jack's party who is silently looking on.

'Where's everyone gone, Brian?'

'Did you ever see that film, *Seven Brides for Seven Brothers*? Well it has the potential for a remake. Nine Italian men for nine English women.'

'What do you mean?'

'No need to worry, Jack. You get on with it and I'll see you back at the hotel.'

'Are you sure you don't mind, Brian?'

'It'll be interesting to see who turns up and with who, won't it.' Brian smiles, turns and heads off.

'Let's do the full tourist bit, coffee at the most expensive place in Italy,' Jack says, pointing to a rare empty table with a starched white tablecloth at the café in the prime location on the piazza.

'Due cappuccini, per favour,' Jack orders when the waitress has approached them.

'E un pezzo di torta,' Jill adds in perfect Italian.

'And would you like something with your coffee?' the waitress asks in competitively perfect English as she looks across to Jack.

'No grazie,' he retaliates.

For a while they're silent, looking at the hordes cutting across the square from all directions.

Jack is first to speak. 'Do you remember…?'

'Of course I bloody remember. Every time I come here I remember.'

'Me too.'

Jill is angry because she can feel tears on her cheeks. 'Well, it's not a competition.'

Jack takes hold of her hand. 'I love you, Jill.'

Further words are delayed as the waitress lifts the drinks and plate off her tray and dumps them down onto the table. Jill's coffee spills into her saucer.

'Here, take this one,' Jack says as he swaps them.

'No need.' Jill returns the drinks to their initial positions.

'I love you.'

'You've already said that. Are you expecting me to say I love you too?'

'I don't know what I'm expecting. Seeing you here is such a shock, I'm so glad. I'm simply telling you my foremost thought, that I love you, the one thing I've wanted to say since, since…'

Now Jack is tearful. Jill pulls her hand away and takes hold of her coffee cup. She won't allow physical contact again if he tries to touch her arm. And she won't say the words that Jack so wants to hear.

They watch pigeons swooping down to capture morsels of food left on nearby tables. Other pigeons are strutting between tourists, gathering food dropped onto the square.

The silence seems eternal.

Jack glances at his watch, wary of Jill misinterpreting this as impatience. He is struggling to put together the right words to explain his situation. 'Look, I must go. I don't want to leave you but we've got a flight to catch.'

Jill would like to tell Jack that she doesn't want him to leave. 'No problem. Go. Look after your group.'

'Can I see you again?'

Jill wants that. 'I'm not sure, Jack. We've both moved on. We aren't the same people who fell in love, we were little more than children then.'

'I think I'm the same.'

'Hardly!'

'I wasn't for a while, I know that and I'm deeply sorry. But that awful period is over.'

Jill looks at this lean man with a healthy tan and a sparkle in his eyes, far removed from the puffy-faced overweight husband she left behind. 'How do I know that?'

'You don't, I'll have to prove it. But I do know what has to happen.'

'Well I'm glad you do because I don't.'

There's a scream nearby, a youth is pouring a bottle of water over a girl's head. Friends around them are laughing.

Jack turns back to Jill. 'Please. Please can I have your phone number?'

'Give me yours, I need to think about this,' Jill says.

Jack lifts his large backpack onto the table, opens it and takes out a piece of paper and pen. Jill notices a first aid kit and a wad of tickets inside the bag. He puts down two numbers, a UK and an Italian one. Jill flinches as she watches him, his writing is unchanged from the neat little boy's lettering that she used to tease him about.

He hands her the sheet, puts a twenty Euro note down on the table and stands. 'I'm back in Venice in about three weeks. Call me, give me a chance. Please.'

Jack crouches, rests his hands ever so lightly on Jill's shoulders, draws her close, and chastely kisses her on each cheek. She responds to the second one.

'Take care, Jill,' he says.

She watches him stride across the square.

She hopes he won't turn round to wave.

He doesn't and she's disappointed.

26

Jack's thoughts are in turmoil as he heads back to the hotel. He's fantasised about an encounter with Jill many a time, but never in his wildest dreams did he think this would be in Venice, a city of such significance. It has to be fate he thinks as he walks. He weighs up the option of deserting his group and sprinting back to the piazza to catch Jill before she moves on. If he doesn't do so he might never see her again. Having refused to give him her number, perhaps she doesn't want to and he would understand why because he was a disgrace during their marriage. Rationality prevails, because if he abandons the group ahead of the return journey to England that would be curtains for the business he's built up with such care.

He carries on walking.

Everyone is waiting for him in the lobby. He's late. All he has time to do is dash upstairs to get his suitcase and say a quick thank you and goodbye to the hotel manager.

As they wait for the coach to arrive, Jack is subjected to an interrogation.

Edith: 'Who was that lovely young lady you were talking to?'

Adrienne: 'She's interested in you, I've always been able to sense that sort of thing.'

Jacqueline: 'Is she English, Jack?'

Suzy: 'No, she's Italian isn't she, Jack?'

Jacqueline: 'What makes you think she's Italian?'

Suzy: 'Well, did you see her complexion? That wasn't a one-week tan she's carrying, it's in her genes.'

Jacqueline: 'But I heard her speak, I'm sure she's English. That's right isn't it, Jack.'

Adrienne: 'You two are made for each other. Roberto and I were watching you at the café, love was radiating.'

Rosemary: 'He's blushing, leave him alone. If they'd met yesterday in Verona, at Juliet's Balcony, that would have been something.'

Edith: 'Casa di Giulietta. That's right, isn't it, Jack? Is my accent improving?'

He's desperate to see the back of them, though he recognises the importance of staying polite to maintain the great reviews he's been getting for his business. So he nods, he smiles, half-listening.

'Great, the minibus is here. Come on everyone, let's get moving,' Jack says with a mix of relief and distress.

On the coach there's a welcome distraction to thinking about Jill as he sorts out passports, tickets and evaluation forms. He joins the driver in unloading cases at the terminal building then marches the group along to the check-in desk. They're as needy as early teens away from home for the first time on a school trip.

Once through customs and security, you'd think everyone could be left to their own devices, but it is not to be. Jack would like nothing more than to sit alone in a corner to think, but the airport lounge is no better than the hotel foyer.

Edith: 'Should I use up my euros or pay with a credit card?'

Jacqueline: 'Jack, should I get an Italian SIM card? I'm going to be keeping in touch with Luca, so would that make it cheaper? What do you use to speak to your woman?'

Adrienne: 'How much alcohol are we allowed duty free?'

Suzy: 'Is there time to dash to the loo?'

Rosemary: 'What will the food be like on the plane?'

'Great, it's time to board. Come on everyone, let's get moving,' Jack says with exhaustion.

At last, high in the sky, in relative solitude, he can take in what's happened and consider what he needs to do next. Brian is sitting by his side, quiet and unobtrusive as he tackles what look like extremely complex Sudoku puzzles on his iPad.

He knows he must get back to Venice as quickly as possible, so a first problem for Jack to address concerns Des, the young man he's recently recruited. Des is booked in to lead the next Italy trip and Jack will need to make up a good reason to explain the change of plan. Nothing comes to mind so the topic is put on hold and he switches to thinking about Jill.

Will she be prepared to see him again? What if she doesn't even phone?

'Please, please give me a chance. I'm begging you.'

'What do you mean?' Brian asks.

Jack looks across with no idea what Brian is going on about. He glances down at a puzzle in the shape of a spider

306

with fat legs, rather more complex than the nine by nine squares that Jack occasionally tries to solve.

'You asked me to give you a chance,' Brian tells him.

'Did I? I must have dozed, it was a dream.' It probably is no more than a dream, Jack thinks, he's had his chance with Jill and messed up. He watches Brian race through puzzles until the plane lands, his own mind blank.

Thankfully the responsibility for looking after the group will soon end, having reached the airport. Jack's final task is to make sure luggage has arrived safely in the reclaim area. He watches as the holidaymakers lift their cases off the carrousel, one at a time saying their goodbyes before making their way out of his life.

Edith: 'Wonderful, wonderful, Jack. A holiday of a lifetime.'

Adrienne: 'Thank you so much. I'll be posting a review on Trip Advisor.'

Jacqueline: 'Who knows, I might see you back in Italy, I'm sure Luca and I will be meeting up before long.'

Suzy: 'Should I take my suitcase with me to the loo or is it safe to leave it here?'

Rosemary: 'Lovely trip, thanks Jack. Do you know if there's a supermarket in the terminal? My cupboards at home are empty.'

Brian: 'Thank you, Jack. Most enjoyable even though it was a bit strange being the only male. That woman today, I don't know what the situation is but there's something strong between you. She's a stunner, too.'

Having seen the last of this needy group head off, Jack passes through customs and sits in a coffee bar to weigh up events of the past hours. Only a matter of hours. Six hours ago he was with Jill in Venice! Brian's few words have stuck with him. Even a stranger could recognise the deep-rooted bond between them. And what a stunner, as Brian had put it, she still is, life in Italy was clearly suiting her. But might she be in a relationship? Maybe with one of her students.

He's exhausted as a consequence of the emotional strain of meeting Jill. But the trip itself was draining, too, his earlier decision to no longer run the holidays himself had been a wise one. That day's events changed everything though – nothing was going to stop him returning to Italy on the next tour. And if need be, the next and the next. Because if Jill didn't call him, he'd stand in the piazza day and night in search of her. He'd seek the location of all the language schools in Venice. If necessary, he'd march up and down every single street in the city until he found her.

~

Jill remains at the café in the square until Jack is out of view and then she stays still longer, her mind blank. There should be emotion, be it anger, indecision or affection, but there's nothing.

Finally she stands and heads off towards her apartment, her mind fixing on what she'll cook that evening. A porcini risotto. She stops to buy a bottle of white wine.

Her flat is tiny, the rooms barely big enough to merit their names – bedroom, open plan kitchen, lounge and dining room. She has few possessions so the size works for her and it does have the advantage of a great location. It suits her as the perfect "here for a while and soon moving on" place, except that she's lived in this flat for approaching two years and has no plan for what to do next. Teaching businessmen pays the bills, provides additional money to enable travel, and is easy. It's quite enjoyable, too, but there's little challenge, no buzz to it.

She opens the bottle of locally produced Soave and fills a glass. Only now does her mind settle on Jack and she has to admit that her first emotion is that she misses him. A lot. Mind you, she thought he was wonderful when they first met and look what happened, though there were happy years before the awful ones.

He looks well, trimmer than when she'd last seen him, tanned, nicely dressed. She wonders whether his addictions are still there, but if appearances are anything to go by, perhaps not. She refills her glass to the brim, aware of the irony of this act against her thoughts of Jack and his alcohol.

The piece of notepaper with his phone numbers rests on the coffee table in front of her. She enters them on her phone. It's only when the task is complete that she realises she's done this for fear of misplacing the scrap of paper. She's lonely in Venice. The teaching isn't like a school where there would be loads of colleagues to socialise with. It's just her in one of two classrooms in a small house, working irregular hours, occasionally bumping into one of the other freelancers. She doesn't even know their names, she hasn't got past a nodded greeting.

What would be wrong if she met Jack when he next visited Venice? That's too negative, wouldn't it be nice to meet up with him? Just as friends though, definitely nothing more.

God, how he messed up her life. Since him, except for Ryan, she'd shied away from a proper relationship. Over two years there'd been two short affairs with Italian businessmen, both starting on the night of their last class. One was married, his wedding band still on as they made love. Both relationships were fun though were never going to be long-lasting. There have been more offers, probably in every one of her classes, but she's turned them all down. Now that she's reflecting, she wonders whether she weighs up every man against the Jack she first knew. No one has come close to matching him. Mind you, that's the old Jack, not the one of the last months of their marriage.

Jill pours the final wine from the bottle and drinks at speed. She collects the limoncello from the fridge and tips some into her wine glass. Is it the alcohol that's driving her to resent Jack so much for appearing out of the blue and making her want him back?

She wakes early morning with a serious hangover. However much Jack drank, he never seemed to have one. One minute she's thinking of him in a positive light, the next remembering the tortuous times together, though increasingly it's the laughter, passion and good times that are on her mind.

~

Jack arrives back in England on the Sunday with Des due to start work the following day. That will make it three in *The Real Italy* company, with Des joining Troya, his ever-faithful administrator. Their office is in Hammersmith, three rooms in an unattractive sixties concrete block located a long walk or short drive away from Jack's flat in Ealing. He likes to walk or sometimes even jog to and from work, travelling through side streets remarkably devoid of traffic despite being so close to the congested and polluted main roads. He uses the journey to plan his day, but on this

310

Monday, as he turns into Bartholomew Drive and approaches the building, he hasn't even been able to address what is top of the agenda, the difficulty concerning Des. When he'd offered him the job, Jack had told him to keep mid-August free for his first tour. There was no way that was going to be the case now.

He settles Des into his office, avoiding mention of the Venice trip because he wants to discuss the situation with Troya first. She's good at coming up with ideas and she doesn't let him down, her suggestion brilliant. While Jack was away she's been busy promoting the tour to Naples and Sorrento, there having been a danger of cancellation due to lack of takers. Now it is viable so he has his solution.

Jack calls Des into his office. 'I've been thinking. It's probably sensible for you to settle in a bit before dashing off to lead a tour. Rather than starting with the Verona and Venice one, I'd like you to lead the Naples and Sorrento holiday in seven weeks' time.'

'That's fine by me. I've been to Pompeii a couple of times and love the place. I'd enjoy telling the story.'

'Great. During the interview you mentioned an interest in marketing so the change of plans will give you time to start thinking about that, too.'

'I already have.' Des talks about updating the website, building up their Facebook profile and setting up a YouTube channel.

Jack hears the words but is barely listening. He's preoccupied with the thought of seeing Jill again. That is, if she calls.

He can't concentrate. When Troya asks him something he tells her to make the decision herself.

311

'Is everything OK, Jack?' she asks.

'Yes, fine. I trust you, I want to delegate more.'

'But you forget what I've said a nanosecond after I've said it.'

'Sorry, Troya. It's tied up with needing to go to Venice again, but if you don't mind, I'd like to leave it at that.'

'A woman?'

'The only woman.'

Beyond will-she-won't-she-call, something else is bothering him. What had made him become so despicable? Did it stem from his family background? From his time at school? Was it the City culture? It would be all too easy to use these as excuses, but if it were his innate personality that was the cause of the nastiness, then what hope was there that from now on he would be the man Jill deserved?

~

There are only two days to go before his trip to Italy. Jack is jogging to work when the song on his iPhone is interrupted by the signal for an incoming call. He stops, looks at the screen and snatches at the accept call button.

'Jill.'

She's been doing a lot of thinking ahead of making the call. There are doubts about Jack, he was a rat towards the end, but what about her own behaviour. The sharpness, the criticism, deliberately antagonising him. She was no angel – it was a mutual journey to destruction. Why should it be any better now? Admittedly, two things were different, he wasn't working in the City and she didn't have the pressure of teaching, but would those differences be enough to influence how they treated each other? Having deliberated

312

for hours on end, her conclusion continues to fluctuate between absolutely not and surely yes.

By lessening the significance of his request to see her again, her anxiety wanes. Meeting Jack would be just that, merely a catch-up chat, not leading to anything else. She'd lived with the man for seven years and hadn't seen him for two; surely a get-together was tolerable.

'Hi, Jack. I've thought it through and I'm happy to see you when you're next in Venice.'

'That's great and it's soon. I'm in Verona later this week, we could meet there.'

'No, let's wait until you're in Venice.'

'All right. I'm there for four days from the nineteenth. Does that work for you?'

'Is it a tour?'

'Yes, another gang of middle-aged desperados. I think there are twelve this time.'

'I could join you and the group at St Mark's.'

'Or I could leave them to it one evening and we can go out for a meal.'

Jill wonders whether a meal is a step too far. 'No, let's go for St Mark's. It'll be interesting to hear what you tell them, you always were a bullshitter.'

'Thanks!'

'You've got my number now so text to confirm the day and time. See you then.'

'Yeah, see you…'

Jack would like to add that he can't wait to see her again, but she's disconnected.

He sits on a low front garden wall to reflect on the conversation. Jill had hardly been warm but at least she'd phoned and agreed to meet. He'd have to rearrange the itinerary to make St Mark's on the first rather than last day in Venice in the hope that she would be happy to see him more than once. She'd called him a bullshitter which was either the old Jill teasing or a critical view of his character. He couldn't tell. But all in all how could he be anything but happy?

~

'Take a look at this pavement, it's rather special,' Jack says. He looks across at Jill, the tour group all but invisible. 'It was first laid over eight hundred years ago in a herringbone pattern to be replaced in the eighteenth century by what you see today. Some say the new pattern was set to resemble an oriental rug. If you look across, you'll notice how it reinforces the prominence of the Basilica. When you go inside, you'll see it's mirrored between the nave and altar of the cathedral.

'Isn't this a stunning place to be standing? Look around you, soak up the history. It's a scene of such great romance. One story, this one not too far in the distant past, tells of two young lovers who were standing exactly where we are now. The piazza was packed like it is today as the man went down on one knee and proposed. Perhaps he was unaware that he was attracting so much attention from tourists and locals alike or maybe he wanted the whole world to know of his feelings for this woman. A resounding cheer broke out when the woman accepted his proposal. He stood and they kissed to further cheers.'

'What happened to them?' Liz asks.

'Why, they lived happily ever after, of course,' Jack replies.

314

'Jack, you're crying. You're such a sensitive soul,' Deidre exclaims. As Jack wipes away the tears the eleven women gather round to mother him. Gary, the single man in the party, keeps his distance and Jill looks away.

Jack regains his composure and addresses the group. 'You'll be pleased to know that we can avoid the queue for the Basilica, our tickets are pre-booked. I'll take you across to meet Federico, your guide, his English is better than mine.' They laugh, he always gets a laugh with that line. 'There'll be a couple of hours of free time after the tour so you can make your own way back to the hotel. It's easy, follow the signs to the Grand Canal and take the turn to the left by the large yellow building, the gallery. You all have a map just in case. I'll meet you at reception at eight for dinner.'

Jill follows them to the Basilica where Jack meets Federico and introduces him to the group. He watches them enter and gives Jill a watery smile as he moves to her side.

'Nice story,' Jill says. 'I've never heard the one about that couple, who on earth are they?'

'A pair of English eccentrics, it's probably some garbled local mythology. It's the first time I've used it, I think I'll make it a regular from now on, it'll improve my ratings no end. Do you have time for a chat?'

'I do, it's holidays so no work.'

'Let's head somewhere a bit quieter,' Jack suggests, looking round to consider which exit to take out of the square.

'I know where.'

'Of course, you live here.'

They walk on in silence, leaving the tourists and reaching near deserted streets in a matter of minutes. They sit in a café full of locals, it's buzzing with conversation and the hiss of the coffee machine.

'How come you're doing these tours?' Jill asks.

'Actually because of you. When I got sacked I was well and truly lost, then I remembered what you were always telling me. To follow my enjoyment of history rather than my father's obsession with banking. I took a holiday here, my last indulgence before selling the house, and it got me thinking.'

'So how did that lead to this job? Who are you working for?'

'No one. After being fired I needed something, anything, and took a job at a travel agency round the corner from where I live, in Ealing. It was a run of the mill place and not doing that well what with internet bookings. But I thought hang on a minute, there's still a niche market out there for guided tours and I could utilise two interests, history and Italy. With some understanding of business, that's one thing I can thank my father for, I decided to give it a go setting up my own company. It was the right decision, I like the fact that it's all down to me and I get the reward for all the effort I put in.'

'So you're still a capitalist bastard then?'

'Slightly capitalist yes, but not ruthless. I hope not. I love what I do.'

Jill is looking away, pensive.

'I have another great love. You, Jill.'

'Don't.'

'So what's the alternative then, to not say how I feel?'

'How do you know you feel it?'

'Because every day for the last two years I've been thinking of you and regretting what happened, what I did. And when I saw you I – oh, I don't want to sound like in an old movie – but I gasped for breath, I shook in fear that you wouldn't acknowledge me.'

'It wasn't only you who did wrong back then.'

'No, you're right. In fact it was mainly your fault.'

They laugh. Two years apart and they've just shared a connection like during those early days together.

27

Three cups of coffee later and the conversation is drying up. Flippant humour about who was in the wrong hasn't been pursued. Instead, dialogue has been light, talking about their experiences in Italy, Jack's tours and Jill's teaching, together with some news about their families. Jill's parents are back in England, living in Newcastle near her brother Dan and his family; he now has two children. Vanessa is teaching part-time and Paul is working for a small firm of architects with childminding a major additional activity for both of them. Sabrina is still with Anthony and that's going well. There's no contact between Jack and his father or brother.

Any mention of their own futures seems off limits.

'I'd better go, Jack.'

'I suppose I should also be heading off. To check they've survived the afternoon without me.'

'Those women are all over you, you could have the pick of the bunch.'

'Bunch being a more appropriate word than bouquet. But even if they were the finest English roses, I wouldn't be interested.' Jill refuses to make eye contact as he continues. 'When can I see you again?'

'Maybe next time you do a tour.'

'That might not be for ages. What about tomorrow?'

'No, I don't think that's a good idea.'

'Please.'

'No.'

'Please.'

'No.'

'Please. Why are you laughing?'

'Because this reminds me of that *Simpsons* episode we liked, the one when Bart and Lisa wanted to go to a theme park and asked Homer to take them. He said no, they kept asking and he kept saying no.'

'Yes, I remember. And in the next scene they're in the car on their way.'

'We were still at uni when we saw it.'

There is a pause, both remembering that they had been in bed watching it. 'Can we have sex?' Jack had asked.

'No.'

'Please.'

'No.'

'Please.'

'No.'

Of course they did have sex, laughing as they made love.

'Can I see you tomorrow? It's the group's free evening which means I'm also free. We could go out for a meal.'

'All those things you've said about yourself today. No drinking, no drugs, no City culture. The wonderful new man – well done! I suppose you give all your profits to charity and volunteer weekends to work in a food bank.'

Jack stands up. 'It's been nice to have a catch up. Look after yourself. Bye, Jill.'

He turns and sets off.

'Wait!'

Jack faces Jill but doesn't move towards her. 'Why? What's the point? Look, I know I was awful back then and of course I'm hardly Mister Perfect now. I do think I'm OK though.'

'What exactly does thinking you're OK mean? Adolf Hitler probably thought he was OK, Nelson Mandela probably thought he was OK.'

'I'd like to think I'm more like Mandela OK.'

Jill laughs, Jack manages to smile ahead of Jill speaking. 'Can't you see that I'm terrified? Terrified because of how I changed when we were married. My gentle sarcasm turned into vicious mockery. I hated myself and I can't let that happen again.'

'It looks like we're both fearful of that, of what the normal is when we're together, our early years behaviour or what happened later. Couldn't we be friends for now to gauge that and see how things progress?'

Jack is now back by her side. Jill watches as he rearranges their coffee cups and places the sugar bowl exactly halfway between them. 'Is that still an issue?' she asks him.

'No, I'm completely cured.'

She messes things up, taking the cups off the saucers and turning one upside down. 'Just testing.'

She looks up, there's a beaming smile. 'Thanks,' he tells her. 'That's much more artistic.'

'Yes to dinner tomorrow,' her decision coming from nowhere. She writes down her address and Jack is once again in love with her wild sweeping handwriting. She

320

hands him the slip of paper. 'There are loads of good restaurants nearby, I'll book something for nine o'clock.'

Ahead of leaving the café to go their separate ways, they repeat the platonic kissing on each cheek of their first meeting, though possibly with a little more gusto.

~

The next evening Jack is waiting for Jill as she leaves the building. He takes hold of her hand and draws her close, holding eye contact. Those two kisses on the cheeks again, Jack savouring the feel of her lips against his skin. 'Where to?'

'Not far, it's a small family restaurant. Popular with locals so you always have to book.'

It's twilight and Venice looks at its best, the canals glistening as they are touched by the light of a full moon. They stand in front of what looks to be no more than a house with an ancient wooden door and small paned windows with half-length frilly red curtains.

Once inside, Jill is greeted on first-name terms and they are shown to a seat by the window. They are handed the menus.

'Tourists never come here so there's no English version. Do you need help?'

'I can read Italian, I need it for the business. I did night school.'

They both choose Mozzarelline Fritte to start with, followed by Tortelloni Ricotta e Spinaci for Jill and Sarde a Beccafico for Jack.

'You *can* eat meat, Jack, I don't mind,' Jill says as the waiter stands by, notepad at the ready.

'No, I'm fine with this. I don't eat much meat these days.'

Jill lifts the drinks menu. 'What do you fancy? I usually go for Soave.'

'I won't have wine, but please don't let that stop you.'

Jill needs a drink. She opts for a glass, a large one, which Jack orders together with an acqua frizzante in more than adequate Italian. He can sense what she's thinking. 'I didn't need to go to a rehab clinic or sign up to Alcoholics Anonymous. I did it myself. I'm not teetotal, I have an occasional glass of wine or a beer.'

'And the coke?'

'Yes Coca Cola, though only if it's the zero calories one!'

She smiles. Is he telling the truth?

They sit in the restaurant for a couple of hours, conversation flowing freely, though anything about their past is once again off limits. That still leaves plenty of topics – music, art, politics, films, literature, living in Italy and the company Jack has set up.

He explains how he'd researched before founding *The Real Italy*, initially canvassing the clients at the travel agency where he worked.

'My first customers lived around Ealing, so high income, a strong interest in culture, and as I quickly found out, a lot of lonely middle-aged divorcees who were attracted to group holidays with like-minded souls.'

'A holiday dating agency!'

'Hardly, the ratio of customers is about ten to one in favour of women. When I first set up I didn't even bother with a business plan. I had no idea whether it could succeed, but I was the only employee and working from home so had nothing to lose. Six came on my first trip, all acquaintances from the travel agency, I suppose I pinched them really. It's grown from that. I haven't even had to spend much on advertising, it's all been through word of mouth.'

'Is this what you want to do forever?'

'The way it's growing, possibly yes. At first it was to earn enough to pay the bills. Now I have an office, an administrator and a new tour leader. I'm organising at least one tour a month.'

'Good for you, it sounds exciting.'

'The last time I was here was going to be my final trip for a while. I'd recruited Des to run the tours, leaving me in the office to build up the business. But with you here everything has changed.'

Jill considers how to take that. This is their third meeting, two on the same day, so in what way is it a life changer? Does she even want to see him again? If yes, would a once a month meeting in Italy work? Of course she wants to see him, and once a month wouldn't be enough.

The approach of the waiter is a convenient distraction. 'Dolce Jill? Signore?'

'Fancy anything, Jack?'

'They've got profiteroles but I'm not sure I could manage a whole portion.'

'Let's share.'

'A splendid idea,' Jack replies with first date politeness.

Jill orders and the waiter leaves them. 'Yes Jack, I do remember we used to share desserts,' she states to circumvent him asking the question.

'We had such good times together.' Jack takes hold of Jill's hand. She doesn't pull away because his touch is soft and delicate, but everything is moving too fast. She orders another wine.

'Listen, Jill. I called Des today and I've asked him to fly out to take over hosting the tour. He's happy with that and it means we can spend time together.'

'What about your doting ladies?'

'Fuck the ladies.'

'Are you still into that then?'

'Not funny. As it happens, no. I only have one soulmate.'

'That's rubbish, you know it's not true.'

'Actually it is.'

'Are you telling me you haven't had sex with anyone since we separated?'

The waiter arrives. 'Profiteroles con gelato alla vaniglia.' For Jack the setting down of the dessert, two plates, two forks and spoons is taking an eternity. Finally the fussy waiter leaves him in peace to resume a conversation that needs to be had.

'I'm not saying that, but that doesn't diminish my feelings for you. Can I see you tomorrow?'

'No Bart.'

'Please, Homer.'

'I said no, Bart.'

'Please.'

'No.'

'Please.'

They smile as they play act, it's corny, old hat, repetitious, but it serves to ease the tension.

'When then?'

324

'I'll have to meet Des at the airport, introduce him to the group and go through some stuff. I may need to accompany him for a bit to check he can cope, but I'm confident he'll be fine. Perhaps it's best if we leave it until the evening and then I'll be completely free the next day.'

'Who says I'll want to see you the next day?'

'Please Homer.'

'No Bart.'

'Please.'

'No.'

'Shall we stop this before it drives us mad?'

'No.'

'Please.'

'No.'

'Come on, let's pay up and go.'

Jack insists on paying and leaves an over-generous tip. While standing outside the restaurant Jill makes the spontaneous decision to invite him over to her apartment for a meal rather than going to a restaurant again the following evening.

'I'd love that, but on one condition, you let me do the cooking.'

'That's not necessary.'

'Maybe not, but I'd like to. I'm sure I'll be shot of Des at some stage during the afternoon so I'll have time to explore Venetian delis. I'd enjoy that.'

'Actually that would help me. There's a new academic year staff meeting so I wouldn't have loads of time to get food.'

'Then it's settled. I'll buy everything, meet you at your place and you can relax while I cook. What time shall I get to you?'

'About eight?'

'Perfect.'

They are chatting while standing on a narrow bridge. It all feels so romantic as a gondola sails by, distorting the reflection of the moonbeams. There's a gentle lapping of water against the banks. The lights go out in the restaurant. There isn't a single tourist visible, they are quite alone in this city of memories. The step towards each other is simultaneous. The kiss is mutual, it's tender, it's lingering, it feels like true love.

'Jill, I…'

'Don't speak, please don't speak. I'll see you tomorrow.'

Jill turns and walks off at speed, brushing her hand roughly against her cheeks to wipe away the tears.

At home she opens a drawer and from the back, behind her socks and tights, pulls out an album. It's been ages since she last looked at the photos. She flicks through the ones taken during their university years, smiling at the one with Charlotte, Morag, Priya and Annie when they're pretending to tread on Jack who's lying on his back on the grass. She lingers on the one in Venice, they're kissing on a steep-sided bridge with no side railings – is it a bridge she's crossed since? They'd asked a French couple to take a picture and had reciprocated. The four of them had had a drink together and exchanged addresses though there was no follow up. She turns to the photo of them proudly standing by the front door of their new house, they'd got a neighbour to take that one and later had laughed at how long

326

he'd taken to meticulously set it up. "Could you take a short step forwards, Jill? No, maybe not, back to where you were before. Jack, run your hand through your hair to flatten it, will you? Or maybe a brush, have you got one at hand indoors?"

She reaches the photo of their wedding ceremony in the Seychelles, Jack with his beaming smile. Enough. She closes the album and returns it to its hidden home.

28

When Jack reaches the hotel he's pleased to see the lounge empty; all is quiet. He heads off to bed, aware that sleep is probably impossible because his mind is racing. He's worried about that kiss. As wonderful as it was, was it too quick? He had to avoid the risk of scaring Jill off having decided to begin any reconciliation with friendship alone. Mind you, wasn't that kiss as much from her as from him? The prospect of failing to win her back is so scary that he is feeling the pain of loss even though nothing has been resolved. He opens his wallet and from behind a credit card extracts a photo folded into quarters. The pair of them are looking at the camera, deliberately over-posing, their faces touching. It was taken by the waiter at their hotel on the last night of their honeymoon. That night they had shared a reluctance to return to England, to their fast-paced London lifestyle. Little did they know the depths of what was to follow.

Jack reads, or rather turns pages, because he doesn't care who killed who in the novel. There is only one thing on his mind – will he have a second chance with Jill. Sleep is fitful; he wakes up in the morning with the light still on and the book resting on his chest.

At breakfast, drained, he's conscious of the need to focus for the sake of his business. He struggles to be friendly, patient and professional as he gathers his fellow travellers in the lobby to announce that he'll be handing over to another member of his team for the duration of the tour.

'No, there isn't a problem,' he tells them, 'it's always been the plan. I'm sorry if I forgot to say. I guarantee you'll enjoy being with Des.'

'Has this got anything to do with you crying at St Mark's Square yesterday?' Ruth asks. She's a perceptive woman.

'No, absolutely not.'

'You're not ill, are you Jack? Please tell us you aren't ill,' Deidre implores. Is she about to weep?

'I'm as fit as a fiddle. It's just that something's cropped up which I have to deal with.'

'But you said us getting a different tour leader was planned,' Liz says. Another detective.

'That wasn't a hundred percent accurate, it's just that I didn't want anyone to worry. Honestly, it's only a minor hassle. Listen everyone, you will absolutely love Des, he's far more knowledgeable than me and he's nicer. I'm picking him up at the airport this morning so let's shift the visit to Gallerie dell'Accademia to this afternoon and you can have your free time now. Actually that's better if you want to go shopping because everything will be open which isn't always the case afternoons. If you're back here by two I can introduce you to Des.'

Jack travels to the airport and meets Des who is relaxed and looking forward to the opportunity. On their way back Jack briefs him on the afternoon's itinerary and is pleased to note that Des is a walking encyclopaedia on Titian and

Canaletto. Over a coffee at the hotel they wade through the paperwork.

'Why the change of plans?' Des asks.

There's a pause as Jack considers how to answer. He feigns distraction, sorting papers before looking up.

'Sorry, what did you say?'

'I asked why the change of plans?'

'I'm thinking of introducing a Florence tour and I want to check out hotels.'

'Will you be back tonight?'

The lie is extending uncomfortably but he can't bring himself to tell the truth when everything is likely to end in failure. 'I'm not sure. Probably.'

'So you might be with us for dinner?'

'No, I definitely won't be back by then. I'll call when I know my plans for certain.'

'I think extending destinations is a great idea. I've done research on competitors and there are big gaps in the market. It's a pity we're called *The Real Italy* because I suppose that limits us to the one country. Greece and France have huge potential for historical tours.'

At this point Jack really doesn't care, he wants to escape from Des and his tour group. 'We can look into that,' he replies blandly. 'But it's nearly two o'clock, let's meet the gang.'

Any risk of resentment, suspicion or hostility is instantly dissolved as Des charms the travellers with humour, knowledge and a touch of seduction. By the time Jack is ready to depart, they're leaving for the art gallery with everyone smiling as they battle to be the closest to their new guide.

Jack saunters through the centre of Venice, stopping off at tiny delicatessens that don't seem to hold enough stock to have any chance of making a living. Having googled seasonal recipes before setting off, he's decided on pesce spada cooked with olives, artichokes and pecorino.

It's gone seven by the time he nears the hotel, on schedule to shower and get changed, his arrival cleverly planned to avoid the risk of being seen by his group. They would be indoors, their tour of the galleries well and truly over, they'd be getting ready for their evening meal.

Loaded with several bags of food, a bottle of Soave and flowers for Jill, he approaches the hotel from one side of the street just as the group are coming towards him from the other. Several wave as they catch sight of him.

'Great, your back!' Liz shouts.

'I'm not really back,' Jack informs them as they come to rest outside the hotel. 'Well, only for a short while. Did you all enjoy this afternoon?'

'I'll say,' Deidre begins. 'It was wonderful. Des is an absolute mastermind on Italian art, aren't you, Des.'

'We're running a bit late because everyone wanted to go on to another gallery. I hope it was OK to do that.'

'Of course,' Jack replies, struggling not to convey the disappointment that his plan to avoid them has backfired.

'That's it for now folks,' Des announces. 'You haven't got long to freshen up before dinner. Let's meet here at quarter to eight.'

There are twelve effusive thank yous to Des as if he's told them they've won a million on the lottery.

'Are you eating with us tonight then?' Des asks Jack as the group members drift off.

'No, there's been a change of plan and I'm setting off for Florence now. The person I was meant to be meeting had a last-minute appointment this afternoon so we've had to re-arrange to early tomorrow morning. I'm travelling there tonight.'

'A she I take it,' Des asks, looking at the flowers.

'Yes, I thought that would be a nice touch.' Jack holds the bouquet aloft. In the same hand is the bag of fish.

'What's that for?'

'This? It's fish.'

'I can see that from the label. I was only wondering *why* you've got fish.'

'I thought she was quite mad, but she asked if I could get her swordfish because they seem to have run out in Florence. It took me ages to find it, but it all helps to get in her good books if we're going to do business.'

'I suppose so,' came the unconvinced reply. 'So I guess we'll see you sometime tomorrow. I hope it goes well.'

Jack realises he can't stay at the hotel that night, there being a limit to how much he can fabricate. Staying with Jill wasn't going to happen so he'd have to find another hotel.

~

Jill's finding it difficult to decide what to wear. She's gone from sophisticated formal (rejected as being too formal) to laid back casual (rejected as being too casual) and is now wearing a well above the knee dress. She's not happy, it's too flirtatious and she's all set to select a fourth option when the bell rings. It's on the dot of eight.

Jack comes in with far more bags than she would have thought necessary for a single meal. Maybe he's brought

332

tomorrow's breakfast and lunch, too. He hands over the flowers and sets the wine down on the small round table which Jill has adorned with tablecloth and two candles. It's ridiculous, it feels like a first date with uncertainty about how to behave. They've backtracked from the kisses on cheeks of the first meetings and the previous evening's lip to lip kiss; now they are keeping their distance.

He pulls a small bottle out of a paper bag. 'Limoncello. Fancy one? Don't worry,' he adds as he unscrews the top. 'As I said yesterday, I'm not teetotal, I'll be having a glass.'

'I'm not worried,' Jill says as she opens a kitchen cupboard. Jack notes an eclectic mix of glasses, cups and mugs unevenly stacked. They could do with a sort, he thinks.

'Have you rented the place furnished?' he asks as Jill pours.

'Yep, it has everything I need. Actually I'm verging on being possessionless, when I move I'll only need one suitcase.'

'Is moving your plan?'

'I'm not sure. This isn't forever, the job or the place.'

'Shall I get started cooking?'

'Sure, what can I do?'

It turns out to be a jointly produced meal, something they'd done loads of times when at university but rarely when living in London. Jack's become a foodie, a flamboyant cook waving his arms around as he chops and stirs. He reminds Jill of one of the TV chefs, but she can't remember his name. His knowledge of herbs and spices is impressive, he's brought some that she's never used. Packaging, vegetable remains and used pans pile up, Jack

333

oblivious to a mess that surely would have disturbed him in the past.

With the food prepared and ready to be cooked, Jill starts to clear up.

'Perhaps leave that until after we've eaten? Let's sit down for a while. Wine?' Jack asks, holding up the bottle.

'Sure,' Jill says and watches as he takes two glasses from what she appreciates is an embarrassingly random collection for him to select from. He opens the bottle, pours, hands her a glass and sits next to her on the sofa, keeping a generous distance between them. Why so far away, she wonders. It would be nice to feel the warmth of his thigh against hers. Or would it?

They face each other, drinks in hand. 'Cheers,' Jack says and their glasses clink together. 'This is the only one I'll be drinking. Actually I'm not going to announce only one every time, that would be pathetic. You'll have to trust me.'

The funny thing is, despite years of lack of trust followed by years of separation, she does trust him. Is this like the old times, their university years? Or even better because they're more mature now? Or could it end up as a second honeymoon with dreams soon to be shattered as had happened in the past?

'Here's something that will amaze you, Jill. I had a go at meditation.'

'You didn't!'

'Yes, I started after I moved house.'

'Why?'

'To slow down, to gain some understanding about myself. To break away from the Ashley-Lovett culture which I reckon has messed up rather a lot of people over the centuries.'

'How did you get on?'

'I did say tried. I couldn't take to it. I'd just started the business and my mind was racing about what was needed, so that didn't help. Mind you, I'm not convinced it would have been any easier even without the business. I've also had some therapy. Two lots, one for the OCD and the other one for alcohol. Not for long though because I reckoned it was up to me to make the changes and that's what I've done. Successfully.'

'Is this confession time? If I'd known I would have worn my priest's gear.'

'I'd rather see you dressed up as a nun.'

Jill blushes because Jack has glanced down at her exposed thighs as he speaks.

'You are looking well, Jack.'

'Thanks. You're looking well, too. Do you mind if I say fantastic?'

Jill doesn't mind but is unsure what to say next. She opts for the safe bet of sticking to facts. 'I run.'

'Me too. Maybe we can go jogging together?'

'Maybe.' Jill is thinking maybe they should go to bed together, make love, have breakfast together, and only go jogging if there's time after that. She opts for facts again. 'Tell me more about your business.'

'It's at a critical point.' Jack outlines his plans to move from the current small-scale operation to something considerably bigger. Jill is impressed by his enthusiasm.

'Having Des on board will help, not only in running some of the tours, but he's a social media guru with some great ideas.'

'Did he get on well with your women today?'

'A huge hit. It was all a bit embarrassing though.' Jack is all set to recount the humorous early evening encounter but pulls up to avoid having to mention the need to find accommodation that night.

'Why embarrassing?'

'They fell in love with him and I was discarded.' He wants to stay the night, to hold her close and never let go. He changes the subject. 'What about you, have you got lots of classes lined up?'

'As many as I want, but I'm still searching for something more rewarding. Actually that's not true, it's more a case of drifting and waiting for something to appear out of thin air. I loved teaching but not this, I've had enough of talking bollocks English to businessmen. *The products we manufacture are first rate. You will be pleased to know that the Italian retail sector is finally picking up. Here is my business card and I look forward to hearing from you.* Maybe I've had enough of Venice, of Italy, too. Jesus, I'm lost.'

Jill doesn't want to cry. She's crying.

Come back to England with me, Jack wants to say. I'll take care of you, this time forever. He knows she'd ridicule him if he said that because she couldn't trust him after what he's done. She's always been too good for him.

But Jill is still crying, quietly, tears streaming down her cheeks. She turns and faces him full on. Are they tears of anger because of what he's done, how he's fucked up her life? Is it a plea for help, is it his sympathy she wants? Or does love come into it?

Jack's done with analysis. He edges closer to her and takes hold of her hands. She edges sideways until their thighs are at last touching and that warm feeling is as good as she'd hoped for. They're kissing, near painful as their lips press together hungrily after all these years. They move apart, both with a look of shock because of what is about to happen. The fury of the kissing is replaced by delicate touches as clothes are removed.

The buzzer goes on the oven. They laugh; Jill leaps up and switches it off.

A naked Jill is leading a naked Jack to her bedroom. There should be tension after all that's gone on in the past, but instead their lovemaking is mingled with laughter because there's only a single bed in this apartment and they're remembering similar nights in the small bed at university. For both of them it's fine, the opportunity to press their bodies together all night.

~

'What now?' Jill asks in the morning.

'There's only one option. I'm never ever going to let you go.'

'But don't you think…'

'No.'

'After what we've been through wouldn't it be best to...'

'Definitely not.'

'But what if…'

'It won't, I've learnt my lesson…'

'And I've learnt mine, too.'

Postscript

George is sitting on Jack's lap looking at the pictures in the pop-up book and cackling.

'Crown,' he says, pointing.

'And who's that on the ground?'

'It's Mummy, she's fallen over! Again. Read it again, Daddy.'

Jack does as ordered, for the God knows how many time. It's George's favourite; the characters have the same names as his mummy and daddy. He knows the story backwards but summons the enthusiasm to point to the letters, words and pictures as he speaks.

> *Jack and Jill went up the hill*
> *To fetch a pail of water.*
> *Jack fell down and broke his crown,*
> *And Jill came tumbling after.*
> *Up Jack got and home did trot,*
> *As fast as he could caper;*
> *And went to bed and bound his head*
> *With vinegar and brown paper*
> .

It's been quite a day for George, his third birthday party has included a treasure hunt on Ealing Common which has finally taken its toll – he's asleep in Jack's arms.

Jack lays him in his bed, tucks him up and joins Jill in the lounge. The laptop is perched on her knee, she's working on a *The Real Europe* spreadsheet.

She looks up and smiles. 'What a quarter, absolutely brilliant, though except for Russia. We're not covering costs on those tours so maybe we should cancel.'

'We've only been running them for a year, perhaps keep going for a bit before we decide. We can add Russia to next month's management meeting agenda.'

'You can, but remember I'm not here, I'm leading the Roman France tour.'

'I forgot. Poor you, a sunny autumn break in Orange, Nimes and Arles while I'm stuck in miserable grey London.'

'I'll send you a postcard! Is everything sorted with Sabrina for babysitting?'

'Yeah, she's fine except for the Wednesday, but I can work from home then.'

'Are you intending to read this one a story?' Jill asks as she gently pats her protruding belly.

'I didn't even know I'd brought the book down.'

Jack opens to a random page. 'Here we are. *Rock a Bye Baby*.'

'Not that one. I don't want her to hear about her cradle falling out a tree.'

'It's funny how kids love nursery rhymes even though the stories are actually quite scary.'

'Maybe scary, but they soon realise that they're totally unrealistic.'

A bell sounds. 'That's dinner done,' Jill announces. 'Let's eat in here and watch telly, I'm dying to see the last episode.'

'Sure.'

'Do you want vinegar on your chips?'

Also by R J Gould:

The Engagement Party
Eight parents, step-parents and partners; two young lovers; one celebration destined to fail. Can Wayne and Clarissa's relationship survive the trauma of the dysfunctional families meeting for the first time at a lunch to celebrate their engagement?

Mid-life follies
His wife has abandoned him after twenty-three years of blissful marriage. Is she having a midlife crisis? Should he be having one, too? A succession of twists and turns prevent a return to normality, leaving their children to discover that immaturity isn't solely the preserve of the young.

The bench by Cromer beach
As the lives of five people living in a sleepy seaside town intertwine, cracks emerge and restlessness grows in this novel about aspirations & the realities of everyday life.

A Street Café Named Desire
One man's quest for two dreams – a relationship with the gorgeous Bridget and opening an arts café. David meets Bridget at a school reunion and develops a teenagesque passion for her, but he has baggage to overcome ahead of achieving either of his aspirations.

Lightning Source UK Ltd.
Milton Keynes UK
UKHW040632170521
383859UK00001B/245

9 781786 970954